THE FALLEN CHRONICLES:
≡ BOOK 1 ≡

LUCIFER'S FALL

VERUSHA ROBBINS

Published by

Ink 'n Ivory

PO BOX 6321, Rouse Hill, NSW. 2155. Australia

www.inkNivory.com

ISBN: 978-1-922113-60-3 (Paperback)

ISBN: 978-1-922113-61-0 (ePub)

ISBN: 978-1-922113-62-7 (Hardback)

First Printing: 2023

Dedication

To my daughter Alaska Kaya Robbins,
May you pursue your dreams no matter how long
they take, because one day they will come true. But
also, please don't take as long as me.

And don't read this book until you're 18.

Acknowledgements

There are so many people who have helped me get this book off the ground.

Firstly, thank you to my parents who have been the most avid supporters in every stage of this journey. Your faith and belief in my creativity has meant the absolute world.

My brother, Yuvash, who has been the genius behind the world building of this book. Thank you for taking my countless phone calls stressing about the plot and its potential flaws and having weird conversations about Hell at work. I couldn't have done this without you.

To all my amazing fans on Wattpad. There are no words to thank you for the years of support you have given this book as I trudged on year after year only updating once in a purple spotted moon. You still stuck with it and loved it and came back again and again. I thrived on your comments and your obsessive love for the characters. Thank you for being my inspiration to keep writing.

To my home team, the amazing women in my life who put their pom poms on and cheered me the whole way through. I'm so lucky to have you.

My wonderful editor Sierra and Milbart for the gorgeous cover.

Last but most definitely not the least, my other half Aaron. Thank you for the time, the sacrifice and for continuously pushing me to 'just get it done!'. You've been the fire at my back when I've needed it and the proud partner who tells everyone I'm writing a book as I cringe inside. Thank you for making me step away from my shadow and into the light.

We really do make a great team. I love you.

Chapter 1

Temptation... it comes in many forms. It whispers its sweet seduction in your ears, tangling honeyed thoughts with yours like a lovers' embrace.

They say the devil is a master at luring the young and innocent away from the shimmering path of virtue and into dark, slippery sin. He should have embodied that horror. He should have looked ravaged and stained with the smear of fallen souls. The crisp, acidic scent of death should have choked the air around him. With all that he had done, he should have never looked like that.

"Angel," came the silky croon of his voice. Obsidian black wings skimmed the midnight floor, framing his impossible beauty. I had heard about those wings, those night-drenched wings. Seeing them up close was equally terrifying and fascinating.

"Lucifer." Was that parched voice mine? I willed it not to tremble.

We were in Kryptos, the neutral realm of both light and dark beings, which was created for both sides to negotiate and trade without the beginnings of a violent battle. The idea of safe passage was an unspoken rule that had been kept and respected, but that didn't mean it couldn't be broken. And if it was Lucifer – The Death Bringer, The God of Darkness, The Forsaken – who shredded the rules and burnt them to a crisp... well, who was going to challenge him?

Only one Archangel had that power, and he wasn't here. I was alone, and I couldn't leave unless he allowed it.

Hellfire eyes studied me with deliberate sensuality and were set in a face almost indescribably beautiful. Lips curved as he stalked forward like the king of all predators, which I suppose he was.

"Heaven made an interesting choice this time. The last angel bored me with spiritual platitudes. Perhaps he thought I wasn't beyond saving. Do you think so?"

Adathan was the previous angel who had stood in my place. I hadn't seen him return to The City of Light, but I heard he had been in the healing chambers for some time. There were rumours of a missing eye. They said he was lucky to have returned at all.

"I'm not here to indulge in games."

The Devil loved his games. He usually ensnared his prey with sweet, decedent words and enticing promises. Like a butterfly, the seduced were drawn to the lure of the rose, only to discover that underneath those soft, silky petals were razor-sharp teeth. On other occasions, he befuddled your mind until you ended up answering questions you had no intention of responding to.

I had been warned, but warnings could only prepare you so much.

I moved around to keep some distance between us. My steps were light, my body alert, poised to move at the merest hint of danger. Trouble was, I was in danger the moment he entered the room.

"No?" he mocked. There was a cruel cast to his features as he regarded me. His wings flexed once like a heartbeat, and the reddish light of the torches glinted off the burnished gold that wrapped around his arms. "What then, little angel, did you come here for?"

I responded coolly. "You know why. To negotiate." Heaven had failed time and time again, but for some reason, the Archangels thought sending me would move the unmovable. I still failed to grasp why, and now even more so.

Lucifer circled lazily around, and I turned to face his movements. Never show the Devil your back. The room we were in wasn't as large as some of the meeting rooms in Kryptos, but it was the most barren one I had ever been in, lacking any furnishing or decorations. Usually, you could request a room with a specific landscape or setting to make negotiations more comfortable for specific races and beings. Clearly, Lucifer preferred to do the opposite.

Shadowed hands caressed my spirit, looking for any weakness to use against me. "Stop that," I said.

"Why?"

Why? "It's impolite."

Lucifer's teeth glinted in the dim lighting and, with the speed of a corrupt thought, gripped the side of my neck tightly, sending sparks of pain shooting under my skin. I sucked in a sharp breath.

"Is this also impolite?" he asked silkily, the subtle pressure of his hand reminding me how easily he could destroy this form of mine and send my energy back to the heavens.

I was tall in my angelic incarnation, but he was just over a head taller than me. Looking up into those dark eyes, they heated like banked embers and seemed to flare when I raised my hand to close over his wrist. Was it somewhere that I heard that Lucifer's eyes were once a cerulean blue? The thought shifted in and faded out gently.

Suddenly, light pooled out from my fingers, its pure, white essence illuminating the space between us.

Like with all negotiations, one needed to establish a position of power. Lucifer was used to beings submitting out of fear. I would never be able to bargain for anything if I proved to be easy prey. I had to show some spine. Otherwise, this meeting would end even before it really began.

Dark eyes glinted with interest, and lips curved up a fraction.

Love sparked the light between us, flowing from me to him like a flash fire. It was the purest emotion in existence, one that bound every atom, every life force together. It was the origin of every thought and the end of every existence. I fused Light with the love of the Creator, combined with every good feeling I had, every dream realised, and every moment of joy I had felt since my angelic incarnation. The sheer force of it shoved him backwards, breaking the physical contact between us.

Lucifer straightened slowly, and when his gaze snapped on mine, I expected a furious rage. Yes, I saw the anger unravelling in black coils, but another emotion tempered it. An emotion I didn't understand.

Confusion.

When he moved towards me once more, I raised my hand again in warning. Light flared again between my fingers. He ignored me. At the time, I had believed my power was significant, that the slight victory I gained gave me some power over him.

A novice mistake.

Lucifer bent the laws of space with alarming ease, and before I knew it, my Light-filled hand was smothered in his and my jaw clenched in a bruising grip. "That might have worked once, angel, but try it again, and I will crush the Light right out of you."

Fear crept through me, eating away at the courage that brought me here. This was not a being who used empty threats. Could he take my Light from me? I wasn't about to test that theory.

Satisfied at the expressions that flicked through my face, he leaned down even closer until his scent invaded my lungs, smoky and exotic with just the hint of something sweet. Apple?

"Now," Lucifer commanded silkily, "What is your name?"

I swallowed and forced myself to focus. "Sandriel." I tried to jerk my head back, but he held me fast.

"Sandriel..." He rolled my name in his mouth, pronouncing each syllable until it sounded vaguely erotic. His hand released its hold on my face only to slide into my long silvery, blonde hair. Lucifer studied my countenance leisurely but with an intensity I couldn't fathom.

"I came here to negotiate."

He smiled. The effect was devastating and oddly familiar. "And how do you think you are doing, Sandriel?"

Spirits, my name. It sounded like he licked up one side of it and kissed his way down the other. "Stop doing that."

"Stop doing what?" came the velvet reply.

"You know what!"

Desperate, I pushed him with my body, with my will and my Light. It either must have worked, or he let me go because, in the next moment, Lucifer was a good distance away, crossing his arms against his chest. His wings fell around him, concealing parts of his body like a great, ebony cloak.

He frowned at me briefly, and then his expression cleared and cooled like winter's night. "You speak of negotiation. Negotiation for what, little angel?"

It was sudden, the shift from heat to cold. I tried to adjust and straighten myself up to look more composed and less flustered. Suppressing the urge to mirror him and cross my arms, I clasped my hands in front of me and eased the lines of my face into smooth, calm contours.

"I came here to negotiate for Devros, Elindara, and Rushton."

"Ah, the warrior angels."

I nodded. "Yes, for their release."

Lucifer had captured many of our warrior angels in battle. I had heard about the horrible ways some of them had been tortured and transitioned by his hand. He was vicious and effective with the pain he inflicted, and it felt as though many angels took centuries to recover from the time spent in Hell, on the rare occasion they managed to leave.

He flashed me a contemptuous look. "And what is Heaven offering me this time? Another offer of peace?"

"Don't you want peace?"

He laughed, rich and dark. The sound echoed through the room, making me feel like I was surrounded by him. Trapped.

Just make the deal and leave, I told myself. "What do you want, then?" I countered.

His laughter faded, and he paused, tilting his head at me in consideration. It made me nervous. The fire had crept back in.

"What are you willing to give me?"

I stared at him. "Me?"

"Yes, little angel. Is it not you whom I'm negotiating with?"

"On behalf of Heaven," I said firmly.

He shook his head slowly, making the glow of the torches play bewitchingly with the angles of his face. "No, I think not. They sent you, so it is you I will negotiate with."

My eyes narrowed. "That is not how it works."

"If you want to free them, then that is how it's going to work."

How did I think that by making a deal with the Devil, I would come out unscathed? "Fine. What do you want from me, Lucifer?"

"Your time."

I jerked back, startled. My time? "Why?"

Lucifer shrugged indifferently. "My reasons are my own."

Floundering, I responded, "Well, if I don't like your reasons, I might not agree."

He arched an eyebrow. "Really? You would say no and leave the warrior angels you so bravely came all the way down here for just because of my *reasons*?"

I blinked. "Well…"

"As I said, little angel, my reasons are my own. If that's a deal breaker, go back to your City of Light and tell those who sent you to stop wasting my time."

I frowned at him. He was manipulating me. I knew it, yet I lacked the foresight to manoeuvre my way out. For the second time, I wondered why the Archangels sent me. "How… much of my time?"

His voice caressed the space between us. "A week."

"Three hours." This was not happening.

He raised an eyebrow. "Surely a life is worth more than three hours, little angel. Eight hours for each."

"Five for each."

"Done."

My wings drooped slightly. If there had been an ominous sound of thunder after he said that, I wouldn't have been surprised. He had agreed too easily, which obviously meant I was the loser in this negotiation. I just didn't know how. There was nothing I could do now. "Fine, five hours each for the release of the angels."

"Excellent. You will pay off one of your hours tomorrow."

What did I get myself into? My heart started to pound. "Tomorrow?"

"Yes, or would you like to make it sooner? Maybe you would like to stay here a little longer?"

"No," I said quickly. "Tomorrow is fine. Where do I meet you?"

"Here," he crooned softly. "You can meet me here."

"And... what are we going to do?" I stuttered slightly.

His lips lifted, but he said nothing.

I left as fast as the Light could take me.

Chapter 2

I went straight from the darkest of angels to the lightest. The City of Light flew past me in a hazy, white blur as I headed towards the Archangel, who seemed to have all the answers, and, God willing, would help me endure this impossible situation. I ignored the picturesque views that humans only glimpsed in their imagination, skimmed past the healing pools of water, disregarded the beautiful, celestial music that would usually make me pause and absorb the thrumming, light-filled notes.

The darkness had cast its shadow upon me and no matter how much I tried, I couldn't fly fast or far enough.

The doors opened as I approached, and Archangel Michael stood in the centre of the room, waiting for me. Like always, I resisted the urge to drop to my knees before him in absolution. Archangel Michael was everything an angel should be. He was beautiful, incredibly wise, strong, and righteous. I could completely understand why he was said to be the Hand of God. He was the best of us, what we all aspired to be, and from what I heard, the only one powerful enough to battle Lucifer.

They had fought once before, an eon ago. The battle was said to have raged many days and nights, causing the elementals to explode across the heavens and rain down upon the Earth. Suffocating smoke, screaming winds, and acid rain accompanied the flashes of light that cut across the sky and the sound of thunder as their blades crossed.

It was an epic battle, one between two of the most powerful beings that had ever existed. No one knew exactly how it started or how it ended, only that Archangel Michael returned to the heavens, and Lucifer established a new domain in the Underworld.

"Sandriel." His voice was soft and brushed over me like a calming wave.

I walked until I stood before him and bowed my head respectfully. "Archangel Michael."

He looked down at me, face serene and framed by a cloud of rich, golden hair. "Are you well?"

I nodded. "I am now that I am back here, in The City."

He smiled back at me softly. "How did your meeting go?'

Jerking my eyes up to his, I tried to find the right words."I... I don't think I was prepared." I shifted on my feet. "It didn't go the way I thought it would." Involuntarily, my mind flashed back to those inky, black wings and that wicked voice which could tempt a statue to bend to his desires.

"Is Lucifer going to release our warrior angels?"

I twisted my hair and pulled its length in front of me. The air was soothingly cool against the back of my neck. "Yes."

"Then I would consider that an enormous success, beyond what many hoped for. You did well, Sandriel."

"I have to see him again," I blurted out in one breath, like trying to dislodge an obstruction in my throat. "It was part of the negotiation. He wants five hours from me. That is, five hours for each angel released."

Violet blue eyes held my gaze with strength and compassion.

My fear was tempered under the temple's healing vibrations, but I knew once I left The City of Light, it would reach out with thick, rough hands and choke me. "I'm terrified," I whispered. Emotions churned like a brewing storm inside me.

"What terrifies you?"

What didn't terrify me? I swallowed. "Him… and what he wants from me."

There was a soft pause. "And what does he want from you?"

Sandriel… I could hear him whisper my name like a sweet caress. The memory heated my skin like summer's touch, and I waited, almost frantically, for disgust to take its place, but I couldn't feel it. Why couldn't I feel it?

I turned my head slightly and avoided Archangel Michael's eyes, looking instead at one of his broad shoulders. "I'm not exactly sure… he wasn't very specific."

I took a deep breath and tilted my chin up. "Why me? Why did you choose me to negotiate with him?"

He moved then, his royal purple robe brushing the floor slightly as he walked to the side of the room. The wall shimmered and disappeared, and suddenly, I could see The City of Light spread out before me like a glorious carpet of intricately exquisite structures. Some of them pulsed and glowed, creating rainbow hues in the sky.

"Because you are the only one who can." He said it like it carried the weight of something I couldn't understand.

I stared at his back, half concealed by the shiny length of his hair. Archangel Michael's wings were within his form, but I knew if they were stretched out, they would take up the width of the room. White, radiant wings that so many great painters and renowned sculptors had tried in vain to capture.

Archangel Michael knew so many things. Many of us believed he got messages straight from the Source. Was this one of those things? It still made no sense to me.

"Why is this so?" I implored.

He turned back to me, hands clasped behind him. "It will be revealed to you in time, Sandriel. You must trust that the path you are on is meant for you. Have faith that you have the strength needed to walk down it. It wouldn't have been given to you if you didn't."

I wrung my hands together. The strength to deal with the Devil, the Eater of Worlds? Who was I to even attempt such a thing? "But I feel so lost."

Michael's eyes unfocused for a second, as if listening to a song that only he could hear. "Meditate," he finally said. "Perhaps some answers lie there."

***

I closed my eyes in the Crystal Room and started to go through the familiar exercises to prepare my mind and body for meditation. It should have been easy for one such as I, but in my mind, I saw flashing, dark eyes instead of the white light that was supposed to soothe me. It took time and some considerable effort, but finally, I felt myself touch that river of peace that passed through my soul and wound its way through every atom in the Universe.

Connected, weightless, light, free…

The memory surfaced from the depths of my mind like it was waiting for me. Impressions, thoughts and feelings slid through, and they weren't pleasant. Despair, bleak, and unyielding saturated the room I was in, shaking me to my core.

He was in pain. Oh, he was in so much pain. I would have done anything, anything for him, but I could not fix this. I could feel his silent screams, his turbulent rage, and

I knew others would be able to feel it soon. They would come for him. He was not safe. I would have gone to him, but this body would not obey my will. The darkness that seeped through my...

I couldn't bear the agony. I tore past that memory and into another one that was hovering just behind the first.

I pressed my hands to my warm cheeks. I shouldn't be doing this, but still, I peeked out from behind the tree.

He was having a bath. What unattached woman would have been able to turn away? The excuse sounded pitiful even to me. I crouched down low and tried to angle the shrubbery in front of me to conceal my rose-coloured gown. It seemed my dignity had kicked up its heels and fled, and now I had reduced myself to a common Peeping Tom.

My eyes widened, but how glorious he looked.

Water sluiced down hardened muscle over tantalising indents and contours. His skin practically glowed in the fading light. I thought him a dream when I first saw him, but now he was more akin to a wild, untamed fantasy. He stood with most of his back to me, and I could see that the water just barely covered firm... I blushed.

I didn't know a man could possess such a form!

But he wasn't a man, that much I knew. He was so beautiful it almost hurt to look at him. My heart raced in my chest.

I watched as he ducked down into the lake like a creature born from the waters and emerged dripping, running a hand through that silky, dark hair. I often wondered what it would feel like to touch it. Would it feel as soft as it looked? I tugged on my own auburn locks that had now collected bits of foliage.

I knew I shouldn't be indulging in such thoughts, and often I'd force myself to think of God and helping other people, but here I was, crawling through the dirt and... oh my....

He walked out of the water. Naked.

My eyes widened further.

Casually, he draped on the white and gold cloth he wore around his waist. Absently, I wondered how it never managed to get dirty. Otherwise, I would have offered to wash it for him.

Water still glistened off his large shoulders and across the sweeping planes of his chest. The setting sun worshipped his body as it slipped below the horizon. He watched it for a few moments, enjoying the last rays of light before turning and disappearing into the tree line.

I let out a wheezing breath of air I had been holding. I hadn't meant to watch. Really, I hadn't.

"Nadia, you are so, so bad," I whispered to myself.

"Yes, you are," came a smooth, velvet voice.

I screamed and tumbled sideways, looking up. Oh god, no.

Amused, cerulean blue eyes looked down at me. "Did you enjoy the view?"

I managed to get his name out in a strangled, mortified moan. "Lucifer."

Lucifer.

My eyes snapped open.

Chapter 3

I had forgotten about my past lives.

Yes, we have many lives and are called many names. Each life we live is given to us to re-remember that we are spiritual, divine beings living in a human body. We forget that we are capable of so much love and goodness, and some of us slide down a darker path, giving in to anger, fear, and unloving behaviour. Our lifetimes that follow set us up to improve on the areas we were weakest in, so we can continue to grow and become the best version of ourselves.

I knew there was a spiritual harmony in all things, but I was still desperately recovering from the shock that I had known Lucifer in a life where I was called Nadia. Were the events of that lifetime the reason the Creator had placed me on his path now? To the best of my knowledge, angels didn't mix with humans, not in the way that I saw in my vision.

In Archangel Michael's temple, we guided the humans on Earth by sending them thoughts, feelings, and intuitive nudges in answer to their prayers. In very rare cases, we would go down and physically lend a helping hand if it was for their highest good, but only for a few moments and never for an extended period of time.

Nadia, my previous incarnation, seemed to know Lucifer very well. Not many beings remembered what Lucifer was before he descended into the Underworld. He was the first amongst the angels and was said to be the most beautiful example of God's perfection. Nadia's glimpse of him in the lake with that angelic shimmer along his skin and the warm amusement in his vibrant, blue eyes was a complete contrast to the creature I had seen a few hours ago.

Everything in me wanted to deny our connection, but the memories still played out before me, imbued with the fascination I had felt, wonder, and, worst of all, that deep current of attraction.

What in the heavens happened to him?

The presence of another angel in the Crystal Room distracted me from my musings. I looked up to see Lycindra, a healing angel from Archangel Raphael's temple and someone I had grown close to.

Her dark, wavy brown hair caressed the sides of a sweetly shaped face. "Sandriel, I heard you were in here. Are you well?"

There was no simple answer to her question, and I hadn't told her about my mission. Archangel Michael had wanted me to keep it to myself for now. I smiled and stood up slowly. "I was meditating and enjoying the peace of the Crystal Room."

Her green dress swirled around her feet as she stopped. "Oh, I hope I didn't disturb you, but I thought you would want to know that Rushton and the warrior angels are back!" Lycindra's face lit up with joy.

I understood her mood. The warrior angels risked themselves greatly by battling the demonic energies in the realms. Many had to go through long bouts of healing just to eliminate all the negativity absorbed into their energy field. The warriors also knew that if one of them were captured, there was no certainty they would come back for a long time. Many hadn't so far, so this was a rare event.

Lucifer had released the warrior angels as promised, but before our agreement had even begun. He probably knew I wouldn't renege on our deal, no matter how much I yearned to. It was against our nature not to keep our word, though I was surprised that he had kept his. I would even say he was being… generous. That alone should have warned me, like the scent of smoke in the air before your house catches on fire.

"They are? Where? Can I see them?" I asked eagerly.

Her smile dimmed. "They are in the healing chambers. We can look but can't go in until they're finished."

***

I should have known. There was always a catch with the High Lord of Hell.

The warrior angels were spread out on the healing tables, with what was left of their wings also fanned out from their body in ragged pieces. I could see the bones sticking out, piercing the membrane of their wings and cutting through the bloody feathers. Devros only had one of his left. The other had been hacked off, leaving a mutilated stump. Claw marks marred the beauty of his dark skin, slicing deep towards the bone. They had been butchered, there was no other way to describe it.

"Dear Creator…" I whispered. "Can we rebuild his wings?"

Lycindra looked pale, despite being bathed in the warm crystal glow of the healing chamber. "Yes, eventually we can reconstruct their wings back to their original form. It will take time. Damage of this magnitude…" she trailed off for a few seconds. "I'd be more worried about their emotional state. Time moves differently in the Underworld. They could have been down there for years."

"Years?" I echoed. According to Archangel Michael, they had left for Earth two months ago. Sometime during that period they had been captured.

Rushton was closest to where I stood behind the clear, crystal glass. Strips of skin hung off him like peeling wallpaper, revealing raw flesh underneath. I could see the healing angels carefully place them back, waiting for the crystals to take effect. His face was a swollen mess, but his eyes were closed in deep sleep, thankfully not feeling any more pain. Normally, angels could heal almost instantly as our light regenerated us at incredible speeds. The only exception was if we were hurt by dark energy. Somehow the dark energy made our vibration lower, more physical and dense.

I had seen Rushton a few times in The City of Light. He always had a calm, confidence about him and was a well respected warrior of the Earth Angels. It was hard seeing him like this, so broken and hurt.

I noticed another tall, imposing angel enter the other side of the healing chamber that was also cordoned off by clear crystal. With his dark hair tied back and his sharp, princely features, I recognized him instantly as Raznoul, the unofficial leader of the warrior angels. From the little I knew, he was rumoured to work alone, but Archangel Michael appointed him to assist the warrior angels and they seemed to be following his lead. I could also tell he was very powerful. His aura was similar to the Archangels but lacked the colour that associated them with their temple. He wore very little expression on his face, but I knew he must be taking the condition of one of his own very personally.

I looked over to where Elindara was twitching on the table. There were more than a few female warrior angels, and Elindara was a fierce one. Her once beautiful, long red hair was now shorn off, close to her scalp. Nail marks scored over her cheeks and down the slim column of her neck in harsh red lines. She twisted her head from side to side and moaned, arching her back off the quartz slab. Some of the healers glided over to her and channelled a stronger current of healing energy into her body.

"She has been psychically attacked," Lycindra said, her voice shaky. "Look at her aura, I've never seen anything like it."

Lycindra was right, her aura looked like someone doused acid over a rainbow. Black, gaping holes punctured her energy field in various places, warping colours that normally would have blended beautifully together. As an angel, Elindara would be surrounded by white angelic light, but instead, brown streaks dampened her glow like a layer of thick mud. I didn't have a vast knowledge of healing, but I knew the holes in her aura were openings for other demonic energies to seep through, affecting her spirit and mind.

This was a whole new form of torture.

"He is a monster." My fingers curled into a fist.

"Who?" Lycindra asked. She stared at the warrior angels, unable to look away.

"Lucifer," I swallowed. "He did this."

"He is a Fallen," she said as if that explained everything.

I reached out and touched the glass with my fingertips, watching the angels activate a set of prism-shaped crystals above Devros. "He was one of us in the beginning."

Lycindra sighed. "That was a long time ago, Sandriel. Now he hates us."

"Why?" I asked, not really expecting an answer.

She shook her head. "No one knows, or no one I've talked to."

Something must have twisted Lucifer in such epic proportions to make him torture his own kind in such a malevolent fashion. Maybe I was wrong, and this was a warning to me if I disobeyed him. Or maybe he was hinting at what he had planned for me. He didn't say he wouldn't hurt me. Oh, what a novice I was! I never even thought to negotiate that!

"I wish someone would stop him. I don't understand why the other Archangels don't just go down together and make sure this doesn't happen again."

I sighed, thinking about my conversation with Archangel Michael. "It might not be their destiny."

She turned to look at me, full of sorrow. "Then whose is it? Heaven needs to send somebody."

They sent me. Taking in the scene before me, I felt more and more inadequate for the task.

***

I wanted to rest before my first hour with Lucifer began, so I headed to my chamber in Archangel Michael's temple. It was a space that I used to meditate, relax, or contemplate the lessons we had learned. It was a simple room with a bed and a healing pool of water. The water could also be used to check in on our charges on Earth, but currently, all my assignments were on hold until my current 'project' was finished. I hoped that the rest might reveal more of my past life. If I was going to face Lucifer again, I needed to know more about him, and Nadia was the key.

Resting my head on the soft creamy bedding, I allowed myself to drift off into nothingness…

It was going to storm tonight. I peered up into the sky and noticed the thick, grey clouds rolling above. I shouldn't have been dawdling out by the lake, but then I saw the apple tree, and I knew I could make an apple pie from one of my mother's old recipes to sell at the market tomorrow. I almost had enough to buy a goat, so anything extra would help.

The red apples rolled around in the folds of my dress that I had lifted up to make an impromptu sack. I was indecently exposing my legs, but no one came up this path anymore, not since my parents passed away. It had been two years, and I was finally doing well on my own. Humming softly, I could just see the roof of my cottage over the hill. As the first drops of rain hit my arm, I increased my pace. I might just make it before the storm hit.

Just before I started up the hill, an odd sound behind me made me stop. I paused, then continued to walk, dismissing it from my mind. The noise came again, but louder… a slithering sound…

My intuition kicked in, and I knew without a doubt that something terrifying was behind me. My shoulders tensed, and I gripped my dress tighter until my knuckles turned white. Slowly, I turned around.

At first, my mind couldn't grasp what I saw. It looked like a man, tall and shadowy, except for the large tentacles that were rapidly moving towards me, curling through the grass like snakes.

Demon!

I screamed, and the apples hit the ground, tumbling forward. Spinning around, I almost tripped on the hem of my dress as I ran up the hill as fast as my legs would take me. We had heard about demons and creatures that existed in nightmares, but never in my life did I actually believe they were true! Anything I conjured up in my imagination could not equal the manifestation of horror behind me.

Did I call it to myself? What had I done that was so bad?

Terror gave me speed, and the muscles in my legs shrieked as I pushed them harder.

I wasn't fast enough.

A thick, slimy tentacle wrapped around my waist, and pain exploded as I crashed face first into the ground. I tasted blood. My fingers ripped into the ground as thin needles pierced my flesh beneath the demon's limb. A wave of nausea swept through me, and I felt weak and lethargic. I was dragged over grass and twigs at a rapid pace back towards that thing waiting in the dark. I was going to die, and somehow the most distressing thing that came to mind was not making that apple pie.

Lightning flashed, and the sky wept harder around me. It took a minute before I realised I had stopped moving. The choking grasp around me was loose, and I managed, with effort, to shakily roll over on my back. Lifting my head, I looked around with blurred vision and tried to breathe slowly as my heart struggled to escape from my chest.

There had been no lightning; the light I thought I'd seen was coming from a man, or what I thought was a man. He glowed like a bright star, casting the darkness back into its shadowy corners. Enormous white wings swept out behind him in graceful arches as he moved with a fluidity that wasn't human. I watched as he sliced through the demon with a great golden sword, ducking and weaving around its monstrous limbs. He had severed the tentacle that had been wrapped around me, and the amputated limb had shrivelled like a dying vine. The thing hissed and spat spurts of fluid from its mouth, but nothing touched him. I vaguely wondered if I was dreaming.

One second, the demon was upright, and the next, after a glint of gold, its head left its body. It rolled down the hill in the same direction as my apples.

Exhaustion claimed me. Rain ran down my face, soaking my clothes. I couldn't hold my head up any longer, so I let myself sink back down onto the grass. I was cold; it felt like ice had been injected into my veins and was slowly travelling through my body, leaching all the heat.

Something soft skimmed my leg, and I looked up and saw God.

"Are you God?" At least, that's what I thought I said, but it came out more like a strangled moan.

God kneeled down before me. Dark hair framed eyes that were a shade of blue I had never seen before, like crushed sapphires mixed with twilight. He ran his perfect hand over my face, and I felt a warm hum run over my skin. A flash of surprise flickered in his eyes before I turned my face into his palm, seeking more of his touch. The warmth felt like pure bliss. I could stay like this forever.

Are you going to take me to heaven? I thought.

God smiled, and his beauty was blinding. "No, little one." His voice was musical and lovely. The fact that he could hear my thoughts wasn't strange. This was God.

"I'm not God," the winged man said.

You're not? He shook his head.

What are you?

Warm, cerulean blue eyes looked down at me. "An angel," came the silky reply.

I felt myself being lifted, and then I was in his arms, and the rain touched me no more.

I awoke slowly, the memories settling in my head. It took me a while to separate myself from what I had seen. It was like slowly and carefully peeling back a glove, ensuring the fragile material didn't get damaged in the process.

Not moving, I contemplated my recent memory. Lucifer had once saved me from a demon. I could scarcely believe it. I could still feel the overwhelming fear, then the awe and gratitude when I saw him kneeling over me.

Lucifer… in the old tongue, it meant Bringer of Dawn. Now, ironically, one of his many names was Bringer of Death. As I thought about the warrior angels still healing in Raphael's Temple, I couldn't help but agree.

Nadia once thought he was a God, but I knew what he was now. I wondered at the karmic tie that linked us. What debts did I still owe him, or what did he owe me? We clearly had unfinished business in this incarnation, and I dreaded finding out exactly what that was. No good could come from being linked to Lucifer in any way. But unfortunately, I couldn't put off this meeting any longer.

It was time to see the Devil.

Chapter 4

I entered the meeting hall in Kryptos and immediately thought I was in the wrong place. It looked like the inside of an Arabian Palace. Gone were the black marble floors and dusty torches. Instead, rich tapestries draped the walls in sensual designs, beckoning for a closer inspection. A plush-looking carpet of scarlet and gold flowed beneath my feet, and large, decadent pillows were strewn about in a careless fashion. The scent of honey and cinnamon twined together from long incense sticks, and I felt that if I parted my lips just a little, I could actually taste the flavours on my tongue.

It was a lavish feast for the senses.

Unfortunately, the room's splendour could not compete with the creature within.

Lucifer reclined against one of two ornate couches, holding a jewelled goblet in one hand. He wore loose black pants worked with gold thread and a sleeveless carmine vest embellished with jet buttons. Dark hair brushed a high collar and gleamed in the flickering light. I noticed his ebony wings were hidden, folded into his body. He looked exotic and dangerous. Lucifer had dressed like a Persian Prince and I like a virgin sacrifice.

Mind games. I had just walked in, and the game had already begun.

The fallen angel studied me over the rim of his cup, dark eyes piercing. I already felt the pull towards him, an inexplicable thread connecting us. I attributed this to my visions. How was I supposed to look at him knowing what I knew now? My past had linked us, whether he was aware of it or not. I felt a sense of familiarity, which I knew was incredibly unwise.

You approach the Devil with caution, not camaraderie.

Taking a deep breath, I made my way over to the couches. The God of Darkness had no equals, and sitting opposite him invited me to his level. I would have been less surprised if he gestured for me to sit at his feet amongst the many colourful cushions. Not that I would. Though, if he insisted, what would I say? I doubted many beings said no to Lucifer and survived the experience.

Better to play this game of his and see what he reveals.

He continued to watch me as I sat down opposite him and clasped my hands neatly on my lap. We stared at each other for a few long moments. Fear and anticipation licked their way along my spine.

Finally, I broke the silence. "Why does everything look different?"

His eyes ran slowly over my modest white attire, then to my hands. I struggled not to unclasp them and fidget with my dress. "Because I will it so." His voice was soft, almost relaxed, as if he were trying to put me at ease. My fear went up another notch.

All things were made up of energy. As a result, practically anything could be manipulated and changed to form something new. The continual thought and intention on a formless substance could create. It was another name for 'manifesting.' Some people called it magic, but it was just another Law of the Universe. Those who were more adept at this art could take what was already formed and transform it. Lucifer had recreated a whole chamber. It was another demonstration of his power.

"So, I'm here now." My fingers twitched. There was no point in pleasantries, but did I really want to head straight to the main course?

Lucifer glanced back up at me, and the smile didn't quite reach his eyes. "Yes, yes, you are." It sounded alarmingly like a threat.

He took a sip from his goblet and stretched out his long legs. Heaven knew what was in that thing. It could have been blood or fruit juice. I shifted uncomfortably. He noticed, tracking my movements.

"You sent the warrior angels back, " I narrowed my eyes, "in pieces."

"So I did." His lips curved up at the edge. "Are you not glad they are back, little one?"

Little one. Lucifer used that same phrase in my past. My heart jumped in alarm. Did he know who

I was? "Ahhh..." Distracted, I blinked rapidly. "You *tortured* them."

"I've been known to do that from time to time."

"Why?" I questioned with intensity. Maybe I could finally learn how this all happened. "Why do you hurt them? You were one of them."

The air suddenly chilled, and inky black liquid bled across the tapestries, marring their beauty. The splendour of the place dimmed as if the taint underneath was finally revealed. I froze.

Lucifer looked me straight in the eyes and said quietly, "They displeased me."

Everything stilled, and for a few moments, I hardly dared to breathe. Then I whispered, "You cut off Devros' wing."

A razor edge crept into his voice, and he leaned forward in his seat. "Does he need it back?" Lucifer gestured with his hand.

Energy prickled along my skin, and I saw a flash of light accompanied by the scent of something burning. To the left, something hit the floor. It was bloody and white, and it only took a second to recognise the remains of a large, angelic wing.

"By all means, return it to him."

I shot up straight off the couch. "You–"

"Demon? Beast?" His eyes gleamed red. "I am all those things and more."

My mouth opened and closed. Horror, anger, and fear waged a war within me. They were dangerous emotions, moving me further away from my angelic centre.

"Sit down, Sandriel," he said mildly. A side table manifested before him, and he set his cup down.

"What is wrong with you? How did you end up like this?" The words just flew out of my mouth. "You were *never* this way before!" I shouted at him. In the back of my mind, I knew it was suicidal. In our game of chess, I just hurled my pieces on the floor, but with all the feelings churning inside, a part of me didn't care.

In an instant, Lucifer was before me, a hand tangled in my hair, pulling me close. "How would you know what I was like before?" he asked savagely.

And there it was, that feeling of connection, of familiarity. I wanted to hate him. I wanted… I wanted…

"I… they speak about you in The City of Light." I needed to calm down. Taking another deep breath, I let it out slowly, willing serenity to my mind. Sometimes in the dark, you are your own worst enemy, and I was becoming mine. He was riling me up. Deliberate or not, I was stepping away from what I needed to be.

"And what do they say?" Lucifer purred. Those sensual lips grazed my ear, and I shivered involuntarily. His energy didn't harm, but it bound us together in dark, silky threads. Tensing, I brought my hands up against his chest, preparing to push him away.

"That you used to be good. That you saved people."

The hand in my hair softened, and the other slid across my hip. The hold that he had on me turned slowly into an embrace. His rich scent invaded me, entwining seductively with my thoughts. Fire sparked in his eyes, and I couldn't help but watch the light dance.

"There was once an angel who followed the Light, but he soon realised that the Light was filtered and weak." Lucifer brushed my jaw lightly with his knuckles, "The Dark, though… the darkness was wild and untamed, and it didn't discriminate. So, he turned to the Dark, and the darkness welcomed him warmly." His voice caressed my mind like velvet, and I felt his thumb brush the curve of my lower lip. Shivers of heat spiralled down under my skin, and my eyelids drooped. "The Light was beautiful, but it distracted him with all its colours. The angel didn't realise what was underneath its pretty facade until it was stripped away. Whereas the darkness didn't need to hide. It is what it is… powerful, electrifying, and free. You accept it…" Lucifer kissed the side of my neck and left a sweet, pleasurable burn, "and it accepts you."

Sweet Goddess, give me strength.

"Let go of me, " I whispered.

A trail of heat followed his lips as they continued to skim my throat, finally resting on my pulse. "Are you sure, little angel? I can feel your heart racing. Is that fear you feel?"

Yes. No. "Yes."

I felt his lips curve against my skin, "Liar," he crooned.

"What do you want from me?"

He dropped his eyes to my lips. "Well, I wanted you to sit down, but you seemed rather resistant. Do you find your seat uncomfortable? Perhaps you'd rather share mine?" he asked.

"No," I said abruptly. Then followed it with a, "Thank you."

Amusement softened his features in a stunning way, and I struggled not to stare. I took a step back, and surprisingly he let me go. Hastily, I sat down. I didn't like the look he gave me. Which was worse, having the Devil's anger directed at you or his interest? A sudden thought crossed my mind. He couldn't hear what I was thinking like before, could he? No one knew the extent of the powers Lucifer possessed. When he had become a Fallen, he would have collected a whole new range of abilities. Though, he seemed to have this mind-reading skill before. Maybe he had lost it.

I looked up at him with wide eyes. *You can't hear me, can you? Can you?*

Tendrils of fire burnt the carpet in front of me in swirling patterns. Another flash of light and a golden cup suddenly appeared and floated in front of me. "Drink," he commanded. He lowered himself down to the couch and watched me like a coiled panther. I felt a current of alarm run through my body.

I shook my head. "I'd rather not."

"I said drink," Lucifer said very softly. He picked up his own cup and brought it to his lips.

It was a command, and I tempted fate by still resisting. "Why? What's in it?"

"Why don't you try it and find out?" The air chilled slightly. "If I wanted to harm you, little angel, I wouldn't need a drink to do it."

Well, did I really have a choice? I debated my options, and I didn't seem to have very many. I curled my hand around the goblet, and whatever magic held it up disappeared at my touch. The contents were too dark to make out an actual colour. I looked back at him hesitantly. His face was expressionless. Tentatively, I brought it to my lips and took a sip.

Life exploded along my tongue. I tasted Earth's seasons mixed in with sweetly scented flowers and warm, happy thoughts. I took another sip just to be sure, then stared in amazement.

"It's called Ambrosia. It is supposed to taste different for everyone."

"How did you get it?"

"I killed a God."

I started. "You killed God?"

He bared his teeth. "Not the Creator, little one. That would surely be a feat. There is a race of beings that some humans label as God. They have many interesting things tucked up in their realm."

"I'm drinking something from a dead God?"

"And enjoying it from the looks of things." Lucifer stroked the arm of the couch with his fingers. "You are the only angel that has tasted its sweet delights."

I tilted my head at him. "Except you."

"If you think that, Sandriel, I urge you to look again."

I felt bold. "Why do you deny who you were?"

"I don't indulge in denial. My past is irrelevant." He cast me a wicked look from beneath his lashes. "I could describe some things I would like to indulge in."

I blinked at him. How does one respond to that? "Well… no, that is unnecessary," I replied awkwardly and took another sip of Ambrosia. "Are you going to let the other warrior angels go?" I diverted.

"No."

"Not even if we made another agreement?" So far, this meeting hadn't involved any pain. Perhaps I could endure a few more hours for the release of more warrior angels.

"No," came the silky reply.

"Why not?" I asked curiously.

He smiled savagely. "Because I enjoy their pain." Lucifer looked at my expression and laughed. The beautiful sound was almost mocking in light of what he said.

I glared. "Then why bother releasing the angels I asked for? Why bother with any of this!"

Lucifer leaned forward and rested his forearms on the top of his knees. Power rolled out from him in waves, and I realised how much of himself he had held back to make me comfortable. "Because I was curious... and now I've decided I want something else."

I looked at him again and realised my body couldn't move. Air held me immobile."What are you doing?" I hissed.

The room started to shift, and the Arabian splendour shimmered away. I was back in the obsidian hall with its endless marble floors. The only thing that remained were the couches. The goblet disappeared from my hand, and Lucifer moved in front of me.

As I stared into his dark bottomless eyes, I started to feel myself fade into the darkness.

"You're breaking our deal!" I managed to get out.

"Am I?" he asked. "Perhaps you weren't specific."

The air bonds released me, and I sagged on the couch. I attempted to unfurl my wings, but they only fluttered uselessly. My head rolled back, and my blonde hair slid across my face. Gentle fingers pulled them back and curved the strands behind my ear.

"Did you really think this was how it was going to end, little angel?" the Devil whispered. "Welcome to my world."

Chapter 5

In the darkness of my mind, Nadia called to me...

He was waiting by the apple tree.

"Hi, " I said shyly as I made my way towards him.

I had taken my time getting out here, but the idea of meeting Lucifer in my torn grey dress that I had thrown on while I was sweeping the house was unimaginable. I had taken the time to wash my face and run a brush through my long, auburn hair, so it didn't look like the tangled mane I often saw when I glanced in the mirror. I knew it was completely idiotic to fuss about my appearance in the presence of an angel, especially one that looked like him.

The forest green dress I now wore was one of my best, and I had been told it brought out the colour of my eyes. I imagined Lucifer would be too busy thinking about more important things like the state of the world and how to save souls than the colour of my dress.

I had put it on anyway.

We had met twice now by the apple tree since that night he first saved me. Every time I saw him, the urge to get to know him became stronger and stronger. He had no idea, but he had completely ruined me. I used to find many men handsome and charming, and afterwards a spark of interest would follow me home with thoughts of the future.

Then I met him.

There were moments when we were together when I felt the pieces in my life fit together, like I had only started truly living the day I met him. I had bathed in the glory of the sun, so how could I now live a life by candlelight?

"Nadia."

That voice. I would never get used to that voice. Lucifer leaned against the trunk of the apple tree, his large, white wings out. His open robe highlighted his broad shoulders and framed an enticing expanse of golden skin. How was anyone supposed to concentrate on day-to-day chores with this image floating around in their brain?

I stopped a few feet away from him. "I didn't expect you to be back so soon." *That probably didn't sound right.* "Not that I'm disappointed or anything. I'm happy, glad, that you came." *There I went again, tripping over my tongue and sounding like a complete fool.*

He smiled softly. "How are you feeling?"

"Still drained like before, but manageable." *I tucked some hair behind my ear.*

Lucifer's eyes clouded with concern. "You should be feeling better by now."

I gave him a wry smile. "Considering I almost got eaten by a demon, I feel amazing."

Reaching out with his hand, he curled it lightly around my wrist. He didn't touch me often, but when he did, I could feel the warmth flow right through my body, lighting me up from within. Every part of me was aware of those beautiful fingers. His eyes half closed, and a slight frown appeared shortly after. To my disappointment, he pulled his hand away, but his frown remained.

"Is something wrong?" I asked.

He shook his head, dark hair brushing his shoulders. "You have a lingering residue of dark energy." At the alarm on my face, he hastened to reassure me, "It's not unusual after what you've been through, but I shall watch it just in case."

"Watch it?" I asked curiously. "How are you going to watch it?"

He paused. "I suppose I would need to check in on you from time to time."

My smile bloomed. "That would be lovely!" I sounded too excited. "I mean, nice. That would be nice." I cleared my throat. "Do all humans who have been assaulted by demonic forces get this level of angelic service?"

Another pause.

"No, they don't," he said softly, looking into my eyes.

We stared at each other for a humming moment.

My brain stuttered for a few seconds, then I replied. "Well, I'm very grateful. Should I be worried about them coming back? Is it usual for demons to be on Earth?"

"There is chaos in hell. As a result, the barrier between the Underworld and Earth is weak, and fissions can appear. When that happens, stronger demons can escape."

My eyes widened. "Are you saying there is a demonic hole near my house?"

"There was, but I sealed it with Light."

Oh, well then. I breathed out a sigh of relief. "That's good. It took me a whole week to leave my house. I don't want to lock myself back in there."

"You have nothing to fear, Nadia," Lucifer said with such calm confidence that I had to believe him.

He was going to check in on me! I suppressed the urge to dance, as now was not exactly the most appropriate time. I could dance later in my cottage. How could I not feel like the luckiest female alive? He also implied that he didn't check on people very often. Did that mean anything? Of course it didn't mean anything! He is an angel who works for Heaven, and you work at a food stall.

A slight smile graced Lucifer's lips. What was he smiling at? I smiled back.

"So, do you talk to God?"

He laughed. "Yes, I talk to the Creator often, little one."

For some reason, Lucifer had taken to calling me 'little one.' I suppose I was by comparison. I kind of liked it. It sounded affectionate. Dare I even say... endearing? Though, I probably would have liked anything he called me. He could have called me 'chair' and I'd be overjoyed.

Fascinated, I moved closer. "What does he sound like?"

"The Creator is not a He."

I stepped back in shock. "The Creator is a She?"

He shook his head again, amusement lighting his face. "The Creator is neither He nor She, though sometimes we use those terms interchangeably. The Creator is just pure energy. Pure love."

I wrinkled my nose. "Energy? What is that?"

"Energy is everything. Everything is made up of energy."

I looked at him, confused.

"The Creator is everywhere, in everything. In the wind, in the trees, the light of the sun, in the animals, in everything."

Putting a hand on my hip, I stared at him. "So when you said you talked to God, did you mean you talked to the trees and the animals?"

Lucifer smiled again. "No, I can talk to God by meditating or just centering myself. The Creator is also inside me." A warm breeze tickled my skin. "In you, too, little one.

"So, I can talk to God."

He nodded.

Interesting. I talked to myself often – in fact, on a regular basis – but never once did I hear a response. I intended to question him further on the topic, but a beautiful red apple caught my eye, hanging an arm's length away. I caught hold of it and pulled it off the tree. He watched me as I took a bite.

After I swallowed the juicy piece, I spoke. "Do angels eat?"

Still watching me, he replied softly. "Sometimes, if they have been on Earth long enough. Then they develop a craving."

"Have you eaten an apple before?"

He shook his head.

He had never tasted an apple? Apples were my favourite. I stepped closer to him, stretched out my hand, and offered the apple. "Do you want to try?"

Lucifer's eyes trailed down my arm to the glossy, red fruit. After a moment, he cupped his hand over mine and brought the apple to his lips. With my hand still in his, he took a slow bite, chewed, and swallowed. The warm, golden connection between us intensified. We were inches apart, close enough for me to see the glimmer of juice on his bottom lip. Utterly entranced, my breath tangled in my lungs. Surely, he was God's most beautiful creation. Without conscious thought, almost as if I lost any will of my own, I leaned up, bringing our faces closer.

Then I blinked and stopped. By the spirits, what was I doing? I blinked up at him, mortified. I can't believe I almost...

I started to pull back, but warm, sure fingers touched me under my chin, pulling me closer. When I was lost in the warm, drowning blue of his eyes, he kissed me. Lips *caressed mine with a slow sweetness, and I was undone. He explored the curve of my lips with his, and learned its texture and shape as if he had all the time in the world. He tasted like apples and sunlight, and the combination was so potent and addictive that I wanted to roll in it. Drown in it. I trembled from the maelstrom of sensations he created within me. I never wanted it to end, yet I wanted it to stop just so it could begin again.*

When he finally pulled back, I was left reeling. Cerulean blue eyes looked down at me with a curious wonder.

A thumb brushed my cheek. "I should go," he said softly.

I nodded dumbly.

The smile he gave me transformed his face into a work of art. He stepped away and opened up his glorious, white wings.

"By the way," came the smooth, silken voice. "Your dress is lovely."

My mouth dropped open.

Lucifer's voice caressed my mind. ~ You think very loudly. ~

He flexed his wings and launched into the sky. I stared after him until his form got smaller, and I couldn't see him anymore.

"Did that really happen?" I murmured over the erratic beat of my heart. I touched my fingers to my lips dreamily. "I just got kissed by an angel."

My other hand was still holding the apple we had both eaten. I brought it to my mouth and ate some more, closing my eyes and savouring the taste.

I was never going to look at apples the same way again.

***

I woke to the taste of apples and sunshine still lingering on my lips. Smiling, I stretched my arms out on the soft bedding under me and opened my eyes.

Reality hit me like an arctic splash of water.

I was in a room with glowing walls. It seemed to be made of dark stone but with flecks of light embedded within, casting the room in a muted golden glow. From where I was lying, I could see a table in the far corner with a tray of food and a large silver pitcher.

Where in the Heavens was I? Or was I even in Heaven? That was a terrifying thought.

I felt him before I saw him. As soon as I was aware of that electric current running along my skin, I knew. Turning my head slowly to the right, I saw Lucifer sitting on an armchair next to the bed. The strange, golden lights played along his form, unveiling him from where he would have been concealed in the shadows. It seemed the Prince of Darkness had been waiting for me to wake up.

"Pleasant dreams, little angel?" Heat layered his voice like hot coals.

Sitting up cautiously, I moved across the midnight sheets towards the edge of the bed on the other side of him. "Where am I, Lucifer?"

He smiled slowly. "Where do you think?"

I paused with one foot off the bed. *Oh, please, no. Please, please, please, no...* "I'm in Hell! You brought me to Hell!"

"To my realm in Hell."

I took a deep breath and looked around. This wasn't the fiery pit I imagined. My hands tightened into fists as I stood up. "Take me back. Now. This wasn't our deal."

"Now, why would I do that when we haven't completed our bargain?" He gestured casually with his hand. "I've held up my end, you have yet to hold up yours."

"Coming to Hell wasn't in the deal!"

Lucifer's voice purred out."Hmm, yes… a pity."

I glared at him. It wasn't *not* in the deal, either. I had already established I was a terrible negotiator. "And once my fifteen hours are up?"

"Well, then, you are free to go," he replied magnanimously.

I narrowed my eyes. I might not know the multifarious ways his mind worked, but I knew it was never going to be that simple. "So you will take me back?"

He smiled again, and this time the effect was frightening. Lucifer stood up and eclipsed the room with his sheer presence. "Do I look like your transport service?" he crooned.

I gestured wildly with my hand. "So how then am I supposed to get back?"

"There is a portal in my home that can transport you to the centre of Hell. From there, you can make your way to the Underworld. If you get lost, I'm sure Hades can point you in the direction of Earth."

My jaw worked. "You can't do this."

"I already have."

He turned, and the wall opened before him like a black hole. Turning his head to look back at me once more, he said, "By the way, little angel, I'd be careful of the Dragarth if I were you."

Fury burned brightly within me. "What is the Dragarth?" I spat out.

As I said that, the wall suddenly rippled, curving like an enormous snake. Something sinister rolled under the surface along the circumference of the room before sliding back beneath its depths. I stepped back in alarm.

Lucifer's smile flashed like lightning before the black hole he stepped through consumed him.

I was left in my dungeon.

Chapter 6

Time stretched endlessly as I sat and contemplated my predicament. I tried not to let the feeling of hopelessness overwhelm me, as the realisation that I was in Hell finally settled past my skin, down to the depths of my bones.

What in the Heavens was I supposed to do now? Eventually, I stood up and paced around my deceptively comfortable room, making sure I stayed as far away as I possibly could from the walls. The serpentine creature lurking within hadn't emerged again, but I wasn't taking any chances.

My own naivety had been my undoing. I had been ridiculously unprepared to engage with Lucifer from the start. Though, now I knew why Archangel Michael had sent me. What did he expect me to do? Just because I had been infatuated with Lucifer in my past didn't mean I could change him now.

Was that even possible? For aeons, he had terrorised the angels and a host of other beings. His malevolent ripple of darkness infected everything it touched. The burgeoning taint had risen from Hell, rolled like a dark mist through the underworld, and found its way to the surface of Earth. The angels could see the effect Lucifer had on humans, and despite their influence, his song of darkness found many ears.

Lucifer couldn't control men's minds or make them do bad things. People were responsible for their own actions, and their choices were their own. Though, the ones who were fascinated with the dark, who opened up their senses to nighttime's lullaby and embraced their lower desires of ego and self, left an echo of invitation. And it was the Devil that answered.

Those who were predisposed to power, greed, and violence became more ambitious in their grapple for glory. It was a gentle guidance towards their own destruction. He was an unrivalled seducer and a master of manipulation. Those who crossed his path were never the same again.

I, too, had crossed his path a very long time ago. What did that say about me? "But he was different then," I said aloud.

Is that why you kissed him? my inner voice whispered.

Oh yes, that. I'd been unsuccessfully trying to forget the way it had felt. "So," I threw up my hands. "That doesn't have to mean anything." That was Nadia. That was her feelings and her thoughts. It didn't have to be mine.

Are you so sure? my mind countered. *Maybe you don't want to admit it.*

"Admit what?" I knew I was talking to myself, but at the moment, I didn't want to look too closely at that.

That he might have left an imprint on you, too. You know you feel a pull towards him.

I tensed, not happy about where my thoughts were going. "He's Lucifer. That's just him. It's his..." I made circles with my hands.

Seductiveness?

"No!" Appalled at the first word that came to mind, I scrambled for another. "His... his..."

Magnetism?

"His energy!" I finally said, exasperated. "It's just his energy." I crossed my arms over my chest.

He affects you more than that, and you're starting to think you affect him just as much.

Lucifer had been acting completely different from what I had heard about him. No one had managed to bargain with him before. Yet, despite my horrid attempt, he had indulged me. Instead of physically harming me, he had chosen the path of seduction. Instead of throwing me in a torture chamber, he had locked me in his home. This, of course, could change in an instant, but so far, his behaviour was unusual.

Somehow Archangel Michael believed I was his weakness.

"Even if that was true," I implored the imaginary image of my Archangel teacher, "look where I am now. I have achieved nothing."

The silence of my mind spoke again. *You know better. Where there is a will, there is a way. Stop seeing the improbable and start looking for the possible.*

I cast my gaze around the sparse but comfortable quarters. The floor was smooth, polished, and made out of an unfamiliar black stone. It was so shiny it looked like liquid, almost as if I was walking on water. I stomped my foot against the surface. I was getting paranoid, but images of me sinking through the floor flashed in my head. Who knew what was in this house of horrors?

There were also no windows and no door. Lucifer had left through a gaping black hole.

"Ok, Sandriel. Anything is possible, right?" I called a ball of white Light to my palm. Its purity seemed vastly out of place, and I noticed the size of the Light was smaller than normal. I guess being in a realm within Hell seemed to be having an effect.

Steeling myself, I crept towards the spot he had left. I was very, very concerned about the creature inside these walls. The Dragarth, Lucifer called it. Who knew what it was capable of and, more importantly, what would set it off? The ball of light energy might not inflict much damage, but it was my only protection. Very carefully, I placed my right hand against the wall where Lucifer had left, then jumped back a few good feet.

Nothing happened.

I let out a huge breath.

That was good. Touching the wall didn't seem to set off the Dragarth. Slightly more at ease, I moved back and examined the spot. It wasn't warmer than the rest of the wall, and it didn't seem to have any grooves, ridges, or anything else unusual about it.

I chucked my ball of Light at it.

I saw a ripple in the wall, moving fast. I scrambled back, bringing up another ball of white energy. The current made its way sinuously around the perimeter of my quarters before once again disappearing from sight.

I clutched my hand over my chest.

Ok, don't try that again unless I have to.

I let my light dissipate. Frowning, I backed up towards the table in the far corner of the room. I distractedly grabbed a fruit off the platter as I studied the wall. As I brought it to my lips, I almost dropped it when I realised what I had unconsciously selected. I glared at the apple in my hand.

"Not going there again," I muttered and dropped it back into the bowl.

Then it dawned on me. I was feeling hungry. This place was lowering my vibration, making my body denser and more connected to its needs and desires. I pushed the platter further away from me. It would probably be best to hold out as long as I could. The pitcher on the table caught my eye. I stared at it for a few moments, then finally gave into my curiosity and poured some liquid into a silver chalice. The drink was a familiar, dark colouring.

Ambrosia. Was this Lucifer's idea of a joke? I put the pitcher back down and moved the chalice to the other side of the table.

I still couldn't believe he had brought me here. I rubbed my forehead with my fingertips, remembering his touch before I blacked out. If he wanted me here, why didn't he just take me from the very beginning? Why bother to go through the elaborate display of changing the hall into a sumptuous Arabian...

The realisation hit me hard enough that I gripped the edge of the table in response. Lucifer changed the environment by manipulating energy! I gave an assessing glance around the room. What if I tried something similar? I hadn't had a reason to bend energy to my will before, but it didn't mean I couldn't do it. There was also the danger of the Dragarth, but if I didn't take the chance, who knew how long I'd be stuck here? The longer I stayed, the more this realm would have an effect on me.

Excited by my plan, I moved in front of the golden, flecked wall again. I should try something simple. Placing my fingertips against the surface, I closed my eyes.

Manipulating energy was essentially a state of mind. Everything in the Universe was made up of energy. There was nothing different between the table and the floor, except the arrangement of energy particles and vibration. Everything was an illusion, a creation of intention and belief. Even this wall.

I asserted my will and imagined that the surface beneath my fingertip was soft and pliable like dough. I created the feeling in my mind of the surface shifting and changing, and my fingers sinking slowly into the wall like quicksand.

After a few moments, I opened my eyes and jerked. My hand was in the wall.

Pulling my hand out slowly, the wall rippled then settled back to its solid state. I stared at my hand and flexed my fingers. It tingled.

A huge smile broke out over my face. I clapped my hands together in glee. "I did it!"

I let myself bask in my success for a few seconds, then calmed myself down. There was a huge risk of not knowing what was on the other side. I might end up in a place a thousand times worse than this room. But what else could I do? I couldn't exactly wait for Lucifer to come back and ask him to let me go. How long did he plan to keep me here? No, right now, he didn't know I could leave. This might be my only opportunity to escape.

Resolved, I tried again. When my hand passed through the surface, I kept going, going, and going until my face and the rest of my body sunk into the wall. I felt cold, chilled… then…

I was in a long, dark hallway. Crimson drapes hung from the wall in sections on either side of me. I turned my head and saw the solid wall I had come from.

Well now… this wasn't so bad.

It was eerily quiet as I walked across the smooth, liquid floor. At the end of the hall was a set of elaborately carved double doors that seemed to be made out of dark wood. I peered a little closer at the designs. There were angels carved in the sides, fighting battles with demons and violently losing. I shook my head. If the rest of this place was going to follow a similar theme I might as well get used to it now.

I pushed open the doors and prayed they didn't creak. They opened smoothly to an opulent lounge room. It was also sensually designed with black velvet chaises and gilded gold mirrors all along one wall. There were several enormous, golden statues of hands with claws tipping the ends, starting from the floor and reaching two thirds of the way to the ceiling. Within the claws danced reddish blue flames in an unholy rhythm. On either side of the room I noticed another set of double doors.

This wasn't the decor I imagined Lucifer having. With all the stories I heard about him, I almost expected a throne made out of bones. Well, I hadn't exactly explored the rest of the place, so I couldn't rule that out yet. This wasn't as elaborate as the Arabian setting but it definitely had a lavish elegance about it.

As I moved around the lounges, the mirrors caught my eye. Instead of casting my reflection back at me, they looked cloudy, like fine mist swirling beneath the glass.

"Now, what is this?" I inched closer.

The mirrors, two head spans taller than me, were also four times my width. Their frames were beautiful, spiralling out with swirling designs and inlaid with stones and carved symbols. Hesitantly, I reached out and touched the surface of the mirror closest to me. The mist beneath the glass glowed white before parting to reveal an image within.

It looked like the inside of a cave. A very peculiar cave that had stairs leading down into the inky darkness.

Interesting.

My curiosity piqued, and I moved to the next one.

When the mist parted from the second mirror, my eyes widened as I saw the hall. It was my meeting place with Lucifer.

"Dear Goddess… these are portals!" Hope fired within me in a blazing inferno. I could escape!

Emboldened by my discovery, I cast a quick look around me. Lucifer could emerge from his hellish activities at any moment.

It was almost too easy, and that should have tipped me off. Unfortunately, my desire for escape muted my rational mind.

I raised my right hand and flexed my fingers. "Ok, I can do this." Reaching out, I touched the glass and watched my fingers go through. It was much easier this time. I wasn't manipulating reality, I was just accessing what was already there.

I was so absorbed with what I was doing I didn't see the Dragarth until it was too late.

The wall bent out, and something large, scaly, and covered in razor spines snapped out of the wall and hit me. I flew through the air and crashed into a solid table, toppling it over and smashing the glass goblets and pitcher. Pain stabbed through me as shattered glass pierced my skin. I moaned, shocked. This was the first time in my angelic incarnation that I had experienced severe pain. I didn't like it.

A hissing sound snapped my dazed mind to attention. Dear God, it had three heads. Black scales obstructed my vision of the mirrors, and red eyes stared at me with intense hatred. The Dragarth was an enormous three-headed snake with spikes. One of the snake heads hissed at me again, and the other darted forward and back, its forked tongue flickering in a rapid motion. The last one opened its jaws and revealed sharp fangs dripping with a yellowish substance.

Wonderful, just wonderful.

Blood coated my hands as I pulled myself up into a sitting position. When my leg didn't move properly, I suspected it was broken. I didn't know how long it would take to heal, but I wasn't going to wait. The glass tinkled as I moved through it, inching my way to the set of double doors behind me. I generated a ball of white Light in my hand, just in case. One of the serpents' heads looked at it with interest and moved closer.

Oh, please don't.

I knew if I threw my Light, it could just enrage it further. It was a couple of metres from me by the time I reached the door. With a speed born of self-preservation, I hauled myself up on one leg and slammed the doors open.

Immediately, I wanted to go back out and face the killer three-headed serpent with my tiny mothball of light.

I was in Lucifer's bedroom.

He was standing and talking to another creature out of someone's nightmare. A demon. Its horns arched high above its head, and I could see serrated teeth lining a vicious-looking mouth. Muscles bunched onto muscles in grotesque shapes, and the ridges on its face moulded a hideous set of features. The demon stared at me with black, bottomless eyes, and the evil in them made me shiver with fear.

And yet, I was still more terrified of the fallen angel that turned his head slowly towards me.

"Angel," he said with terrible softness.

Movement caught his eye behind me, and he moved his head slightly in a dismissive gesture. There was a slithering sound, another tinkle of glass, and then nothing. I didn't dare turn my head away. He had been here the whole time.

The demon growled at me with hunger. "Annngggeelll....." its voice grated out. Its claws flexed, and it lunged towards me. Then it froze and was lifted in the air like a child. The demon flailed its arms, still desperate to get near me. Suddenly, it howled with such pain that it made what I was feeling equivalent to a bee sting.

Lucifer's voice coiled out with deadly power. "Oh, no, Volac, that one is mine." A black hole opened up beneath him, and whatever magic was holding the creature vanished. Still screaming in agony, it dropped into the abyss. I watched as the floor became smooth once again.

Now I had his full attention. His beautiful face revealed nothing as he took in my appearance. I realised I was dripping blood on his floor.

"I'm sorry, " I stuttered. "I think I got lost."

I turned to flee, and the double doors slammed closed in my face.

His voice was smokey and dark. "You came in here, little angel, and now you have to stay."

Chapter 7

My back stiffened, and the fragments of glass pierced further into my skin. Sucking in a breath, I turned to face my captor.

The Ruler of Hell stared back at me with those fathomless dark eyes. He looked like a barely tamed barbarian with his hair tied back and his muscled, bronzed chest gleaming in the firelight. Loose black pants sculptured over long legs, leaving his feet bare.

It was hard to gauge his mood. Was he going to portray the elegant host as he had on previous occasions? Or the savage warlord I could see smouldering beneath? Either way, this was his domain, and the rules could be held or obliterated in his hands.

Out of all the rooms in this God-forsaken place, I had to pick this one. The irony was not lost on me.

Now that my escape route was blocked, I couldn't help but notice how spectacular it looked. Fire ran across the walls in grooves casting the room in a sensual glow. There was a large ornate mirror against one side of the wall that broke the line of fire, just like the ones in the lounge room. Another portal to an unknown destination.

A large four-poster bed was the centrepiece, draped with similar black sheets as the one in my room. The bed alone was surprising since I couldn't imagine him laying there meditating or contemplating the mysteries of the Universe. Angels didn't need to sleep, but perhaps this realm, with its denser vibration, induced one to feel the need to slumber.

Or he could be doing something else entirely on that bed, my mind supplied helpfully. I fought the urge to smack myself in the head.

Above the bed was one of the most beautiful works of art that I had ever seen. A dome made out of stained glass and crystal fragments arched high above the ceiling. It was an elaborate mandala that drew the eye and captivated your attention with its array of jewelled colours. The design was intricate and flawless, and I imagined the view would be even more impressive if lying in the centre of the bed.

It was such an odd thing for Lucifer to possess. This was something beautiful, something that appealed to my higher awareness, and he had it in his inner sanctum. If this Fallen Angel could appreciate such a wonder, did that mean he was capable of something greater? Did he yearn for his former days?

"Come here," he said softly.

Fear churned sickly in my stomach. Was he going to punish me? I did try to escape. I opened my mouth to quickly apologise, then stopped. No, I wasn't going to apologise. "Why?" I asked instead, my jaw set.

I felt myself being lifted and pulled towards him. Instinctively, I started to pull my wings out, but the burning sensation in my back stopped me. The straps of my dress crossed at the back so my wings could have room to come out if needed. If they had been out, they would have buffeted most of the shattered glass. Unfortunately, I had pulled them in.

Lucifer set me down in front of him and closed his hands around my upper arms. I caught that scent again, dark and intoxicating. Hunger stirred, with a different bounty in mind. I wrestled with the feeling and forced it back down. Barely.

"You tried to leave." His voice was deceptively mild.

I tilted my chin up. "Of course. What else did you think I was going to do?"

His lips curved. "I warned you about the Dragarth."

"So you did," I acknowledged.

Lucifer released one of my arms, and I felt his fingertips run down the centre of my back. Sharp, needle points of pain followed the path he made. I gritted my teeth and tried not to flinch. He drew his fingers back, and I could see them covered in blood.

Lucifer shook his head at me, the smile still faintly on his lips. "Foolish angel."

Power wrapped around me, and I found myself moving past him towards the bed.

I panicked. "What are you doing?"

"Assisting you," came the smooth voice.

"I don't need your assistance."

"I think that's up to perspective, little one."

The bed loomed closer, and I noticed the posters adjoined to the bed frame were carved snakes entwined intimately together. I tried to look behind me. "I can heal on my own." Panic seeped slowly in.

"But how will you remove the glass to do so?"

Well, yes, that would be difficult. "I... I..." I was lowered onto the bed face down against the cool, black sheets. Immediately, I tried to push myself back up, but a firm hand pressed me down by the back of my neck. I had to turn my head, so I could still breathe. "Let me go, Lucifer."

The bed dipped on either side of my hips, and that dark scent drifted tantalisingly closer. "I was surprised you made it out of your room at all." The warm weight of my hair left my back.

"What? I... I just moved through the wall." Could I use my Light and blast him off me?

"It's not a skill many angels possess." Lucifer's voice caressed the side of my face with a touch of heat.

I lost my train of thought. "What's not–"

His hands took a leisurely course down either side of my back. "Manipulating energy. It's not a common skill." Warmth penetrated my skin in a lazy wave, loosening my muscles and making me sink deeper into the bed. It was like I had laid outside during the afternoon sun for an hour. I could barely feel the pain, just a slow, comfortable heat.

"It's not?" I should be stopping him. What was he doing? Taking out the glass. He must be taking out the glass. That was alright. Wasn't it?

"No. Neither is using Light." His voice had turned soft and soothing like it was enveloped in a smoky haze. His fingers ran along the length of my back, stopping here and there.

I frowned slowly as I struggled to register his words. "It isn't?"

A husky laugh. "Didn't your City of Light tell you? Angels have elemental abilities; fire, wind, water, and earth. A select few can use more than one, and even less can use Light."

This was news to me. "You used to. You used to use Light."

Lips brushed a hot trail down the back of my neck. My eyes widened in shock. Pleasure flared in response, winding tightly within me, aching for release. "I used to be many things, little angel," he murmured against my skin. "Now I'm so much better." Lucifer captured my hands on the bed on either side of my head, entwining our fingers together. I could feel him leaning over me, the smooth planes of his chest just barely brushing my back.

"What are you doing?" I managed to get out.

"What do you want me to do?" he purred.

"Release me?"

Lucifer's lips played along the sensitive skin behind my ear. "That's a question, little angel. One that even you're not sure of." His husky voice brushed down my spine like sensual fur.

My resistance was weakening from the onslaught of earthly pleasure I had never experienced before and the haunting familiarity. It was a heady combination that threatened to overwhelm me. "It's not like I can stop you. If you want something, you'll take it." I gasped out.

"Does it make you feel better to think I'd force you? You think you can hide behind your virtue and convince yourself I took something you had no intention of giving. That you could never want, desire, *need* something as unholy as me. You would shake your head and say the Light couldn't possibly crave the Dark." With ease, Lucifer turned me over, and I was slammed with his cruel beauty, that stunning face and form edged with shadows. His hands wrapped around my wrists, and his midnight eyes locked on mine. "I don't need to force you. I know desire, little angel. I can recognise it in its basest, purest form. You can dress it up and call it what you like. You can hide it from yourself, but you can't hide it from *me*."

As the energy sizzled between us, I stared at him.

"Maybe you're right," I finally said. "I might feel it, but I don't have to act on it."

"Why? Afraid you'll like it?" The muscled length of his thigh slid between my legs. He watched my face as he did it, capturing every shift and nuance of expression.

"No," I said, barely managing to keep my voice even. My pulse rocketed out of control. "But I would regret it."

A subtle shift, a slight press forward, and I was on fire. My eyes involuntarily closed, then opened. "Regrets are for those who don't take responsibility for their actions," his voice stroked the flames higher.

Drowning. I was drowning. I had to do something. Sandriel, think of something before you do something utterly insane! "Negotiate!" I said loudly. Too loudly. I tried to lower the decibels. "Let's negotiate."

Lucifer paused. His sensual lips quirked up. "Oh, I'm all ears."

"Stop trying to seduce me, and I will... I will... halt my attempts to escape for now." Oh yes, reveal your mind-blowing negotiating skills.

He laughed. "You can try to escape all you want, little angel. Though, the Dragarth might decide to take a bite next time." Amusement simmered in his eyes, but I wasn't sure he was joking. If the Dragarth took a bite out of me, I'd be gone.

"How about this," his voice dipped low and silky. "I'll let you leave this room if you stop resisting yourself for one minute."

I frowned. "What do you mean resisting myself?"

"You are trying to tell yourself how you should feel." His gaze dropped to my lips. "Instead, just feel."

"No..." I said slowly. "I know who you are."

"How fortunate. I'm honoured."

"This is just another one of your elaborate manipulations."

"I would hardly call it elaborate."

"You didn't deny it was a manipulation."

"Did I need to?"

I huffed out a breath, dislodging a few strands of hair that had fallen on the side of my face. "No. The answer is no."

"Well then," he purred and stretched out my arms higher above my head. "You best make yourself comfortable. Perhaps I shall make these your quarters? I'm sure we'll get to know each other very well."

He wasn't serious... was he? "You're lying."

His expression cooled. "Am I?"

I glared at him. "Fine. Then I'm free to leave."

"This room, you're free to leave this room. Is that a deal?"

"Yes, but–"

He stopped my words with his lips. It wasn't with the sweet, gentleness of his past, it was with the raw, flaming inferno of his present. He kissed me with impatience and a hint of anger. Then slowly, those feelings changed, rolled into a stormy whirlpool of lust. My words died in my mouth. I forgot what I was saying. I forgot my name. He demanded with his lips, pressing me into the bed with such heat I forgot to breathe. My world narrowed to his mouth and the devastating things it was doing. His tongue was a lash of fire, and I wanted more. I kissed him back with the same raging fire and felt a moment of relief. Of not having to deny anything at all.

Something unlocked within me, and I knew him. Feelings I didn't understand surfaced like forgotten landscapes beneath the ocean. I knew this angel like I knew the deepest part of myself. I had kissed this mouth a thousand times, felt the silken steel of his skin as if it was my own. Where had he gone?

Lucifer, my mind whispered his name with such sorrow I tore my lips away with an aching pain.

A beast stared back at me with hellfire blazing in his eyes. This was not the angel I had known. This creature before me was a nightmare, a collection of horrors sent to torment the world. Dangerous, merciless, and cruel, he would use whatever weapon he had to break me and relish in the experience.

A chaotic jumble of emotions swirled beneath my skin, but I gripped them hard, holding them tight to me. "I believe my minute is up." My breathing was harsh. "We made a deal."

The Devil released my wrist and eased back, a dangerous expression on his face. "So we did."

As he moved, the mandala came into view. I was speechless. "It's beautiful. How can you have something so beautiful?" I whispered, distraught.

Lucifer's expression shuttered, his tone dismissive. "Go, little angel. Your window of opportunity is closing."

I didn't hesitate. Barely holding onto my sanity, I left.

Chapter 8

I didn't know how I managed to make it back down the hallway towards my room. My leg had healed marginally. The pain of walking on it could not eclipse the storm of emotions thundering through me. They swelled and rolled like a turbulent sea, threatening to take me under with them. I braced my hand against the wall that led to my room, almost buckling under the strain. My hair fell forward around my face as I took a shuddering breath in.

"Come on, come on," I whispered hoarsely. Tears slipped down my skin, and I desperately tried to reign them in. I attempted to merge my hand with the wall, but failed. Tried again. Failed. I slapped my hand against the surface so hard it stung. "Come on!" Gritting my teeth, I forced myself to concentrate. The wall gave. I slipped through.

As soon as I was inside my knees hit the floor. I wrapped my arms around myself and cried. Pain flooded through me, so strong I felt torn inside. It wasn't a physical wound, but an emotional one. An ancient wound that had been buried so deep, it had never fully healed. Another woman's emotions, another woman's agony. I cried, hot tears running down my face. I cried, not fully understanding why I cried, but simply that I had to.

Emotions battered at me. Anger, grief, heartache, and loss were fists pounding their way out of my skin. It all centred around him. Lucifer.

I gripped my head. "Who am I!"

The memory grabbed, pulled...

He was in pain. Oh, he was in so much pain. I would have done anything, anything for him, but I could not fix this. I could feel his silent screams, his turbulent rage, and knew others would be able to feel it soon. They would come for him. He was not safe. I would have gone to him, but this body would not obey my will. The darkness that seeped through my veins was both alien and terrifying. It was a battle for my soul. A battle I was losing.

I snapped out of the memory like a rubber band, still clutching my head. It was the same one as before, yet now it made even less sense. What battle for my soul? My head throbbed dully. Sitting back on my heels, I rubbed my forehead then wiped away the tear stains from my face. I felt like I was going insane.

If I had been asked a short while ago who I was, I would have been able to answer with a firm certainty. I was an angel in Archangel Michael's temple who guided mortals towards their highest purpose. I loved watching the muses inspire artists and writers to create incredible things. I appreciated my conversations with Lycindra on healing and energy in her healing chambers, and one of my favourite things to do was to fly high above The City of Light and marvel at its beauty and peacefulness.

Now, that foundation had been shaken.

My past was mixing with my future. It was a past I couldn't begin to understand and a part of me didn't want to. What good would come from knowing my life had been entwined with the Prince of Darkness? He had clearly meant something to me and that, quite simply, was terrifying. What angel would want to be associated with Lucifer? I couldn't trust myself. I couldn't trust these feelings that I didn't have any context for. They were clouding my mind, making me linger where I shouldn't.

Pushing myself up off the floor, I sat down gingerly on the edge of the bed. I had to get out of here. I had to find a way. If I stayed any longer, I would go mad.

My leg throbbed and I realised that, before another escape plan could be hatched, I needed to make sure I could move. Closing my eyes, I sensed the area of my leg that was causing me pain. Intuitively, I knew the broken bone was still healing, and without seeing my leg I could tell there was swelling and bruising. I was surprised that was the extent of my injuries. The pain had been shocking. I was still getting used to all these new feelings. Peace had been all I had known and now I seemed to be experiencing a range of the opposite.

Using a technique that Lycindra taught me, I weaved green and white Light together in my mind and channelled it through to my leg. Green was the colour of healing and was commonly used with a number of crystals to repair emotional and physical injuries. Combined with the purity of white Light, it made a powerful healing conduct. My abilities weren't as strong in this realm, but eventually my bones knitted together. I reached out my senses to the wounds on my back and was surprised to discover nothing remained. Lucifer *had* taken out the glass... maybe the cuts weren't that deep?

Reaching my hand back, I touched the smooth skin. My fingers slowly travelled up the back of my neck, and across the side of my check to linger lightly on my lips. They tingled.

That familiar feeling shifted through the cracks in my mind. I shook my head. Yes, it was time to leave.

I sat on the bed facing the wall, watching how the golden threads of light played across the room. What could I do? What were my options? Minutes dragged into hours, but slowly an idea started to form, then steadily began to take root. Holding out my hand, I let a ball of Light manifest about the size of my palm. It swirled in different directions, brightening further when I added more power to it.

Then I hurled it at the wall in front of me.

It only took a few seconds.

The ripple came from my right. The Dragarth moved with deadly speed within the wall until it hit the spot where my Light had touched, then disappeared.

My lips curved up in a grim smile. "You're stronger than me... but are you faster?"

Time would tell. I couldn't enact my plan now as there was a strong chance Lucifer was still in residence. It would have to wait until he left. I knew there would be no chance of escaping if he was around.

My stomach rumbled and I gave in to my hunger and got something to eat from the table. I sampled some grapes and devoured a peach, scrupulously avoiding the apple. My hunger momentarily satisfied, I crawled across the bed and curled in the centre amongst the dark pillows. Their softness enveloped me, and I let out a sigh.

My emotions had drained me and I longed for the sweet release of sleep. Even as I felt myself slip away, I knew my dreams would haunt me.

"It wasn't my intention to spy on you while you were having your bath." I blushed furiously, desperate to explain. *"I mean, I know I was crouching in the bush and it must have looked like I had been there a long time..."* I glanced up at him where he was leaning against the tree.

Did he look mad? I couldn't tell. He had a curious expression on his face I couldn't quite decipher. I could tell he hadn't completely dried off from his dip in the lake. Oh God, stop ogling him! It's not helping your case! "I just saw you flying above and thought I'd come out and see you." I shifted my eyes to the right and gestured with my hands. "And then I saw you..."

Lucifer looked down, smiled, then raised his eyes back up at me.

"Are you... are you mad?" I asked. My heart clenched painfully. I didn't think I could have handled it if I had made him angry.

He shook his head. "No." The sun had just dipped below the horizon and twilight cast soft shadows around us. "I knew you were there."

My eyes rounded. "You did? The whole time?"

"Yes, I could sense you." His smile grew as he reached out and plucked some crushed leaves from my hair.

Flustered, I couldn't immediately think of what to say. Did he want me to spy on him? I blinked, confused.

When I didn't say anything, Lucifer continued, "It's getting late. You should head home."

"Oh, yes." I was feeling tired. It was strange because I had woken up later than usual this morning and had to rush with all my chores. While drying out some clothes, I had seen a flash of white and a hint of feathers trailing across the sky and landing not too far from me. I couldn't contain the rush of nervous pleasure. After the day that Lucifer kissed me by the apple tree, I could think of little else.

Would he do it again? Maybe it was an experiment? Maybe he just wanted to see what it would feel like. Maybe I'm just a complete utter fool. Lightning never strikes in the same place twice. He's an angel and you're the lump on the ground. Vast difference.

I nervously brushed off any excess dirt from the sides of my dress. "Well, I better go. It was nice seeing you again." I tried not to think exactly how much I had seen.

Lucifer reached out again and grabbed my hand, pulling me to him. His smile held a hint of mischief. "Why walk when you can fly?"

The damp skin of his muscled upper body pressed against the palm of my hand and I felt the warm hum of energy between us. I looked up at him, managing one word. "Fly?"

Lucifer leaned down and picked me up, holding me close to his chest. Cerulean blue eyes regarded me in a warm way that made my stomach flutter. "Yes, fly."

He stretched out his massive wings that glowed a shimmery white in the dark. They were so beautiful up close and looked incredibly soft. Each feather was flawless and layered on top of each other right to the tips.

My fingers twitched. Lucifer tilted his head down and whispered in my ear. "Hold on tight."

With a powerful beat of his wings we shot through the trees and into the endless sky. I gasped at the sheer speed of our ascent and wrapped my arms around his neck. The ground became smaller under me and the night stretched out before us like a velvet blanket. The wind blew my hair back as we glided above the trees.

It should have been terrifying but all I felt was exhilarated and powerfully free. The world was so much larger than I'd imagined, my life a tiny thread in the weaving of creation. With the stars twinkling at me from above I felt like a contradiction; insignificant, yet so much more than I'd imagined.

We dipped down as we got closer to my cottage and I couldn't help the laughter that bubbled out from my lips. He let my feet touch the ground as we glided to a stop.

"That was incredible!" I looked up at Lucifer in awed wonder. "That is the most amazing thing I have ever done."

Lucifer smiled at my obvious joy. "You're welcome."

I beamed up at him and then slowly became aware of how close we were. My heart started to pound in a different rhythm.

He brushed some hair away from my face. "Nadia."

"Ah... yes.."

"This is not an experiment."

My eyes widened slightly but his lips covered mine before I could speak. Golden warmth hummed in my blood and my breath tangled with his. By the Spirits, it felt so right. The kiss banished the cobwebs of doubt and replaced it with something else. Something delicate and new.

His lips caressed mine softly before he pulled back and brushed his thumb down my cheek. "Goodnight, Nadia," he said in that low melodious voice.

I stared up at him, and felt something my heart soften and glow like it was infused with light. "Goodnight, Lucifer."

My dreams shifted into flashes of warm summer weather, spiralling peaks of crystal temples and finally oblivion.

***

I woke up later feeling rested and in better spirits. I unwound my arms from the pillow I had been hugging for the duration of my sleep and placed it neatly amongst the others. The memory of white wings and a starry sky drifted up in my thoughts, but I ruthlessly shoved it away. Today, I would enact my battle plan.

As I rolled out of the bed and had another bite to eat from the fruit platter, my mind ticked over the possibilities and the potential obstacles. First, I needed to check if Lucifer was around. That was probably the most frightening aspect of my plan, and considering what else I might be up against was saying a lot. There were so many ways this could go horribly wrong, but nothing could be achieved by sitting around and wishing to escape.

"Those who take great risks, reap great rewards," I said to myself.

I didn't consider myself to be a warrior in any aspect. Having never trained in combat skills, the only thing I knew to do with my hands was pray. I had never held a weapon in my life and the only encounters I had with demons resulted with me trying to crawl away. Strength wasn't all physical, it was also about will. If I could survive my meetings with Lucifer then perhaps I could find a way out of here.

I remembered what Lucifer said about my Light. If it were true, I wished I knew more about it. Archangel Michael had been aware of my gifts but he never led me to believe they were unusual or rare. I never had the opportunity to use Light in The City, so I had just assumed many people had the same ability.

Light was a powerful weapon against the dark. If I managed to figure out how to fully access this ability then it would serve me well here and in the future.

Readying myself, I took a deep breath and moved through the wall. I made my way down the hallway and pushed open the double doors that led to the lounge room. Everything looked neat and orderly as if the Dragarth had never emerged and threw me into the furniture. Even the pitcher was back on the table. I eyed the walls wearily as I cautiously approached Lucifer's room.

With my heart beating in my chest, I cracked open the door and peeked inside.

The room was empty.

"Lucifer?" I called out softly. Then abruptly realised how stupid I sounded. Yes, sure, call out for the Devil to see if he was around. I might as well paint suspicious across my forehead.

When there was an absence of black holes and thunder claps, I tentatively assumed he wasn't here. Well, he wasn't in his room. He could be lurking anywhere really. I guess I just had to take that chance.

I made my way to the side of the lounge, where I could see past the open double doors all the way back down to the wall that separated my room from the hallway. I needed to give myself as much distance as I could for this to work. Or for me to survive. Turning my head to the left, I could see the portal mirrors lined up, the swirling mists within beckoning eerily. It was the second mirror that led to the place in Kryptos where I had first met Lucifer. That was my goal.

Now I had to test my range.

I called Light into my hand. It glowed softly, and woefully small. Taking another deep, calming breath, I aimed down the hall and threw my Light. It flew straight and true, then faltered a third of the way down and dissipated.

"You can do this," I encouraged myself. I sent a quick prayer out to the Heavens and generated more Light. Squashing my nerves, I threw the light down the hall. It shot out in front of me and then faded into nothing at the same distance.

I threw again. It dissipated.

Gritting my teeth I threw again. Failed.

Again. Failed.

Oh for the love of the Creator! I cannot fail. I cannot stay here!

I took another breath and threw the light as hard as I could. It curved through the air and evaporated like the last remnants of hope I had inside me.

"Arrrgh!" Upset, I turned around and hurled my Light across the lounge room in frustration. It slammed against the opposite side, white light spilling against the wall like liquid. I stood shocked, then stepped quickly back when I saw the tell tale ripple moving beneath the wall's surface. My heart hammered as the Dragarth eased around the spot where I had sent my Light. The tip of its tail flickered out of the wall, its spikes glinting in the light. Then it disappeared.

Relief flooded through me when it didn't emerge. *That was close. Too close.*

I frowned, staring at my hand and then back at the wall. This whole time I had been trying to calm myself down before accessing my abilities. Was that the problem? Maybe I should stop blocking how I feel and just let it all out. I didn't like keeping anger and pain within me, but squashing it down wasn't exactly healthy either. I wasn't dealing with my emotions and perhaps that made me weaker.

Drawing the Light back into my hand I channelled some of my confusion and fear. This time when I let my Light go, it flew through the air like a bright star and faded just short of the wall. A smile stretched across my face, and I let out a light, happy laugh. I did it once more just to be sure it wasn't an accident.

Now for the hard part.

I needed to distract the Dragarth long enough to access the portal without being attacked. That meant it needed to be the furthest away from me so I had more time to escape. Thinking about this plan was one thing, but acting it out was petrifying. Fear shivered inside me and I resisted the urge to push it aside. This time I'd use it.

It was now or never.

Channelling a little bit of Light into my palm, I lobbed it against the wall next to the portal mirrors. As soon as the Dragarth rippled around to that spot, I pulled all my fear and anxiety into the next Light ball and slammed it down the hall to the other end. I saw a flash of bright light, but I didn't turn to look if it hit the mark.

I knew it would and I knew the Dragarth would follow.

I ran desperately to the second portal, aware of each second that passed. As I did, I heard the blast of Light hit the wall with a loud sizzle. I hurriedly touched the smoky mirror, waiting for it to reveal the Hall in Kryptos. Then I heard it, the fast slithering sound of something large moving in my direction.

Come on, come on, come on…

The mist cleared and I saw a rocky tunnel leading into darkness. This wasn't the Hall! Frantically, I looked behind me. I saw the Dragarth slide its serpentine body into the lounge area, crushing into the chaise and destroying a large table with mad swipes. Three reptilian heads locked onto me with terrible focus. It was going to kill me.

I turned back. I didn't have a choice. I had to take the risk.

Not knowing where I was going, I plunged into the portal to the unknown and prayed I was going to survive.

***

The Fallen stood around the raised dias in perfect, curved lines. Their dark wings fanned out behind their armour and dropped to the floor like thick, luscious capes on forgotten kings. They resembled the jagged rocks that enclosed them; harsh, barren, and unyielding. Though the light had all but fled from their blood stained hands and brutal pleasures, its absence couldn't erase what they once were, stars in the heavens, and that incandescent beauty was still imprinted upon their cold, empty flesh.

Some were newly turned and still exploring the abilities the darkness had gifted them, while others were veterans, their names a whisper of terror in the realms above. They were only a small number in comparison to the armies of the human world. A general might laugh when confronted with their size across the battlefield, and then watch their armies crushed and their cities burned by just one of their kind.

They were beautiful and deadly, powerful predators that could not be controlled... except by one.

He moved through them like an arctic breeze, a vessel of lightning storms and end of days. They didn't kneel when he passed, and he didn't want them to. This wasn't a court, this was a war, a war they had been waging for as long as they had been turned. Warriors didn't kneel, they stood straight and strong as the weapons they were.

Lucifer ascended the dias and turned to face them, gold bands around his arms glowing faintly in the dark. He spoke one word in cool, crisp tones. "Report."

It was Ezriel who stepped forward, a shadow amongst shadows. Even the Fallen had a hierarchy within their ranks. "Two Level One demons have managed to escape into the Underworld, their location is unknown. We have their descriptions and energy signatures and will commence a tracking expedition. There has been another summoning from the Earth plane, this time it was a Third Level demon by the name of Aldinach. He has not yet returned."

"Find the location of the breach on Level One and let me know. When Aldinach returns, bring him in for questioning," Lucifer instructed.

Ezriel inclined his head.

"Upper level descents?"

A feminine voice answered. "We found twelve demons from Level Two that had descended into Level Three and eight demons from Level Three to Level Four."

"And you did what?" Lucifer asked.

Selaphiel blinked slowly as if remembering a fond dream. "I bled them dry. Then I staked their empty husks on the borderline to remind them when they eventually reform of what their empty eye sockets look like."

"Good," Lucifer purred. "Rumours?"

"There were a few that slipped into the Sixth Level," Selaphiel cut in, her voice sharpening eagerly, "we could…"

"The Sixth and Seventh levels are out of bounds. As a group they'd be too powerful for you to control. I'll deal with them."

Selaphiel's eyes darkened, but she wisely discontinued the subject. "Philotanus is raving on about the next eclipse, that his powers will grow so he can create a hole in reality and escape to find thirteen virgin priestesses to sacrifice. I don't believe we need to be concerned."

"He is not that strong," Ezriel agreed.

Selaphiel smirked. "That and there is no such thing as a virgin priestess."

Lucifer held up his hand. "Nevertheless, I want you to keep an eye on him. He'll cause trouble just by believing his own story." He cast his eye over another one of his Fallen in the front with hair the colour of a silver blade. "Nadiel, what are Hades' movements?"

Nadiel took a step forward and slapped a fist across his chest. "My Lord, Persephone has only just recently left her cycle in the Underworld. Hades' attention will now be focused on quelling any disturbances in his realm, so we can now use our resources on other missions."

The Devil closed his eyes and extended his senses upwards into the Earth plane. His eyes slowly opened, the whites now completely black like theirs.

No one knew why there were subtle differences between Lucifer and the rest of the Fallen. When an angel embraced the dark, it was the Darkness that controlled them. It consumed their soul, eclipsed their minds, and, as a physical manifestation, bled into their eyes and wings. With Lucifer, the Darkness responded differently. Sometimes his eyes blazed red, as if the fires of Hell were trapped within them reflecting his rage, and other times it was his irises that dragged you into a dark, soulless pit and kept you there. The Fallen attributed the anomaly to him being the First Son of Light... and the First Son of Dark. There were even rumours that he controlled the Dark and not the other way round.

"A new manifestation of Rakshasa demons have formed in the middle west of the Earth plane where there is war amongst the tribes. There will be possessions. Send a team to retrieve them."

"The City of Light will most likely be sending a team as well to banish the Rakshasa. We should all go in force and capture as many of them as we can," Ezriel ventured. "We can grow our ranks and become stronger."

"That is not the objective."

"We could do both."

"Our resources are needed elsewhere." Lucifer gave Enziel a piercing look. "If during the course of your mission your team captures some warrior angels, so be it. But if you come back with warrior angels and no Rakshasa demons, you and I will be having a conversation."

Enzriel's jaw clenched, understanding what a conversation with the Devil would entail. He nodded. "Of course, it will be as you wish."

"Good, now go."

The Fallen turned as one and filed out the room. A couple of them lingered, waiting to report on individual missions that had been assigned to them. Selaphiel fell into step with Enziel, her gaze straight ahead. She said under her breath, "That was risky."

"It needed to be said," he said harshly.

"Now is not the time to be pushing our agenda, brother," Nadiel said from his other side. "You're just asking for pain."

"I don't care," he growled. "We miss opportunity after opportunity. It needed to be said."

"Reign it in," Selaphiel snapped. "The time will come soon enough."

"It better. I grow tired of waiting."

Chapter 9

A thick, icy substance rolled over my skin as I pushed through the portal to the other side. As soon as my feet hit the rocky terrain, I took a few great leaps forward, then spun around with another ball of Light, preparing to face the Dragarth.

But there was no portal. Where I expected to see a gilded mirror was just empty space that led further into darkness.

"Not sure if this is a good or bad thing," I murmured to myself. While the Dragarth couldn't follow me, I was now stuck in this place without another way out. I shook my head. I had spent all this time trying to escape, and now I was worried I wouldn't be able to get back to Lucifer's house in Hell. "Focus, Sandriel."

I rolled my shoulders back and scanned my surroundings. The Light I conjured let me see a few feet around me, but beyond that, it was just emptiness. I twisted my lips thoughtfully, then threw the ball of Light out into the dark. Rocky walls were illuminated on either side in a narrow passageway. When my Light faded, the tunnel had not ended. As far as I knew, it could have gone on forever.

I had no idea where I was. I tried to use my abilities to shift back to The City of Light, but there was a heavy weight of resistance.

"Well, that rules out the Earth realm." So far, my luck had taken a fair beating. If I was on Earth, it would have been easy to leave and transport myself back to the heavenly realm. My only relief was that it didn't look like a fiery pit of doom.

No one really knew much about Hell. The handful of warrior angels that had come back from Lucifer's ministrations all said it looked different. One claimed Hell was a tiny box that increasingly became smaller until your bones were slowly crushed. Another said her flesh was eaten by insects, then she regenerated and had the whole process repeated. The other account was more of what I imagined Hell to be like. The warrior said he was thrown into a pit of fire, and every time he tried to escape, horrifying, skinless creatures pulled him back.

As I wasn't experiencing constant, unrelenting agony, I got the feeling I had fortunately bypassed Hell. Seeing no other option, I cautiously made my way down the tunnel. The air was chill and damp, almost as if I was under the ocean. It was also eerily quiet. I couldn't hear anything beyond my own footsteps, not even the sound of dripping water.

The floor was uneven, and my feet, covered in thin white slippers, had to constantly adjust to my weight so I could keep my footing. I continued forward for what seemed like an hour before the tunnel split off in two different directions.

"Left or right?" Hesitating for a few seconds, I swivelled my body to the left and continued down another tunnel. This time it curved gently and gravitated downwards.

After a few minutes, the passage broke into three new directions. There was a set of roughly cut stairs in the middle that spoke of a steep climb and the other two twisted off on either side.

"What is this? A labyrinth?" I muttered under my breath. Bewildered, I stared at the stairs. "Maybe it leads to the surface?"

You wouldn't build stairs unless it was leading somewhere. The only question was if it was somewhere good. I wished I could fly to the top, but the tunnel was too narrow to stretch my wings. I braced my hand on one side of the wall and peered up into the dark, holding out my Light. "No, just more stairs."

Keeping my Light in front, I began my arduous climb. As time passed, I could feel my legs protest in pain. I stopped for a minute to catch my breath. A twinge of fear skittered along my spine as I realised the implications. If I was feeling physical discomfort, I was still in one of the lower realms. In the higher or neutral realms, my vibration would have been too elevated to experience pain.

There were quite a few lower realms in existence, and all of them had their dangers to contend with. Who knew where these tunnels were leading me? I wasn't exactly dressed for camouflage with my white shift and Light waving around in front of me.

I continued on. Eventually, after another long span of time, the ceiling of the tunnel ended, and the stairs continued to go up. *Finally!* I hastened my climb, eager to leave the narrow space I had been confined in.

My mouth dropped open.

Oh yes, the stairs continued, but they continued across a vast, empty space of nothingness. They swept across without any foundation underneath, like they were frozen in the air. I couldn't see where they led, and I couldn't see what was beneath them. I suspected one slip whilst climbing, and it would be a long fall into the dark. Luckily, there seemed to be enough room here to fly.

I turned my head and looked back at the way I came. I wondered where the other tunnels led. Did I make the wrong choice? I shook my head. No point in second-guessing now. I took a few steps up and spread out my wings. My angelic glow made them shine a little in the dark.

Please don't let me be a beacon for bad things.

I leapt off the ground and let my wings carry me up. They stroked the air with two powerful beats, and I launched upwards. I flew above the stairs, keeping quite close in case I crashed into an unknown formation above. Who knew what was hanging from the ceiling? If there was a ceiling.

The stairs seemed to go on forever until finally, they came to a flat landing that also seemed to run on indefinitely.

"Whoever has to walk through this place must be exhausted," I murmured.

Then, I saw them.

They drifted aimlessly across the rocky platform, flickering with a misty, silver-blue light. The light blurred out their feet, so they looked like they were floating an inch above the ground. The lines of their limbs and clothes were just a hazy outline, like someone had sketched them with a blue and grey pencil but forgot to colour them in. Their clothing, shapes, and sizes were varied like a mixed bag from different eras. It was their eyes that were the most disturbing, empty and dead, without any will or purpose.

I now knew where I had landed. I was looking at spirits.

I was in the Underworld.

The Underworld wasn't Hell. It was a place in-between, like Purgatory, where restless spirits roamed until they were pulled into the higher or lower realms. It wasn't the best place to be, but it also meant that somewhere here I could access the Elysian Fields, a beautiful higher realm that souls could enter and rest if they had done well during their lifetime.

Of course, I could also run into Hades, the Lord of the Underworld, or a Hell Gate. Not sure which one was worse.

Unsure of how the spirits would react to my presence, I flew cautiously above them, keeping enough distance between us. They didn't seem to notice me. The platform ended after another few minutes of flying and I saw a spirit disappear into a large, gaping hole in the wall. I guessed this was my stop.

Landing, I managed to just avoid direct contact with one walking past. The silver-blue light mingled with my glow, and for just a second, the spirit, in the vague form of an older man, paused as if he sensed something around him. A sliver of awareness shifted in and he tilted his head this way and that as if he were trying to get a lock on me. I held my breath and kept statue still on the side of the walkway. After a few tense seconds, the unfocused glaze crept back into its eyes and it kept on moving.

Phew! Another close call. I didn't know what would happen, but I'd rather not find out. I quickly ducked into the tunnel opening.

I won't tell you how many tunnels I entered and how many different paths I had to choose. There were many. I lost count of the turns I took and how many spirits I had to nimbly avoid. It felt like days had passed and I was starving. My Light had dimmed to a muted glow as the energy to maintain it took its toll. My feet ached constantly and I didn't know what I would give to crawl into a corner and take a nap. I felt so… human.

The trouble began when I decided to rest upon a small boulder. It felt so good to sit down, even though the indents and grooves made it extremely uncomfortable. I took off one of my slippers and tried to massage my foot. As I was considering a way I could lay down, two men entered the rocky chamber I was in.

Except they weren't exactly men.

From my higher position on top of the boulder, it took me a second to see there was something *wrong* with their faces. Their eyes were completely black. Even the whites around their eyes were black. The inky colour spilled out from the corners in dark veins that patterned themselves across the sides of their faces. From a distance it would look like they were wearing web-like masks to shield their eyes. A smoky grey breast plate covered their chests, welded on to show every contour and muscle definition.

Another detail I noticed in those shocked moments, was that one held a wickedly curved blade with many jagged edges and the other a gauntlet on his left hand where thin blades curved out from the top like claws.

They also oozed with an energy that told me to run screaming in the opposite direction. The hairs on my *everything* stood up.

They stared at me, equally surprised to see me perched on top of the boulder, with one leg dangling off the edge and my shoe in my left hand. I doubt I made a very formidable sight.

My eyes rounded and then survival instinct finally kicked in. Hurling my dim Light at them, I took a blind leap off the boulder. Pain shot through my knee as I hit the ground. As soon as my Light faded, we plunged into darkness. I heard an angry, deep snarl vibrate through the air and I quickly generated another ball of Light. Scrambling back up, I raced in the other direction.

I didn't even have time to put my shoe back on.

A frantic look behind revealed my attackers advancing towards me, hunger and anger stamped blatantly across their face. I couldn't fight them; I couldn't even defend myself properly. The only thing I could do was run as fast as my feet would carry me. If only I could get to a place where I could fly, then perhaps I could stay out of reach.

Laughter followed me as I rounded a bend and darted through a tunnel to my right. "I do love it when they run," the grating voice echoed behind me. Closer.

"Ruuunnnn, little rabbit. Ruuuuuunnnn! Your flesh will taste all the sweeter when I strip it off you." The second voice rubbed along my inner ears like sandpaper.

My breath squeezed out of my lungs in painful pants. My Light wasn't concealing me, but acting as a lovely glowing trail for them to follow. If I dissolved it then I wouldn't be able to see. I had to find a place to hide! They were catching up. I needed more time.

I spun around, channelled my fear from my tired body, and blasted it behind me just as I ducked through a small opening in front... and fell down a small hole. I let out a startled scream. My Light disappeared as I desperately tried to find something to slow my rapid descent. My fingernails clawed into the hard dirt but I continued to plummet down… down… down…

Splash! Icy water closed over my head, pulling me down into its suffocating embrace. I kicked violently with my legs and came up to the surface with a gasp. Pitch black greeted me and a loud roaring sound. I held up my hand quickly and called more Light. I was in a little cavern with running water and a narrow pathway. The roaring sound was coming from my right.

Just as I was about to move, a tumble of small stones hit my head from the hole I had fallen from.

Oh no, they were coming.

I lurched to the edge and hauled myself up. Dripping, with my dress clinging onto me like a second skin, I stumbled through the opening to the right. I just managed to avoid a spirit as I saw a larger chamber with a waterfall crashing down on the side. Water spat at my face and I moved further in to avoid the spray. I couldn't see how far the chamber extended, but there were numerous boulders emerging from the ground like oddly shaped eggs. There were also quite a few spirits.

I made it part of the way down, weaving through the rocks, when I heard a voice echo just slightly above the roar of the water, "Which… go?"

Immediately, I shut down my Light and ducked behind a boulder. I still glowed dimly but I fervently hoped the rock would conceal me from view.

"You go... I'll... right. Make... scream... find her." I could only hear bits, but the conversation didn't sound like fun times ahead.

I held my position, my body trembling from cold and terror. I wouldn't be able to hear footsteps. I just hoped they'd pass me and keep going.

Then, a spirit approached. It was a young woman with a frilly bonnet and a conservative long sleeve dress. My mouth parted with horror as her blue-grey figure glided absently towards me. I pressed myself against the boulder so hard I felt the rough surface leave indents in my back. Holding my breath, I prayed it wouldn't notice me.

I wasn't that lucky.

Her fingertips brushed through my angelic light.

She paused. I froze.

She turned her head and *saw* me.

Her gaze was wild as it held on to mine. "Hhhhheeeelllllpppppp meee..." she moaned in breezy low tones.

Oh sweet Goddess! I shook my head frantically and tried to inch away.

"Hhheeeeelllllpppppmeeeee..." she groaned again. One of her hands reached out as if to grasp my

108

shoulder but instead went right through me. I felt pressure then a chill. I moved slightly again, but the spirit followed my movement, her other hand trying to latch onto my dress.

My heart beat in a frenzied dance then almost stopped as very real, hard fingers closed around my throat in a brutal grip. The cold metal of a breast plate pressed against my chest, grinding me into the stone.

I let out a strangled gasp.

"My, my, my, aren't you *delicious*," the voice rasped. I could just make out the evil twin's features in my dim light. The edge of his serrated blade slid up my leg, leaving behind a fine line of white hot pain.

My hand grasped around his wrist, trying to loosen his grip. I might as well have playfully battered at him with my feathers.

"Heeeeeeeelllppp meeee," the spirit wailed again.

The evil twin snapped his head around and blew some sort of dark, oily mist at the spirit with his mouth. It had the same effect as throwing acid. The spirit let out a torturous scream as gaping holes appeared on her face, eroding her energy. She turned around and fled.

"Now, where were we?" His tongue lashed out and ran up the length of my cheek to my temple. I cringed. "I wonder what your bones will taste like."

Calling up the last dregs of my strength and the clamour of emotions I was feeling, I summoned my ball of Light. It pulsed in white waves and illuminated the area around us. His dark orbs glanced down.

With a gurgling shout, I blasted my Light right into his face. His scream made the spirit's pain sound like a child's giggle. It rocketed off the cavern walls as he let go of my throat and clutched his face, howling.

I did the only sane thing and ran. Light flickered weakly along my fingertips, just barely giving me enough to see. I could still hear his screams. They crawled along the walls in shrilly pitches, following me. I raced along for another few minutes, tripping a few times until I came to a fork in my path.

This time, I felt an energetic pull towards my right. Not the encouraging pull that your gut gives you when you're heading towards something good. It was an energetic pull that moved me physically, turning me towards it like tainted coils wrapping around my limbs. I forced my feet back.

"Uhuh." There was no way something good was down there. Spinning around, intending to go in the other direction, my face crashed into something hard and I fell to the ground in a daze. My Light flicked off. I groaned and felt something wet trickle from my nose.

"What do we have here?" said a sinister voice. "A present, I think."

A hand tangled cruelly in my hair and I screamed as I was dragged backwards towards the tunnel I had tried to escape from. I twisted and turned, and my head felt like it was on fire. I even tried to summon more Light, but I was tapped out, exhausted.

Suddenly, I was thrown out in front by my hair. I rolled and came to a stop on my back. My vision blurred for a few seconds. The pull was stronger now, screaming at me to come closer. Malevolent whispers slid its tendrils in my mind, urging me to get up and follow. I rolled weakly to the side and looked up.

She was horridly beautiful. Long chestnut hair framed a sensual face and cascaded down a generously curved body covered in patches of red, gleaming scales. The scales flowed over one breast in a sinuous wave, then over her navel like small, ruby jewels. It appeared again in glittery flashes over her thighs, feet and arms. She looked like a snake who had shed parts of its skin only to reveal a stunning creature underneath.

Then I noticed the Hell Gate behind her. It was a stormy black whirlpool in the wall, suffocating me with its strength. I screamed inside in sheer terror.

"I found her nearby," the male voice said behind me.

The snake woman parted her luscious red lips in a sharp smile. Her dark eyes glinted as they skimmed over my crumpled heap. "An angel! How fascinating! Just when I was getting bored with my last toy." She lifted her eyes from me. "Bring her."

The snake woman turned and disappeared in the swirling vortex.

"No!" I screamed and struggled against the hands that dragged me up. Black veiny eyes stared malignantly back at me.

He walked forward and dragged me into Hell.

Chapter 10

Darkness and negativity hit me with the force of a mountain. Fire scorched along my nerve endings, burning them until they bubbled and popped. Pressure swelled inside my head, pounding against the inside of my skull in violent waves. I couldn't scream out the pain. My throat locked up as the muscles went into a series of fits.

Such was the experience of going through a Hell Gate.

Then I was thrown into a misty darkness. I landed on all fours, my head ringing, my body trembling as it tried to recover from the pain. Looking up, I saw the snake woman with her back to me, rolling her shoulders in ecstasy. The scales glittered as her skin shifted, pulling over muscles and curves.

"Mmmm… much better," she hissed in low tones, enouncing each syllable with pleasure.

Awareness prickled and I turned my head sharply to see the evil twin emerge from the swirly smoke surrounding us, eyes fixed intently on me.

"I'm hungry," he growled, moving around my body with predatory steps. When I continued to stare, shifting so I kept facing him, he opened his mouth. The bones in his jaw cracked and snapped as they shifted and then elongated. Razor edged teeth burst through gums and pierced the dark cavity of his mouth. His face had transformed to match the creature I had sensed within. The demon had captured his prey and now he planned to dine.

"Now, now Mardith. Let's not gobble up something that has to be savoured." I flinched at her voice, so close to me. I turned my head ever so slowly, still trying to keep the evil twin in my periphery vision.

Her almost bare legs knelt down before me and her hand caught my jaw, lightning fast, before I could move away. She tilted up my chin, straining my neck in a brutal angle. Her nails, which I didn't notice before, were long, sharp and blackened at the edges. They bit into my skin as she brought my face close. I tried to conjure my Light, but the attempt brought me another exquisite wave of pain that I had to blink back tears.

"Such a pretty little thing," she said, her red lips forming a sensual smirk. "And so very, very afraid." She closed her eyes briefly and breathed in like she was inhaling candy. Her voice deepened, "Yesssss... you, my toy, shall keep me *very* entertained."

"Lucifer is looking for me," I managed to get out in a gasp. "We made a deal. He'll be looking for me."

The snake woman burst out into laughter. "You!" Her eyes lit briefly with amusement. "How desperate you must be to call upon his name."

"We made a deal. He released the warrior angels for my time." I gripped onto her wrist, trying to ease the pressure on my neck.

"Did he now? I suppose that's why you were wandering around the Underworld like a lost, little lamb." She cut off my next protest by digging her nails further into my skin. "My dear love. You will be far better off in my care than in his. Now…" her eyes glowed, "we are all very hungry."

We? I caught movement in the mist around us. Dark shapes of all sizes shifted through the smoke, hovering at the edge of our circle. I was surrounded. Despair blanketed me with its heavy weight. Was this it? Was this to be my fate?

I caught a flash of fangs from the snake woman's mouth, like blades glinting in the dark. I was too slow to put up my hands. My neck and shoulder ripped apart in a river of agony.

My world shifted and suddenly I was alone.

There was also an odd pulsating sound in the air. It was like I was inside someone's chest and I could hear their heart beating in a deep, steady rhythm. I jerked myself up and looked around, every sense on high alert. My shaking fingers went to my neck, surprised to feel the skin whole. I could have sworn I felt my blood running down my chest.

A sudden movement caught my attention.

I wasn't alone.

A figure moved out from the shadows. Her dress was made out of rich black satin and lace. It left her creamy shoulders bare and covered the length of her slim, toned arms. Black satin fit her chest and waist like a glove, highlighting the subtle curves beneath. The material parted at mid thigh, revealing long, slender legs as it hit the floor in a midnight pool. White blonde hair fell in a thick, tumble of waves, contrasting against the dress and the black wings that framed her body. Dark eyes watched me in a delicate face.

My face.

Dear spirits…

The woman with my face was a Fallen Angel.

My other, darker self moved with a sensual grace that I certainly didn't possess until she stood a few feet away. She smirked at me, a twist of expression I was unfamiliar with. "You look like Hell."

Completely disturbed, I took a step back and shook my head in denial. "This isn't real."

"In this place, anything is real."

My lips tightened. "You're not me." They were playing games. They had to be.

My other self arched an eyebrow and looked at me with a glimmer of disgust. "Not the way you are now. Look at you, you're pathetic, weak…" Her lip curled. "You can't even save yourself. You're practically a demon snack."

I sucked in a breath. "I'm not a warrior."

She leaned her upper body forward, her dark eyes capturing mine. "Oh, that's abundantly clear. You're *nothing*." Straightening up, my darker self stretched out a black wing, following the movement with her eyes. "Don't you get tired of being utterly useless?"

I shouldn't have felt offended. She wasn't even me. "I'm not useless."

Snapping her wing back in place, my other self smiled slowly. "You won't be."

I eyed her warily. "What's that supposed to mean?"

"It means you will evolve from the thing that crawls along the floor, vulnerable to anything that might peck at it." She eyed me contemptuously. "You will go inside the dark, cool cocoon that you have been so stupidly avoiding and strip away all that dead flesh. Then, you will emerge and fly amongst the dragons."

I stared at her, my heart picking up speed. "If you think I'll be anything like you, you're wrong."

She laughed at me, my own voice echoing mockingly. My darker self crossed her lace covered arms beneath her chest and shifted to one hip. "Too late. I am already your future. I am what you will become."

"No," I shook my head. "*No,*" I said stronger. "I have a choice. I choose my future. This…" I gestured towards her and the smoky darkness surrounding us, "is a lie."

"Is it?" she asked, raising an eyebrow. "Just because you fear it doesn't make it any less true. You are already on the path of darkness. To him."

My breath knotted in my lungs.

Her smile grew and she stalked around me in a wide circle. "Finally, we are getting somewhere. Lucifer… isn't he just all the seven deadly sins wrapped in one glorious package?" She paused at my left shoulder and whispered, "And my do we take every opportunity to sin."

"I would not!"

"Oh, don't be such a prude. You'll get over that sooner or later. Thank the Devil." Her lips curved.

"Stop telling me what I would do!"

"What you have *done*." Her dark eyes held mine. A stranger's eyes. "It will be so much better, I promise you. You have so much more potential than you realise. You won't have to snivel and crawl in front of them. You'll *rule* them." Her teeth flashed in the dark. "Let me show you how we can make them beg."

My eyes widened in alarm as my other self streaked towards me in a dark blur. I braced myself for the impact, then froze in shock as she went into me. For a few seconds, I couldn't breathe. Something alien settled in me, flexing their limbs beneath my skin.

There was a coolness to the energy, a depth that eclipsed mine.

How much fun we shall have. The usual self-deprecating and sometimes helpful voice in my head was replaced with an insidious whisper.

"Get out of me!" I tried to force the energy out, but it easily squashed my attempts.

Your weakness is an insult to us both. Let me show you how it is done.

The dark mists parted in front of me and I saw a demonic creature emerge. It was hairless and grey, with arms too long for its body. When it saw me it screeched, and blunt yellow teeth snapped at me.

It ran, hunger on its face. Long, gangly limbs ate up the distance with surprising speed. My hand moved with a will of its own and a stream of dark energy lashed around the creature's neck like a whip. My arm moved out in a slow arch, then jerked viciously down. The creature followed suit. It lifted high in the air, then cracked down upon the floor with a sickening splat.

The voice inside my head laughed.

My eyes widened in fear at the darkness spilling out of me, and yet some part enjoyed the power to render harm to the beings that tormented me.

Dark energy lifted the demon back up off the floor like a noose suspended in mid air. I noticed a black ooze seeping out from various lacerations on its face and body. Part of its skull had been crushed in, but it was still aware, still looking at me with pure, utter hatred. Though, now I could see a tiny glimmer of fear.

Look at it. It would be tearing you apart right now, and you would have screamed and screamed and there would have been no one to save you. Now it's scared of you.

My body moved over towards it.

"What are you doing?" I tried to force myself to stop, but my legs kept going. I didn't want to go anywhere near that thing, but my control had been stripped away and I was a puppet in another set of hands. "No..."

The demon tried to grab me, but my body deftly moved out of the way, weaving fluidly around like a silken ribbon. The creature seemed uncoordinated in comparison. My small hands grabbed its arm with strength that I didn't possess then... *twist... tear... snap...*

Black ichor sprayed over my face and across my white dress. I trembled inside as my hand held up the demon's limb, detached from its body. The demon screamed, a scraping, raspy sound that hurt my ears.

"Stop this! I don't want to do this!" I cried out.

You will. You'll do this all the time.

"No!" I tried to fight. I tried to stop myself, but as the demon flailed around in pain I ripped off its other arm. I screamed as more black liquid ran over me, coating me like paint. The smell was awful, like rotten fruit left out in the sun. "Stop, stop, stop! Please, I don't want to do this. I'm not like this!"

You are, you just don't know it.

I tore into that demon like he was a piece of meat. I screamed and cried at the horror and pain I was causing, even to one so damned. The warrior angels destroyed demons to save Earth, they didn't torture them for the pleasure of it. But my hands didn't stop. They took their time, savouring, making it last as long as possible until only gurgling noises remained and finally... nothing.

A moan left my lips. There was a pile of flesh on the floor. Some pieces still twitched, others lay there as still as stone. I felt battered and bruised inside as if my soul had taken a beating.

This wasn't me. It couldn't be me.

My hands lifted in front of my face so I could see the stains that coated them. My nails were covered in gore, and it felt like the demon blood had seeped into my skin invading my blood. Invading me.

I gagged, a dry coughing sound.

Look at the power we wield. This is only the tip of the mountain. There is so much more beneath.

"Stop... please..."

A pause. *Oh, look at what we have here.*

I turned my head to see another demon emerge from the mist. This one had bat wings and horns that curled on top of its head like a ram. It was also big and muscular with hands the size of my face. It growled low and menacingly.

The voice in my head laughed with delight. *Now this one is more of a challenge.*

I strung the demon up first like a piece of morbid art, my dark coils of energy holding him still. His bat wings went first. I shredded through them like they were paper. He managed to get a few good tosses of his horns, attempting to impale me, but the dark presence that rode my body was too quick, too strong. I snapped them off and shoved them in his chest.

On and on it went. More demons came and more fell in a bloody pool at my feet. I stopped screaming after a while. I could only watch as my hands and body did terrible, violent things. Things I knew would haunt me forever.

Are you getting bored?

I couldn't speak. I couldn't...

Awww... don't be like that. You wouldn't be so upset if you knew the things they have done, or the things they thought about doing to you. You should be thanking me for putting an end to them.

Black gore dripped down from the ends of my hair.

Strength is the only thing respected here. Do you understand? Or do I need to teach you another lesson?

"Sandriel?"

My heart clenched in my chest. I turned my head towards the sound and saw Rushton, one of the warrior angels I had bargained for.

He looked like he had been in a fight. A few slices marred the perfection of his tanned skin, one particularly close to his eye. He wore loose white pants that were stained with dirt, not the oily, black substance that saturated my clothes. His handsome, angelic face studied me with growing concern.

"Rushton…" I whispered.

Holding his sword tightly in one hand, he looked around, his golden eyes trained on the darkness around us, looking for danger. Tension ran through his muscles as he waited for a few heartbeats before finally settling his gaze back on me.

"What happened to you?" he asked, moving swiftly closer.

I panicked. "No, stop! Stay where you are!"

He halted at the shrill sound of my voice. "Why? What's wrong?"

"You have to leave Rushton," I pleaded desperately. "Go now before I hurt you."

He frowned softly. "Why would you hurt..." I saw him take in the demon remains on the ground. Hesitating, he asked, "Did you do this?"

My voice trembled, "Yes. Please, please, you have to go now. Quickly!"

Rushton shook his head, the sable strands of his hair falling across his brow. "It will be ok. I'm not leaving you here."

See, he doesn't want to leave. He wants to stay and play.

"NO! Don't! Please let him go!"

Rushton took a tentative step closer. "Who are you talking to, Sandriel?"

"Go, Rushton, go," I begged him, half sobbing. I couldn't move. My dark self still had control over my body.

We both know he's not going anywhere.

Dark energy lashed out at him. He barely managed to avoid it, rolling out of the way.

He is quick, my dark self murmured.

I screamed in my mind as I flung more dark coils out in deadly slices.

"Sandriel! Stop!" Rushton yelled, ducking and weaving. "I'm trying to help you!" One of my midnight ropes of energy managed to curve around his leg. I yanked my hand back in a sharp movement and he slammed to the ground, grinding his teeth in pain as the darkness burned into his flesh.

Now I knew what Hell was. I was a monster. I was a demon. I was everything I despised. I would have preferred to be roasted in the fires of Hell. I would have welcomed the pounding of fists against my skin. Anything. *Anything* but this.

Just as I hoisted him up in the air, voices intruded. Not my darker self in my head, but others that echoed all around me.

The world shifted.

More screams surrounded me. Things broken and dying.

"…apologies, my Lord, I did not know…"

My eyelids were heavy but I managed to crack them open. I was lying on the cold ground. Dark mist flowed over me as I shivered uncontrollably. My neck and shoulder felt like they were on fire.

I saw the snake woman on her knees, not too far from me. Her head was bowed in submission, the rest of her body rigid.

"Didn't you?" The frozen silk of his voice swept over me. I knew that voice. I struggled to turn my head but it felt too heavy.

I suddenly realised I had control over my limbs. Was she gone? My dark, terrible self? The things I did…

"If I knew, I wouldn't have touched her, my Lord. I wouldn't have dared," came the feminine hiss.

There was a strange, dark pile of ash near my leg. On top was a familiar looking breast plate, black scorch marks trailing across the front. Now that I had noticed, I realised there were piles of ash everywhere. Some were small and others were significantly larger.

A dangerous note entered his velvet voice. "I don't know about that, Kumaya, but you certainly won't now. If anyone comes across her again, let them know what happens when she is not returned to me. Untouched. Do you understand?"

There was a hissing sound of pain, a gurgling scream.

"Do you understand," he crooned.

"Yessss… yessss, my Lord!"

Where was Rushton? Wasn't he here somewhere? My head swam dizzily. Was it all a dream?

Familiar arms wrapped around me and I was picked up off the floor against a smooth muscular chest. I looked up at Lucifer, blinking slowly. Happiness spread over me at the sight of his beautiful face. Where was our link? That golden hum that always passed between us?

I smiled at him as he looked at me with those dark, dark eyes. "Luce, you came," I said softly.

He flinched. It was the slightest of movements, but I caught it. That confused me. I frowned. There was also something not right with his eyes. Why weren't they blue?

I felt a sudden turbulent swell of energy. Rolling my head, I saw a black hole open up in front of us. As we stepped through, I caught sight of my hands. Black stains marred my skin, vivid against my pale skin.

No, not a dream.

Then darkness engulfed me.

Chapter 11

Nightmares made out of twisted horrors and drenched with blood chased me.

I ran down endless corridors with terror snapping and salivating at my heels like a rabid wolf. Sometimes I would be a hairs breath too slow and they would be on me, tearing into my flesh with claws and teeth. Other times I would turn, face them, and grow fangs myself. Rage burned through me, searing my thoughts until only one remained – *kill, kill them all.*

I relished their scream until I looked down at my hands and saw not black demon blood but pure white feathers splashed with crimson.

The nightmare repeated, taunting me with visions of gruesome deaths, mine and theirs. I felt trapped, suffocated, and alone. I struggled to find a way out, struggling… fighting… pushing…

Something intruded outside my dreams. A familiar touch that made my blood sing. I grabbed onto it like a lifeline.

Then… *shift…*

We sat underneath the dappled sunlight, facing each other on the cherry red picnic blanket. His long legs stretched out to the side as he leaned back on one hand, sampling a piece of date cake I had made earlier that morning. It was a joy to watch the shifting expressions play across his exquisite face. First, there was curiosity, then a shimmer of anticipation, followed by wonder and pleasure as the textures and flavours flowed over his tongue. I could have sat there and watched him without eating a thing.

"Do you like it?" I asked.

Lucifer nodded with a half smile. "I like it."

Absurdly pleased, I started to make him a chicken roll. I normally wouldn't be having such luxury items like chicken, but for some reason I'd find packages of food and spices on my doorstep every other day. I never said anything to Lucifer and I was never given an explanation. To thank him, I decided to arrange a picnic for him to enjoy.

"Nadia, where are your parents?"

I looked up from my roll making. The question surprised me, as did the dull aching sorrow that swiftly followed. I didn't usually talk about my parents. In town, people kept to themselves, reluctant to awaken memories of the dead. The silence didn't bother me, but sometimes it made me feel even more isolated, like they weren't just gone, but forgotten.

"My mother passed away after I was born." I tucked some hair behind my ear. "I grew up with my father. It wasn't easy for him to look after me by himself. But he did it. He did a great job."

Cerulean eyes softened and hints of gold broke through the blue like sun rays. "What happened to him?"

"One day, he came back from the town and he found it hard to breathe. Then the next thing I know he collapsed, clutching his chest and telling me to get the doctor. By the time I raced to town and got back... he didn't make it." I handed Lucifer the roll and our fingers touched. That warm golden hum flowed between us and our gazes met and locked.

"What happens to people when they pass?" I asked softly, breaking that slight, thrumming tension between us.

He pulled his hand back. "They usually go to a place you call Heaven."

"Usually?" I queried.

"It depends on how the soul has passed. Sometimes a violent passing can transition a soul to a different realm, but most of the time souls end up in Heaven."

"So what if you do bad things?"

His lips quirked. "Bad things?

I made a gesture upwards. "You know, hurt someone, lie, and cheat. Bad things."

"If a soul steps out of alignment of their purer self and gives in to negative emotions, then..."

"Then..." I prompted.

Lucifer leisurely took a bite of his roll and took a moment to absorb this new treat before he answered. "They go to Heaven."

"What! That doesn't make any sense!"

He responded with a mysterious smile as the wind shifted teasingly through his dark hair.

I brandished a bread roll at him and frowned suspiciously. "You're teasing me, aren't you?"

"No."

"So I could go to town tomorrow and hit Mr Johnson, our baker, with a chair and I would still go to Heaven?"

"Well we might make an exception for you."

Now he was teasing me. I huffed out a breath and looked at him expectantly.

"I would feel very sorry for Mr. Johnson for your unprovoked attack, but yes, you would still go to Heaven."

I leaned closer to him, both fascinated and disturbed by his meaning. "So, you are saying I could do anything I want and there would be no consequences for my actions?"

Lucifer brushed the tip of his index finger down the curve of my cheek. "I didn't say that."

Trying not to become completely distracted by his caress, I pushed, "What do you mean?"

He intertwined his finger lazily around a lock of my hair. "There is always an effect to every action and a balance that must be maintained. When a soul leaves the body and goes to Heaven, it reviews its life and all the choices it has made. If it has hurt another in that lifetime, then that balance needs to be paid in another life. Sometimes with the same soul it hurt."

My mouth dropped open. "There are other lifetimes?"

His teeth flashed. "Most definitely."

He continued, "I'll give you an example. A wealthy man who lets greed and ego dominate his actions to the point in which he subjugates the poor, might decide to come back in the next life as a person born in unfortunate circumstances. The soul's goal might be to experience and appreciate the feelings of being without all the luxuries money can buy and hope to overcome ego and greed with a more simple life. Or the soul might choose a wealthy life again, but with parents who came from simple beginnings so the soul has a broader perspective growing up and perhaps use their money to help the poor."

I frowned, picking at the red blanket and noticing how close my fingers were to the white material of his leg. "But how can we choose? Wouldn't we just pick good lives for ourselves over and over?"

He tugged on my hair until I met his eyes. "No matter what you've done in this life, your soul is always pure. When it leaves your body it will make choices out of love. Love for itself and love for others."

"Then why... what's the purpose of us even being here?" His eyes seemed to glow with blue fire and I found myself distracted again. What were we talking about? The tempting line of his jaw beckoned, and I traced the line with my fingertips. Sparks erupted under my skin.

God, he was beautiful. Sitting amongst the trees with his white open vest revealing more hardened muscles under gold dusted skin was causing my pulse to race like a wild horse. His dark, silky hair was left loose and gleamed in the afternoon sun. Thoughts I wouldn't have ever dreamed of voicing slipped teasingly into my mind. Like, what would it be like to run my hands all over that silky, hard, skin.

Oh my god. Stop.

"That, I think," Lucifer murmured softly, a slight smile brushing his lips, "is an answer for another time."

His hand slid around my waist, pulling me close against him, and our lips met as if they had been dying to touch. Heat moved through me in a way it had never done before. I clung onto him as if he was the only solid thing in this world and everything else swept away in a rush beneath my feet. The kiss wasn't hard or rough, but had an intensity and depth that left me breathless. Then there was that golden hum. That beautiful golden hum whenever we touched. It intensified like strands of sunlight woven in a glorious pattern, pulling us inextricably closer and binding us in a molten glow.

What is that? I thought. My hand slid down the strong column of his throat to the top of his chest.

~ Our link? It's our soulmate connection. ~

I pulled back slightly, startled. "What?"

"You're my opposite. My balance," he murmured, his eyes gazing into mine.

My world trembled. "Me?"

His lips curved then brushed gently against mine once more. ~ Yes, you. ~

Stunned, I tried to comprehend what he was saying. "What does that mean?"

~ It means you belong with me. ~

***

I woke up, my whole body aching like I had been slammed into the ground multiple times by a giant troll. Letting out a small hiss of pain, I cracked my eyes open to see a jewelled mandala above me. It sparkled, cascading coloured lights down upon my skin in exquisite patterns. It felt like a soothing balm across all the pain. I struggled to remember where I had seen this before.

Looking down, I noticed silken, black sheets draped over me like a pool of shadows. I was also wearing a soft, black shirt that was entirely too large and fell off one of my shoulders. There was a scent that clung to the material, something exotic and heady that made me feel flushed and restless. I breathed it in and wondered who it belonged to.

I sat up and winced. The room I was in was enormous. Fire ran along the edges, heating the room to a comfortable temperature. With effort, I moved off the bed. My feet hit the cool floor and I wobbled just a bit before steadying myself. The shirt slid down my thighs like a cool caress until it fell to my knees. A large man's shirt.

A face flashed in my minds' eye. Stunningly beautiful with a hint of something savage underneath. Wow. I looked down at the shirt and then looked back at the bed. That opened up a few more questions.

I padded slowly across the room to the ornate double doors. Pulling the doors open was a challenge and my body protested loudly. I considered going back to bed but I wondered if anyone was around. Curiosity got the best of me.

The next room was furnished quite decadently. I ran my hand over sumptuous material and carved wood.

"Hello?" I called out. My voice sounded hoarse. Odd. "Is anyone here?"

Smoky mirrors caught my eye and I stared at them. Fragments of memory shifted in place.

A monstrous serpent. Boulders. Running. Demons. Underworld.

An icy chill washed over me, followed by an intense desire to run. I had to get out of here. This place wasn't safe. How did I get back here? I had to leave. *Now.*

I spotted another set of elaborately carved double doors on the other side of the room and ran towards them, pushing them open. In my haste, I almost fell into a rectangular pool of water.

It was a bath, but it was like no bath I had ever seen. There were four pillars at each corner of the large rectangular pool. Each pillar had fire flickering up its length, bathing the water in red gold light, making it look as if it, too, were burning. The walls were a deep crimson and there were paintings of creatures I had never knew existed. It was masterfully done in a spectrum of colours. Some were monstrous and others were achingly beautiful.

I knelt by the edge of the water and dipped my hand in. It felt warm and silky against my skin. I cupped a handful and let it slide back down my fingers in a trickle. It was then I noticed a young woman looking back at me from the water. Her long, white blonde hair framed her face in waves and tangles. For some reason, I felt that she should be smiling, the curves of her face serene and peaceful.

She looked haunted instead.

My fingers came up to touch my face. She mirrored me. I peered closer and the fire light played in her eyes, making them look dark and lit up within with an unholy glow. Just like that, she transformed into something sinister and my nightmares came back to me with crushing force.

Hell. Violence. Joyful tearing and slicing. Power. Delicious scent of fear. Blood. Blood everywhere. Rushton.

Oh my god, Rushton…

A sound escaped my lips, high and breathy, and I jerked back. I looked down at my hands; it was as if I could see the blood coating my fingers and palms, sinking into my skin, mixing with my blood and becoming a part of me.

"No, no... I have to get it off. Get it off!" I plunged my hands into the water and scrubbed viciously. I scraped my skin with my nails. I couldn't tell how deep inside the demon blood had gone.

I pulled my hands out, my skin red and still stained black, but this time it had spread further, coating my wrists. I sucked in a panicked breath. "No, no, no, no..."

My hand went back in and I rubbed furiously. My skin burned, but it felt cleansing. It felt good. The blood needed to get out.

"Get out, get out, get out, getoutgetoutgetout..."

To my horror, the taint started to spread. I watched, my eyes wide as it crawled up my arms in black tendrils, wrapping around my pale skin like vines, seeping inside and becoming another network of veins that pumped darkness through my body.

I half slid, half tumbled into the water, clawing at my arms. I pushed myself to the surface and the water came up to my chest. I could feel it. I could feel it in me. Why wouldn't it wash off? WHY WOULDN'T IT WASH OFF?

"Sandriel." I heard that voice. The voice that belonged to both my saviour and my tormentor. I remembered him now. I remembered everything.

"Sandriel, look at me." That sleepy, seductive voice was closer now. I kept scrubbing. I wanted to look. He made me want to look. How could anything not obey his will? The stars would fall out of the sky just to please him. Who was I to deny him? I was just an angel. A weak, pathetic angel. A creature he could crush with a fingertip of effort.

No. I was more than that. I was his soulmate.

"Nadia," the voice said with an edge.

My head snapped up and locked on Lucifer standing at the edge of the pool wearing nothing but loose black pants and gold armbands. His hair was loose and untamed and so was his expression. The knowledge was there, burning in the dark, depths of his eyes.

He knew. God help me, he knew.

Chapter 12

We stared at each other across that small, suffocating space. The walls closed in, making my heartbeat sound abnormally loud, like cymbals clanging in my ears. I looked up at him, the wet strands of my hair sticking to my face like cobwebs.

"You…" I swallowed and started again, "You know."

His mouth thinned, and shadows shifted in his eyes. "Get out."

"Wh…what?" I asked, confused.

The fire that curled around the columns dimmed, then flared back brighter and hotter than before. "Get out of the water. I won't ask again." His voice held no threat, but the calm delivery had me gripping the marble edge of the pool, readying to haul myself out.

With will, I peeled my fingers back from the edge. Maybe I was suicidal, but some part of me was too tired to be afraid. Too tired to care. "Or what?"

The air drained away, leaving flimsy wisps that I valiantly struggled to swallow. His knees became level with my eyes as he crouched by the water.

Knuckles grazed the curving edge of my cheekbone, the gentle touch at odds with the hardness of his eyes. "Or maybe I'll join you. After all... it's been such a long time."

I flinched back from his touch. Now that I knew it should have been there, the lack of golden fire humming over my skin was disturbing. As I moved out of his reach, he grabbed my wrist so fast I barely had time to register it, stood up, and dragged me up out of the water. The cold air bit into my skin in tiny pinpricks as the water fell from my body. My feet slipped on the midnight tiles, but Lucifer's steely grip kept me upright.

His dark eyes slid from my face to the wrist he held captive in his hand. I followed his gaze and saw the raw flesh I had exposed with my nails. It throbbed with a dull pain, but all I really felt was relief. The demon blood had vanished. I was clean again.

"I believe one removes their clothes first before taking a bath."

I felt the intensity of his gaze run over my skin. Suppressing a shiver, I replied, "I wasn't taking a bath."

Firelight edged him in red and gold, giving him, a fallen angel, an aura of light. I couldn't quite read his expression. It was so cool, harsh, and unyielding. It said, 'Your life is infinitesimal, and I'm still deciding whether to let you breathe.' Yet... intuition told me that it was a mask. There was a current of emotion lying just below the surface, as hot and turbulent as a river of molten lava. I didn't know if I was grateful for the mask or if I wanted to tear it off and stomp on it.

"This is the fourth time I've found you here clawing at yourself." His grip tightened a fraction. "I'm finding the repetition tedious."

"Fourth time? This is the first time I've seen this room."

"No, it's not." Lucifer tilted his head slightly to the right, his dark hair sliding across his shoulder. "Though, you seem more lucid today." His voice took a silky edge, "I was beginning to think I might have to chain you to my bed."

"How about letting me go instead?"

He pulled my wrist slowly towards him, so my hand rested against the smooth, hard plane of his chest. "Now, why would I do that?" He leaned closer until his dark scent curled wantonly around me. "Especially since you've been saying my name so urgently in the middle of the night."

My face burned. I tried to jerk my hand away and failed. "I have not!"

"Yes, you have," he purred.

His insinuation ran through my blood like a trail of fire. I was suddenly very aware that I was standing in front of him, wearing only his wet, black shirt.

"My nightmares," I whispered.

A fingertip grazed the underside of my chin. "And your dreams."

I stared into his midnight eyes. "It doesn't matter. You have to let me go." I pushed at him again, agitated. "I'm tainted, I have... darkness inside me." I stared into his eyes, pleading, "I need to go back to The City of Light and be healed. I need to get it out before it consumes me."

I glimpsed the flash of impatience. "You don't have any darkness in you." Lucifer's voice deepened, "I would know if you did."

He would, wouldn't he?

"But I did things," I whispered.

"Did you?"

I shook my head, confused as images blurred and melded together in a melting pot of harsh colours infused with screaming... so much screaming. I pressed my other hand to my head as it started to pound, a dim echo of that horrible place, that dark pulsating...

"Look at me."

This time, there was no tone of command rippling through his voice but the seductive pull of a velvet cord that had me lifting my eyes to his.

As his eyes captured mine, I felt like I was falling, drifting in a swirling darkness that wrapped itself wantonly around my thoughts. He did it with ease as if he had done it before. My already fragile mind barely resisted, and I was captured in his power. I felt that tremble of fear as I dimly realised he had complete and utter control and my will could be bent as easily as a ribbon drifting in the wind.

I expected the worst, more darkness to engulf me, eating away at my soul, but slowly, I was drawn away from the horrors that lurked at the edges. There was a strength around me, formidable and sure, navigating me through the night like someone only forged in its depths could. Other memories crept in like filtered light. White wings, flying, the healing glow of a beautiful mandala, and apples…

I slowly came back to myself, feeling calmer and more settled in my skin. We stared at each other, our breaths mingling by the edge of the pool.

There was a strange sort of tension in the air. He had seen inside of me, and in a way, by doing so, he had also revealed a part of himself.

"I remember what you were before," I whispered. My voice sounded so intimate in the small space between us.

"Do you?" he murmured back, running his long fingers down my damp hair. The firelight reflected in his dark eyes, almost masking the emotions flickering within. His hand slid across my lower back and pushed me slowly forward. I pressed against the muscular contours of his body and found myself locked there, trapped against the heat of his skin.

With a tone of liquid silk he asked, "What do you remember exactly? Do you remember this?" His lips cruised along the side of my neck in a slow, sensual sweep. My eyelids fluttered in response, and I felt my skin shiver.

"Or this?" he said in smokier tones, just before his lips captured mine. I took a sharp breath through my nose as his flavour teased along my tongue. It was exotic and addictive… like him. His lips played sensually with mine, captivating my mind with a different sort of power. A more dangerous one. His hand curved around the back of my neck as he deepened the kiss an erotic inch more.

I let out a sound at the feelings stirring hungrily within me, at the touch of his body against mine, then felt the world shift as my back pressed against a wall. "Or this," he whispered against my lips as he let go of my wrist and ran his palm deliberately up my thigh, caressing my flesh.

Sweet Goddess… I burned…

He took me under again with a hot, drugging kiss. I kissed him back, chasing the pleasure he offered. His metal armbands filled my hands as I gripped them tightly. Desire stabbed through me as he lifted my thigh up and curved it around his. I gasped into his mouth, and he drank in the sound.

Instinctively, my mind reached out to his, seeking a deeper connection. I wanted to feel his energy blend into mine, our souls intertwine in the way they used to. I wanted to feel that hum come alive like wildfire.

I wanted to feel his thoughts the way he felt mine. I wanted to feel *him*.

I felt nothing. A cavern of emptiness greeted me, dark and cold.

My eyes flared open, and I jerked my head back, smacking it against the wall painfully. It briefly broke the lust-filled haze I had been under. His eyelashes slowly lifted as he regarded me with the look of a lazy lion enjoying its meal. I could see the hunger in them and the control barely leashed.

I managed to rasp out unsteadily, "Our link. I remember our link. Where... where is it?"

He smiled. My heart lurched, then raced faster. It wasn't a warm smile. The fire of the moment died slowly from his eyes, and I was faced with winter snow.

Lucifer let go of my leg and pressed his palms against the wall on either side of my head. "Our soulmate link?" He leaned down and brushed his perfect jaw against mine. "I would need to have a soul first."

The air hummed with danger. "You do have a soul," I whispered.

Lucifer eased back away from me. "Do I?" His large, midnight wings swept out from his back and stretched out across the room, making me feel impossibly smaller. Fallen angels had black wings, a marker that they lost their light. But did that mean they lost their souls?

I had seen firsthand what he had done. His actions were as dark and horrid as I had ever seen, and yet...

"I think you do."

"And why is that, little angel?" he crooned.

I don't know. It's a feeling I have. "You did save me..."

Lucifer let out a harsh, derisive laugh. His eyes flashed with contempt. "Is that what you think? You think I *saved* you?" He leaned closer until his face was a breath away and said distinctly, "I took you back because I *own* you. You foolishly made a bargain without reading the fine print, and now you are stuck here, at my mercy. Make no mistake, little angel, you are my property, and I can discard or keep you at my will."

His words angered me. "I'm not your *little angel*, I'm your soulmate!" Despite whether I wanted to be or not.

"You'll be whatever I *want* you to be."

Some part of me curled up in a ball and rocked itself. Another part snapped. I blasted him back with Light. "Stop threatening me!" I shouted.

Instead of the usual ball of diminutive size, a large horizontal bar of light appeared before my hands and shot out, hitting him in the chest. Lucifer flew back a few metres before his wings countered the force of my power. Light sizzled over his body like oil before dripping to the ground and melting into the inky floor.

My mouth dropped open.

The room plunged into darkness. Silence spread through the air, making my spine tingle with warning. Red eyes glowed in front of me from the shadows.

"Little angel, you have a death wish."

Oh no.

My eyes widened. "Uh… sorry… I didn't mean to… it just came out." I looked around, trying to see how far away the door would be.

I yelped as thick ropes of air lashed around me and yanked me into the dark. There was nothing to latch onto, nothing to prevent me from heading towards the lion's jaws. Those red eyes drew closer, and I was lifted up to meet them, my feet dangling off the floor.

My throat dried up. I could feel his anger like a palpable, living thing, pulsing around him in waves. A low, rattling sound vibrated through the air. It took me a second, then I realised that sound was coming from him.

Even though I was partly terrified, another part knew what to do.

Reaching out slowly, my hand came in contact with his shoulder. The sound intensified. I felt my way up until I cupped the side of his face.

"I'm sorry, Luce," I whispered.

The rattling stopped, and I was pushed away from him. I stumbled when my feet hit the floor and dropped to one knee. I conjured up a ball of light, which illuminated part of the room.

He was gone.

Chapter 13

Sepheroth stood on a pile of bones in the lowest level of Hell. Most of the bones were demons who had dared to challenge him. He wiped the blood from his chin with the back of his hand and let his sword disappear in a cloud of smoke. He preferred to dine on a different sort of cuisine, but for the moment, he had to be content with what this realm offered. He could afford to be patient… for now, at least.

Even demons had a hierarchy. To command the demon army was a long and vicious battle, but why spend energy wading through worthless meat when you could just pick the prime ribs from the top? He had bided his time, letting the arrogant and the ambitious feel confident enough to take the crown, fighting amongst themselves. While they squabbled and attacked each other with claws and fangs, he watched for the sly ones hiding in the darkness, building their strength and alliance slowly but surely. It was those he disposed of first.

With nothing to hold them together, alliances broke, and it was only a matter of time to bend the lesser to his will. He had hidden his bloody trail amongst his seven forms, each different and powerful in their own way. His rivals had no idea that a singular entity was working against them until it was too late.

And now the throne was his.

Soon, he could wage the war he truly wanted. There was only one being between him and the Earth realm. Even if he broke through the prison walls that kept him here, which was challenging but not impossible, he knew he couldn't engage the Warden of Hell directly.

Once he broke through the seventh level of Hell, combat was inevitable. Even with an army behind him, the outcome would still be uncertain. He needed something more, and he had been searching for a long, long time.

His patience served him well. Rumours began to filter down; interesting, enticing rumours that were overfull with possibilities. So, he sent messages to his allies in the upper levels to find out more.

Change was coming.

He clenched his fingers into fists. Soon… soon…

***

I didn't see Lucifer for a few days.

The master of the house had been absent, doing whatever nefarious things that amused him. That, or he was avoiding me. It was a ridiculous thought to assume I had somehow pierced that welded armour to whatever lay beneath. But as I replayed our last encounter, a part of me hoped.

Finding out he was a soulmate changed things. Yet, in the deepest part of myself, I knew he was more than just a soulmate. He was my Flame.

We have many soulmates in our lifetimes, people we are born with that we feel an inexplicable connection to. They can incarnate as lovers or even the best of friends. You are always drawn to each other as the wheel of time rolls on.

Flames were something different. They were your strongest soul connection, your mirrors, your other half reflecting the best and worst of you. They were catalysts, the ones who shattered and remade your world.

You can't ignore them.

Encountering them could bring you unimaginable bliss or exquisite torment. It all depended on how balanced you were within yourself.

I had seen Flames in The City of Light. Two people in harmony were exquisitely beautiful. Each other's strengths and weaknesses balancing out, and both growing together for their highest good. In that kind of unity, jealousy and selfishness didn't exist. Only love.

Ones who weren't balanced brought misery and pain to each other and to every person the couple touched. I didn't have to think long and hard to know which category I fell in.

My Flame was Lucifer. *Lucifer*. Lucifer was my Flame.

Somehow, my soul was meant to balance his out. It didn't matter how I said it, it still sounded crazy.

But that's where that irritating sliver of hope came in. Like a bright butterfly tormenting a swamp creature, I couldn't quite catch it and cease its fluttering. It paraded itself in front of me, teasing me with bright colours I had no right to see.

Being his other half meant that I did have some power over him like he had over me. That meant to a certain extent, we were exposed to each other. Eventually, the fissures in his armour would show, and I had a choice to exploit them or potentially heal them.

Being an angel, the idea of helping my Flame, who had spent the better part of eternity in Hell, seeped in all its rotting horrors, was a dangerous siren song. Trying to navigate those waters would mean I could crash and Fall, too.

Literally.

I couldn't stop being cautious, and I certainly couldn't let my guard down. Like a sentinel, I had to watch myself for weakness.

Another disturbing realisation was that Lucifer's absence made the nightmares worse. I realised now that his energy, as dark as it was, soothed me. Maybe on some instinctual level, my soul recognised him, despite the absence of our link. Somehow, he kept the rest of the darkness away, which seemed to be constantly circling around me like birds of prey looking for weak flesh. Since he left, the nightmares had been worse. Most of the time, I was afraid to sleep, sure my darker self would find me and continue our games of torture and terror.

Usually, I was right.

The dreams left me drained like I had been up for days without any rest. I longed to go back to The City of Light and restore my spirit in the healing chambers. After my recent adventure, I hadn't dared make another attempt to escape.

Thinking about The City of Light, I wondered if they had sent anyone looking for me. Part of me hoped they did, and another was afraid that they did. If Lucifer wanted to keep me here, no one was going to get me out. I had to find my own way out.

Rushton. I felt a stab of fear. I forgot to ask Lucifer during our last encounter. I still had so many questions. Was anything that happened to me real? I shook my head. I had to talk to my fallen soulmate.

I pushed open the doors to Lucifer's bedroom and tensed, half expecting him to be standing there, but the room was absent of his presence. My head throbbed thickly behind my eyes, and I reached up to rub my forehead. I paused midway and stared at my hands. They trembled slightly. I remembered the dark blood running down my fingers and the large bar of light that flashed out of them.

How in the Heavens did I conjure up that much Light? I had assumed in this place of darkness, my Light would dim, but it seemed to be growing instead.

How powerful was I?

In The City of Light, I barely used any abilities. I mainly carried messages from Archangel Michael's temple to other angels in The City. I was hardly ever in any danger, and if I was travelling I usually had a warrior angel accompanying me. Except, of course, that night I met Lucifer. When there were unexpected guests in the Devil's presence, he tended to get violently creative in showing them the exit.

If they managed to leave at all.

My stomach gave a low rumble, reminding me that I hadn't eaten. It seemed the Lord of the Manor intended to stay away for a while.

"Whattss are you lookingss for?" came the low hiss.

I let out an embarrassing shriek and spun around, white light flaring in my hands. A dark, hooded spectre hovered sombrely before me. Its features weren't solid but made up of black mist, shifting and changing in rolling waves. The only other movements were the wisps at the end of its cloak, fluttering in the air beneath it.

"Get back," I said, flexing my hand and readying myself to blast the spirit thing.

It didn't move.

After a couple of tense seconds, I said, "What do you want? This is Lucifer's room." *Oh, what, are you the guardian of his room now?*

"Whattss are you lookingss for?"

I frowned, my body still taut like a bow quivering for release. If this thing was here, I rationalised to myself, then Lucifer *must* know. Right? "What am I looking for? Um… clothes… food… a way out?" I ventured slowly. My Light flickered. I was too tired to hold it much longer.

The spectre floated eerily, then replied in that low, hissing tone, "Sussstenancce and clothingss will be left in the room youss arrived in." It paused. "Youss knows the ways out."

"Through the mirrors?"

"Yessss that iss one waysss out."

I blinked. Hang on. "Are there other ways out of here?"

"Yessss," came the hissing reply.

My heart rate sped up. "Where?" I asked urgently.

"Askss the master."

Master? Was this thing a servant of some sort? "Ahh… thanks, I'd rather not." I edged around the room towards the door. "Is it your job to follow me and make sure I don't leave?" I got out once, maybe Lucifer had taken further measures to make sure I obeyed the second time.

Its wispy form turned to face me as I moved around. "Youss are free to leave whenever youss wantsss," it replied.

"Uhuh." Sure, it made it sound so easy. I eyed the walls wearily, then looked back at the spirit. "Well, thank you. I'll be leaving now." I slipped through the doors.

Please don't follow me.

My Light winked out halfway to my room. I experienced a moment of panic, expecting the spectre to appear and attack me, but it had stayed in Lucifer's room. Or disappeared. Whatever that thing was, its intention wasn't to harm me... yet.

I merged through the wall and into my room and immediately spied the dress laid out for me on the bed. That was quick. To my eternal relief, it wasn't black with lace, but white. A beautiful white dress.

I picked it up off the bed and held it in my hands. It felt so soft and silky between my fingers. Hesitantly, I slipped off Lucifer's large shirt I'd been wearing for a few days, and put it on. The straps were simple, and the cut modest, but it clung to my skin like a silken spider web. The material shimmered and hugged my form down to my hips, then fell lightly to my knees.

Picking up his shirt, I draped it over the back of the chair and shoved some nut bread that had appeared on the table into my mouth. It felt so good to ease that gnawing ache in the pit of my stomach.

Eyeing the walls again, I hesitated. What if the spirit thing came back?

Well, there is nothing you can do about it anyway. You can't summon up any more Light. And if Lucifer wanted to harm you, there would be nothing you could do to stop him.

***

I dreamt of days long past…

I could hear them outside my window.

He was arguing with someone. The sound of Lucifer's melodious voice, taut with strain, made me raise my head off my pillow. I blinked, confused at where I was. Did I collapse again?

"…it's too late; the demon blood has spread too far," came a smooth, light-filled voice. "Your presence is the only thing that has been slowing it down. I'm surprised she's lasted this long."

"I know you can heal her, Raphael," Lucifer said urgently. "It's why I sent for you."

"I wish I could, brother, but I can't. It's not part of her fate."

His voice rose. "If she dies by a demon, she will go to the Demantos realms. You can't tell me that is to be her fate!"

I sat up a bit further, my heart hammering. I'm dying?

"Her destiny is written. I don't know where it leads, only that healing her is against the pattern. I'm sorry."

"Do it anyway!" His voice turned unusually fierce. "She could end up in Hell. I won't allow that to happen!"

I slapped a hand over my mouth to stifle the sound and reach for our link. Fear and anger burned through his usual calm, centred emotions.

"I know you care for her, but you need to let her go. There is no other way."

"Don't say that to me. She is my soulmate, Raphael. My Flame. Would you let yours go to Hell so easily?"

There was a pause.

His voice was steel. "I didn't think so."

"I don't know what I would do, Lucifer. You can't be with her. She is human, not in her evolved form. Her life would be a breath compared to yours."

"Then I would wait for her next incarnation! If she ends up lost in Demantos, or worse, in Hell, her soul won't incarnate. You know this, Raphael, so help me!"

"There is a chance she could be pulled into the higher realms. Maybe she won't end up in the Underworld."

An angry sound. "That is a slim chance, and you know it. I won't lose her this way. I'm asking you to help me."

The voice was soft and full of regret. "I can't."

The anger deepened through our link. "You mean you won't."

A sigh. "I know you don't understand, Lucifer. You've been on Earth for far too long; that's why you can't see this from a higher perspective. You need to come back to The City of Light and recharge. Then we can discuss this again. The demons have been breaking through from the Underworld in several places. The rest of the humans need your help."

"Tell Michael to help them. I'm not leaving her." I could hear the bitterness in his tone. "If you are not here to help, Raphael, then leave. I'll do this myself."

"Lucifer-"

"Go and don't come back here."

***

Dreams shifted like smoke, trailing through barren, foreboding lands.

I was lost in darkness. I stumbled blindly over rocks and tree roots, running from something. The feeling of dread was like a knot of ice, weighing me down. Whatever I was trying to run from was close behind. Its malevolent presence hovered over me like a dark moon, impossible to escape.

I tried anyway and almost tripped over her.

"Lycindra!" My friend from The City of Light was sprawled on the ground, unmoving. Her long, brown

locks blended in the dark, so all I could see was her still, oval face. Quickly, I knelt down and tried to rouse her.

"Lycindra, are you… are you…" I trailed off as I felt wetness against my palms. I looked further down her chest and screamed, falling back on the ground.

Her abdomen had been ripped open.

"No…" Something from above caught my eye, and I looked up to see another body strung up like a sacrifice between the trees. White feathers scattered the ground beneath him. I couldn't see his face. I wasn't sure I wanted to.

Getting up slowly, I spied more white feathers on the ground. There were bodies everywhere, hidden in the foliage, glimpsed behind trees like a horrifying treasure hunt designed specifically for me. Angels, all of them. Only the Creator knew where their souls were.

I screamed in rage. In anger. It tore through me, calling for blood.

"You don't like my present?"

I spun around, and there she was. My darker self watched me, amused at my pain. She was wearing a black shirt that was clearly too big for her. I knew whose it was.

I blasted a bolt of Light at her. She moved fluidly, avoiding my blow. I fired at her again and again, white fire crackling between my fingers. She ducked and weaved, her steps light and easy. I started timing my hits, anticipating where she would be before she moved.

She laughed and brought up a black energy shield, absorbing my power. "My, my, we are angry tonight." Smiling, pleased, she added, "Did the bodies of your friends upset you? They didn't give me much of a fight."

I didn't answer her. I wanted to destroy her. It was a need that consumed me until I couldn't think of anything else. My Light filled both my hands. I waited and let it intensify, and become stronger.

"Especially that one," my darker self looked pointedly at Lycindra in pieces on the ground. "She just wailed and ran like a little rabbit. I thought her heart may stop before I actually had any fun with her." She shook her head in disgust. "Healers."

I combined the Light together in my hands and, instead of throwing it, shot it at her in a stream. It almost blinded me. Our magic clashed together like thunder. She was doing the same with darkness. I gritted my teeth and pushed harder. Suddenly, the resistance stopped, and I stumbled forward.

"You'll never be strong enough to defeat me." I turned around as she slammed her hands inside my body. Dark energy crackled through me, fusing to my bones and bringing unimaginable pain. It melted my insides, burning my brain to ash. Liquid spilled out of my mouth. I couldn't breathe. I was dying, dying…

***

I slammed to the floor, shaking uncontrollably. I was in pain. I wasn't in pain?

"Get up," the voice was cold and harsh but warmly familiar.

Blinking, I stared at the floor, feeling disorientated as my dreams merged with my present. I tried and willed myself to move, but my body wouldn't obey me.

"Get up. I won't help you."

Tears threatened to show themselves, but I held them back. Instead, I struggled to my knees and glared up at him. I hadn't seen him in days, and now, when I did, I wanted to blast him again with Light.

Lucifer crouched down in front of me, his obsidian eyes hard. "Your fear is suffocating this room. Control it."

My nails bit into my palms. "You don't... understand." I managed to get out.

"I understand plenty." His gaze flickered dispassionately over me. "Stop fighting your fear and accept it. Otherwise, you won't survive this place."

"And how exactly do I do that?" I yelled at him.

He dragged me up by the elbows and turned me to face the wall. It shimmered, and a large, floor-length mirror appeared in front of me. I could see him behind me. His dark robe, which he wore over his bare skin, contrasted against the white of my dress.

"Hell is different for each soul. It shows you what you fear the most, and you live it over and over again." His eyes met mine in the mirror. "What do you fear?"

I let out a breath. "Turning dark," I said.

"You can. It's a possibility."

I clenched my jaw. "I won't!"

"Fighting the idea is foolish. You can, and it will be by your choice."

"I won't choose that!" I tried to turn and face him, but he locked me in place, forcing me to look at myself.

Lucifer raised an eyebrow mockingly and replied, "Then why are you so afraid?"

I opened my mouth and closed it. *He's right. I'm afraid of making that choice.*

"You can turn dark, but you're not yet. Not today. Accept it, and it won't have control over you." His eyes glowed with faint fire. "Every warrior accepts he can fall."

I pondered this, then asked boldly. "And what was your Hell? What fear did you have to conquer?"

His smile was a touch sinister. "Little angel, I lost my soul long before I entered Hell. I had nothing to fear."

"And how did you end up here, Lucifer?" I asked softly.

His fingers curled around my upper arms, and his face came closer in the mirror. I could feel the currents of energy swirl around in the room. "How did I end up here? I chose to." His tone was mocking. "Stop looking for something that isn't there."

"And what do you think I'm looking for?"

"My soul."

I clenched my teeth and swallowed. He was lying, or… did he really believe he had no soul? "Then how did you lose your soul?"

His fingers ran up to the back of my neck, sending shivers down my spine. "Are you interrogating me, little angel?"

I was balancing on the edge of a blade here. "I'm merely curious since you claim to have lost something that I feel is impossible to lose."

His obsidian eyes gleamed in the low light, and his hand tightened on the back of my neck, just a hair's breadth from being painful. "And do you think a soul could do the things that I have done and relish every second of it?"

"I don't know everything you've done," I whispered.

"Is that an invitation to show you?"

Suddenly, I remembered. "Rushton!" I blurted out, eyes wide. "I saw Rushton in Hell. Was that real?"

Lucifer let go of me, and I turned to face him. His beautiful face was marble. Everything was cold again except for the vicious fire burning in his eyes. "Come see for yourself," he crooned.

Chapter 14

I followed Lucifer into the room with the bathing pool. I was confused as to why we were there, but I waited to see what he would show me. Things might not make sense to me, but it was likely paved with perfect clarity in Lucifer's mind. Seeing the water, a pool of dark liquid lapping gently at the edges of the marble, made my skin itch. The urge to wash my hands flowed over me again; it was a hard battle to temper the need. The memory of my darker self was still fresh, and I needed to be clean of her.

Lucifer had mentioned that I had been to this room before, apparently out of my mind. I wondered what had happened while I was here. I glanced at his black robe, shifting loosely over his tall, muscular frame. What happened after he found me? As always with this angel, every piece I collected of him brought even more questions until I realised the piece I had was merely a grain of sand on the ocean floor. I knew something, and yet at the same time, I knew nothing at all.

Maybe I should just ask him and see what he says.

As I contemplated this new disastrous line of thinking, Lucifer stopped at the edge of the pool. He lifted his hands, palms facing together, then moved them slowly apart. There was a loud churning sound, then the water started to part as if an invisible blade ran down the middle. I already had seen him use the element of air with masterful ease, it seemed his ability to manipulate water was just as strong.

I watched as liquid rose high, yet not one drop spilled over to the smooth marble that surrounded it. A set of stairs that I hadn't noticed before appeared at the centre of the bath and led to the dark floor at the bottom.

Without casting a glance in my direction, Lucifer gilded down the stairs, the edge of his robe blending so well with the floor it looked as if he had emerged from the depths of the water himself. As soon as he stopped in the middle, there was a grinding of stone against stone. I watched as a square section of marble floor slid seamlessly beneath another piece. Another use of power, this time earth.

He then turned just slightly towards me, the shadow and light playing with his exotic profile. His dark eyes lifted up to my face and a sardonic smile flickered across his lips, before he turned back and descended below ground.

I moved and hesitated at the edge of the pool, eying the wall of water on either side. Wherever he had gone, it had to do Rushton, so I had no choice but to follow. Quickly, conscious that the vertical state of the water could be time sensitive, I stepped across the slippery surface to the place Lucifer had disappeared from.

I peered down. I couldn't see anything.

Was I supposed to jump down into a dark pit of nothingness? Actually, that could be exactly what the Ruler of Hell expected me to do. I called a bright ball of Light into my hand and thankfully managed to see another set of stairs. Walking down, I held the ball of Light in front of me like a shield. Almost as if my thoughts shaped it, the Light started to thin out and spread until it resembled a small disc.

I stared. Huh. Interesting.

The glow of fire beckoned me closer. I came upon a narrow tunnel with smooth dark walls only broken periodically by ornamental sconces. In some cultures on Earth, fire represented warmth, life, purification, and new beginnings. In others, it was a symbol of chaos, endings, and terrible destruction. I couldn't imagine Lucifer using fire to warm his hands in the chill of these halls but more as a source he could draw power from.

Like all the other archangels, Lucifer wielded all four elements, which included fire. It took great strength to manifest the elements at will without an external source. I knew Lucifer had that strength in abundance, but why use it when you didn't have to? Maybe that was why there was so much fire in this place. Fire was the most destructive element, even the strongest castle needed its own defences. Well, besides the three-headed serpent that resided within the walls.

The tunnel continued far ahead until I could see an opening that framed the fallen angel in an infernal border.

"Lucifer?" I called out. He wasn't facing me. It seemed his attention was fixed on what was in front of him.

More than a little uneasy, I made my way towards him. I should have felt weary of the possible dangers that could lay around me like unseen traps of serrated steel and wicked fangs, yet knowing that I was with the most vicious creature in existence made me feel oddly … safe.

Nothing could reach me if they had to go through him.

There was a slight pause in my step. Dear spirits, was I feeling a sense of *pride*? I *really* needed to return to The City of Light for some healing.

Then I heard him. "...been bored. You might as well get on to what you've planned, Dark One, before I die of old age." The voice was low and defiant, and it belonged to Rushton.

With a sharp intake of breath, I all but ran towards the sound. Rushton was here. Rushton was *here*. A hundred questions went in and out of my head in a stormy whirlwind. I threw myself forward, past Lucifer's solid, unmoving form, and stumbled into the room beyond.

He was in a cage in the centre of a large room. It wasn't an ordinary cage made out of materials such as stone or metal. I could tell instantly by looking at it that those black pulsating lines that barred his escape were formed from dark, crackling energy.

There was no fire in this room, but like above ground, the walls seemed to glow like molten veins running through ink. Rushton stood tall and proud in the middle of the cage, though his hair was mussed as if he had run his hands through it several times, and his natural angelic glow was dim and muted. The dark energy seemed to be draining his strength, and it showed in the tightening of his face and the hardness in those golden eyes. His wings were folded into his body, and the warrior uniform of white loose pants and closed vest was only missing his sword.

As soon as I stepped forward, his eyes narrowed at me. "Sandriel?" Rushton looked at me as if he wasn't quite sure if I was real or a trick of the mind. In this place, I guess anything was possible.

Did this mean that the things that happened to me in Hell… were real? Illusions and truth. It was hard to tell the difference in this place.

"Sandriel?" Rushton said again, reaching out as if to touch the bars but pausing before he did. "Is that you?"

I nodded. Did he remember me from before? "Yes… I… it's a long story." I took a step closer. "Are you okay, Rushton? Are you hurt?"

Rushton stared at me, frowning. I could feel his intense gaze rake over my form, analysing me and the situation. "What are you doing here?" he asked slowly. I could see his gaze flicker behind me to Lucifer. The fact that I was willingly putting my back to the Devil must be saying something, and I assumed it wasn't good.

I spun around and faced Lucifer, flinging my hand out behind me. "What is he *doing* here, Lucifer?" I shouted.

Lucifer folded his arms nonchalantly, the firelight flickering behind him. "Oh, I didn't bring him here."

I glared at him, my lips pressed together. "Who else but you would bring him here?"

"Me."

I turned around to see Rushton's head snap to the left. "Gregori," he uttered with a mingled look of distress and concern.

Suddenly, there was another angel in the room. Dark blonde hair flowed over strong shoulders like burnished copper. He wore a similar outfit to Rushton, except his was all black. So were his eyes. Even the white parts. Even his wings.

A fallen.

I stumbled back, then kept backing up until I collided with Lucifer's chest. "Lucifer..." I whispered, "there is a fallen angel in the room."

A thread of amusement curled through his voice like smoke. "Actually, little one, there are two."

I flinched at that and manoeuvred a little bit away from him, though still keeping close. "Who is he?" my voice stressed out.

"Turn him back!" Rushton snarled.

"Why would I do that?" Lucifer responded calmly. "He chose his path."

"You mean you tortured him until he had no choice!"

Lucifer shrugged. "Some angels' faith in the Light are less than others."

"Did you torture him?" I asked.

Lucifer gave me a half-lidded look. "Oh yes," he purred. "Most definitely."

"Shouldn't have come after me, old friend," Gregori mocked lightly. "You took the bait a little too easily. I'm actually disappointed."

"You were killing people," Rushton gritted out.

Gregori raised an eyebrow. "So?" he smirked and leaned closer. "Now look where you are. I would almost think you liked this place."

"Lucifer," I hissed. "Let him go."

Lucifer ignored me.

Gregori turned at the sound of my voice, his upper lip curling. "You have no place here to make demands, *angel*."

It was shocking to see the drastic transformation of another angel from the light to the dark. Gregori all but radiated violence and animosity.

"I bargained for his release," I said coolly, catching the look of surprise on Rushton's face.

Gregori stepped closer to me. "Oh, yes, I heard about that. Unfortunately for you, I recaptured him." His eyes took a dark glint. "I might be willing to negotiate his release for a price. I wouldn't be against having the taste of your blood on my lips."

Gregori looked past me to Lucifer and flinched. I didn't dare turn around to look, but the other fallen's face went from pale to snow.

"She doesn't belong here," Rushton interjected quietly. "Taking warriors is one thing, Dark One. At least we can fight back, but taking angels like her…" he shook his head, "seems there is no standard of low the Devil can't fall to."

I winced. "Rushton, you don't understand."

"Oh, I think he understands perfectly." Lucifer moved forward, his long black robe brushing the ground behind him. "He knows what manner of creature I am and has an idea of the depths I can sink to." Lucifer trailed his fingers across the bars. The dark energy that it was made up of unfurled out like a flower and caressed his hands like an obedient pet. "But only an idea."

He stopped walking, only to tilt his head towards me. "With such a salient reputation, it's a wonder why Archangel Michael sent her down to me in the first place." The corner of his sensual mouth lifted, but the look was directed at Rushton. "Almost like a sacrifice… or an offering."

What game was he playing? I opened my mouth to speak but found my tongue held by some invisible force. My eyes widened and then narrowed as I glared at Lucifer. *Why that black-winged…*

Rushton frowned. "You're lying."

"Am I? You heard it from her yourself. She bargained for your release." His voice took a velvet tone, "Sandriel is from Archangel Michael's temple, is she not? Do you think she would be here without him knowing?"

"If he did send her, it must have been for a reason," Rushton countered, but I could see the confusion growing on his face. Though Lucifer wasn't speaking the whole truth, the words he did speak were true, and Rushton seemed to be able to sense that. Only warrior angels went down to deal with the darker forces, not angels like me.

"Oh, it was. And now I have her, and now I have you." I could see Gregori smirking in the background as he listened to the exchange.

"Well, I don't see her in a cage."

Lucifer raised an eyebrow. "Yes, being the seasoned warrior that she is, she certainly needs one," he mocked. "Sandriel knows that if she attempts to leave, I'll pluck her wings off." Lucifer smiled and added, "Much like Devros."

Rushton's face darkened at the obvious taunt. Lucifer's words angered me, and I wanted to conjure up a sphere of light and blast it in his face, but instinct held me back. It wasn't because of Lucifer's reaction, but Gregori's. For some reason, my gut told me to keep my abilities to myself. For now, at least.

"More will come to face you, Dark One. In the end, the Light always wins."

Lucifer leaned closer and purred, "Does it feel like it's winning now?"

Rushton gestured towards Gregori. "Are you planning to try and turn all of us? Then what? You can't be so egotistical to think you can destroy The City of Light?"

"Is it less egotistical for you to think you can destroy the Dark?" Lucifer countered mildly.

Gregori spread his wings. "My power has doubled since my transformation. You would be a fool to think you can defeat us."

Rushton stared at Gregori for a few moments before he answered. I could see the undercurrent of pain it caused him to see Gregori touched by the dark. He said quietly, "We don't need to defeat all of you." He turned his head to look at Lucifer. "Just him. Then everything here will crumble."

Lucifer laughed, his teeth flashing white in the gold lighting. "Yes, and not in the way you would imagine."

"What does that mean?"

"You'll have plenty of time to ponder my meaning down here. Gregori," Lucifer said mildly as he turned back towards me.

"Yes, my Lord?"

"You have things to do."

Gregori flicked his eyes to Rushton, then nodded and disappeared. Literally, in a blink of an eye, he was gone.

Lucifer took a sensual gait towards me. I still couldn't speak, so I crossed my arms and continued to glare at him. "It's time to leave, little angel."

My eyes narrowed, and a spark of white fire crackled between my fingers.

Lucifer's mouth lifted as he caught my expression. "Oh, I wouldn't want to stay. I don't think you'd enjoy the company."

My eyebrow twitched in confusion, but then I heard the snarls. *Oh no, now what?* Black mist faded from two ferocious-looking hounds on either side of Rushton's cage. I saw Rushton move away from the bars, eying the demon dogs warily and clenching his fist as if he wished he was holding something long and pointy.

Yes, I knew what these creatures were called, even though I had never seen them before now.

Hell Hounds.

Blood-red eyes dripped with hatred from a muscular body the size of a pony. Their coat admittedly was beautiful ebony, shiny, and velvety, and occasionally punctuated by sharp protruding spines all along their back. Saliva dripped steadily from their mouths, pooling to the ground and steaming the surface of the floor.

They didn't look very friendly, especially when they snapped their teeth together and started stalking towards me like I was dinner with wings. Like chicken. That's what humans called it. Chicken.

I did not want to be chicken.

"Stay," Lucifer said sharply without looking. The hounds stopped instantly, their nails scraping against the floor as if an invisible leash pulled them taut.

Lucifer brushed past me and said, "You have a few seconds before they try and acquaint themselves with you." I heard him start to walk down the hall.

The force holding my tongue disappeared. I hesitated, staring at Rushton and then looking at the Hell Hounds watching me with avid interest. I turned my head towards Lucifer's retreating back. *He wouldn't, would he?*

"Go," Rushton urged. "Go, Sandriel, before it's too late."

"But I don't think…"

"Go!" he commanded.

The hounds started growling at me, their eyes becoming fever bright. I took a hesitant step backwards.

"Sandriel. Be strong. Don't let him corrupt you."

I flicked my gaze up to Rushton's golden ones. "I'm going to get you out of here," I promised.

I turned and ran down the hall.

***

I followed Lucifer into the large sitting room before I let loose. It took me that long because I had barely managed to leave the pool before the water came crashing down like two gigantic tidal waves.

I was surprised he had talked to Rushton for as long as he did. This current version of him didn't seem the type to engage in idle conversation unless there was a point to it.

"Lucifer," I called out. He kept walking past the opulent furniture, ignoring me.

"Lucifer!" I blasted a ball of Light just past his right shoulder. It hit the opposite wall and exploded into tiny sparks. I clenched my jaw and stared him down, which was a little difficult considering how tall he was. Out of the corner of my eye, I could see a tell-tale ripple in the wall.

A little voice in the back of my mind whispered, *What in God's name are you doing, Sandriel?*

He turned slowly, black robe flaring out, and gave me a sleepy look from beneath his dark lashes. That look, that look was a warning. Even in my furious state, I still couldn't help but notice how truly beautiful he was. Which, of course, only made me more angry.

I gritted my teeth. "Let him go."

"Now, why would I do that?" he asked silkily.

Why indeed? I knew any reasoning to appeal to his higher self was a fruitless endeavour. So maybe it was business. "What do you want for him?"

"Nothing," he replied coolly, folding his arms. "He remains here."

"There must be something you want!" I argued.

Shadows moved along the walls in strange patterns, and his voice took on a cruel edge. "Nothing that you have, angel."

I took a step towards him and said tightly. "Really? I am your soulmate, after all. It seems I am *everything* you're lacking."

Ice shivered through his voice, sharpening the tones to frigid points. "You say that word as if it's supposed to mean something. It doesn't."

My emotions stirred, wanting to be free. "So I suppose I don't matter to you one way or another?"

His eyes glittered. "Were you under the impression that you did?"

My voice rose steadily. "If I matter so little to you, why am I down here without any real purpose? If I matter so little, why did you get me out of Hell when I was taken? If I matter so little, why is it because of *me* that you're down here in the first place!" The last part came from deep inside of me. I realised now that knot inside my chest was guilt. Somehow I knew I was the cause of this. It had always been me.

There was a slight pause in the air. Lucifer regarded me coolly, an impenetrable fortress with no foreseeable way in. "Stop flattering yourself. Hell was and has always been my choice."

I flung my hair back with my hand in frustration. "You're lying. Or you're bending the truth!"

"It clearly fuels your pretty delusions to think so."

I tilted my chin up. "Is that right? What was it that you said? If I attempt to leave you'll pluck off my wings?" I moved around the edge of the room, keeping my gaze on him. "So you'll pluck off my wings, the Hell Hounds will tear me apart, and the Dragarth will use me as a toothpick?"

"Why, are you getting bored, little angel? Shall I make things more exciting?" he offered malignantly.

I turned around and blasted the wall with Light. With all the feelings coursing through me, it was like a miniature explosion. "Well, why wait?" I said fiercely. "We might as well get this over with now."

Dark energy wrapped around him, making his features darker, more dangerous. "Don't test me."

The wall rippled and I blasted it again, this time in a longer stream. "If every step I take is going to lead me to a horrifying end, what am I waiting for?"

I stormed over to the closest mirror and shoved my hand in, not caring what portal it was. "Go on!" I shouted. "This is what you want, isn't it?"

As if on cue, the Dragarth burst out of the wall in all its terrifying glory. The three snake heads weaved together hypnotically and a multitude of hissing sounds filled the air in a petrifying symphony. I swallowed, trying to suppress the terror I felt.

I looked over at Lucifer, and he looked back at me expressionless. The monstrous serpent knocked over half of the furniture in its single minded focus to get to me. For its size it was quick. It came at me in seconds. Its heads reared up at different angles, fangs glistening, preparing to strike, and I almost bolted through the mirror.

I knew I wouldn't make it in time.

I refused to close my eyes as it carved through the air towards me with shocking speed. I refused to conjure Light. I refused to defend myself.

Oh Goddess, I had miscalculated.

Just as that thought entered my brain, the Dragarth froze just a few centimetres from my face. I made a small sound in the back of my throat and looked at Lucifer. Untouched by the destruction around him, Lucifer murmured a few words in a harsh tongue I didn't understand. The Dragarth hissed in displeasure and slid away, melting back into the wall it had come from.

I turned towards my Flame, trying not to shake and stepped towards him. I could see the fury in the depths of his eyes, and something else, something I couldn't quite grasp. I invaded his space the way he so easily invaded mine and leaned up, gripping the edges of his robe and brushing my lips lightly across his. It took me a second to get the words out. "Maybe I do matter after all."

He gripped my chin and held my face close, our breaths mingling together, "Maybe you're right. Perhaps I won't harm you, at least not yet. But you didn't consider one thing, little angel. Your friends aren't off limits to me, and I do have one of them downstairs." Lucifer leaned down and kissed me hard and bruising, yet his hands ran gently down my hair. "Whatever I don't do to you, I shall do to him. And that, little angel, is not a lie but a promise."

There was a slight snap in the air and he was gone.

I should have been afraid for Rushton, and I would have been if there wasn't the slightest hum on my skin that caused my heart to pound in a different way than his lips had done. I almost didn't recognise it, it was so faint it could have been almost anything. But as thin and fragile as it was, I couldn't mistake it for anything else.

Our soulmate link.

It was back.

Chapter 15

Sepheroth watched the tortured soul writhe in agony. Its natural light had dulled as spikes of dark energy pierced it from a multitude of different angles. The soul screamed, and the other demons watched in pleasure and eagerness for their turn. It had become a game of who could make the soul scream the loudest. It was mildly entertaining, but his desires were darker and more vast than the few pleasures offered in Hell.

His lips curled in contempt as he watched the lesser demons squabble and fight amongst themselves over the flickering soul. They were like trapped animals, used to their cages and happy with the scraps thrown at them. Few had the capacity to conceive something greater, something worthy of their stature. And even less had the ambition or the patience to obtain it.

The beast inside him was restless, howling for the hot spray of blood and the taste of flesh between its teeth. His other forms were warring inside, straining to be free, but while he ruled, he preferred to be one entity. He was the most powerful this way and easily crushed those who tried to displace him.

Movement from his right stopped the current train of his thoughts.

"Kumaya," he said from his seat of bones. Sepheroth watched as two lesser demons dragged the snake woman to cower in front of him. Lesser demons could enter the seventh level of Hell, but they rarely did, knowing that they would end up as playthings for those more powerful. He had promised these two safe passage, providing they brought him something useful.

"My lord Sep… Sepheroth," she stuttered, her ruby-flecked eyes darting from him to the sport happening beyond. "I heard you requested my presence."

Her first mistake was appearing weak. Weakness was like blood in the water, and even he felt the desire to rip her apart piece by piece. He could smell the sweet tang of fear, taste it like a drop of honey on the back of his tongue, urging him to drag out more. He might indulge later, but first, he needed information.

"I heard there was an incident in the upper level of Hell, one that you were involved in." Sepheroth's voice, deep and cavernous, echoed around her, penetrating her ears in harsh ragged waves and making them drip with dark demon blood.

Her face contorted with pain, and he felt a slow burn of pleasure at the sight. "Yesssss… my Lord… there was an angel. A young female… not one of those warriors."

His interest escalated as the rumours he heard were confirmed.

Her forked tongue flicked out. "We found her lost, and roaming around in the Underworld, so we took her through a Hell Gate. We… played with her for a while before the Warden claimed her back." Kumaya reached up and grabbed her throat, rubbing it as an unpleasant memory seized her. "He was angry that we touched her and said if we came across her again, we were to return her to him, otherwise…" Her face twisted in fury. "The Warden destroyed many of our forms to make his message clear." She hissed and opened her mouth, displaying her fangs in a laughable, belated display of aggression.

Sepheroth knew that Kumaya would have grovelled so low in front of the Dark One she would have tried to meld her face to the floor. Her posturing did nothing but cement her position as a lesser demon. Her power was a mere flicker in a firestorm. The fact that she managed to command a few of them only fuelled his desire to shatter his prison doors. It would be so easy to control the upper levels of Hell with such weak leaders in charge.

This news, coupled with the information he received about an angel staying in the Dark One's domain, was ripe with promise. He needed to find out more. He wouldn't leave anything to chance.

"I would like to see what happened for myself."

Kumaya cringed as more blood seeped from her nose and ears. The other lesser demons who had brought her here seemed to be suffering the same effect. He could smooth the glass shards that lined the acidic notes of his voice, but he chose not to. Instead, he relaxed the immense control he had over his other forms, just enough to call forth the one he needed.

Dark energy swirled and condensed in a vortex within the centre of his chest and then moved outwards. He watched his skin shift and stretch as his other self emerged, peeling away from his body like a large newborn. Its own unique features slowly took shape as dark power rolled around its form. Not as powerful as his combined self, but strong. Very strong.

The lesser demons flinched. Kumaya cowered back.

Long black hair fell down his other self's back, smooth and straight, all the way down to his thighs. Pale skin stretched over sharp bones, heightened by ebony eyes outlined with kohl. Scarlet lips parted in an enticing smile as he locked on to the snake woman and long ivory fangs protruded.

Go, he commanded with his mind. *Find out what she knows.*

With pleasure.

Kumaya's ruby eyes widened, barely managing to scream as his other self struck at her neck in a whiplash motion.

As her blood flowed and her body convulsed, images shifted through Sepheroth's mind. The scene from Kumaya's perspective unfolded. There was more here than he thought there would be.

He was pleased.

There was a name for this form of his, a name that had slithered through the darkness, cloaking itself in myths and legends as it reached the soft, sweet world above.

Vampir.

When I arise, how unprepared you will be.

***

"Massstter." The demon floated across the room as Lucifer stepped out of the mirror. The Lord of Hell was wreathed in power and dripping with dark demon blood. His twin swords gleamed in the firelight and hummed with unleashed energy. Forged with the darkest of magics, they caused the inhabitants of Hell unimaginable pain should they cross the one who wielded them.

With the amount of blood and power that coated Lucifer, the demon assumed his master had gone to secure the barriers between the levels of Hell. He did this often and sometimes came back smeared with the blood of his brethren, with none of his own to mingle with it.

This first son of Light might be small in stature compared to some of the creatures that lurked in the lower levels, but his power eclipsed theirs tenfold. He commanded the darkness with the same ease he had commanded the Light. Many hated his authority, envied his power, and tried to topple the coveted position he had held for so long.

But slowly they learned…

To underestimate the Fallen One meant unimaginable agony, and for those used to the tormenting crevices of Hell, that was surely a feat. So, his rule was rarely challenged.

Clearly, this time, a foolish demon thought it could test the boundaries.

Lucifer stared at the demon with midnight eyes rimmed with crimson. After a few heartbeats, the crimson faded until all that was left was a dark, bottomless abyss.

"What is it?" the Lord of Hell asked.

"Ssshhe tried again to make it into the tunnelss below."

The corner of his lip curved slightly. His blades disappeared from his hands. "How?"

"Thiss time by merging throughss the floor around the baths."

"What happened?"

"The marbless wass too thick and sshe got sstuck."

This time his master did smile. It was quick and as rare as a merciful thought.

"How long has she been attempting to reach the angel?"

"Three nightss now, Masster."

Lucifer paused thoughtfully, then nodded. "Return, and keep me informed."

The demon nodded and slowly faded from the room.

He was confused by his Master's obsession with the frail one and these games he played. He first thought she was a snack, but as time moved on, she was still alive. He thought she was a bargaining chip, part of a larger plan in the game between shadow and light, but there were no plans to release her. Then he thought she was a passing amusement, but so far the Lord of Hell's interest had not abated but rather increased.

The demon had been here a long time, and every move his Master made was strategic and precise. He allowed no room for error. This was one of the reasons Lucifer held his power as the ruler of Hell.

So there must be a plan for the frail one. It was just a plan he couldn't see.

For what other reason would he keep her?

***

The demon followed his Master's energy to the Underworld. Unusual, he thought, for his Master to be here. He appeared on a rocky plateau and saw Lucifer facing another figure who was glowing with power.

Charcoal grey armour with heavy black accents moulded over the other man like a second skin. Spikes tapered wickedly up to a point on his helmet and covered various parts of his armour. At the slightest contact, the demon imagined those needle tips would shred through flesh straight to the bone.

There was the gleam of a weapon on his back, but with the position of the demon's arrival, he couldn't make out what it was. His face was also covered by a helmet, leaving only a narrow space for the eyes, nose, and mouth.

The posture the man took spoke of power and the arrogance of one used to wielding it. It also commanded the space around him, like he owned it. Of course, this wasn't just a man, he was a God.

Who else would this be but Hades, ruler of the Underworld.

Hades' voice flowed out like frigid water tumbling over jagged rocks. "Take care of your house, Lucifer, and I'll take care of mine."

"Then do a better job, Hades. I can't have dark witches summoning demons out of Hell."

He had underdressed for this meeting. Lucifer wore his dark, loose pants, gold arm bands, and nothing else. There was no weapon in sight. It gave the message that he didn't consider Hades to be a threat, or a significant one at that. An insult, and one that might be true.

The demon knew the Gods were powerful in their own way, and they had no great love for angels. If these two beings decided to war, the chaos would destroy the barriers between the worlds, and Hell would break loose. Knowing that, there was a tenuous alliance, a feeble tolerance for each other's existence.

"Have you forgotten that I control the Underworld, not the activities of dark witches and what they do in their leisure time on Earth? And is that not in the jurisdiction of your pigeon-flying family?"

"It seems you are unaware they ventured down to the Underworld to obtain the information necessary to complete the spell. If you're so ill-informed, Hades, I'd be happy to clean up your blind spots for you." The High Lord of Hell's eyes gleamed.

The God bristled. "Stay on your side of the wall, Lucifer. Your presence here will not be greeted kindly."

"Then take care of it. The witches will be back when they realise they can't summon their demon anymore. They will try and find another to take its place." He stared at Hades calmly. "I will expect they won't be successful."

"I don't answer to you, Lucifer," Hades growled, "but if the witches return, they will find their stay permanent."

Lucifer nodded with a faint curve to his lip. Hades faded slowly from the plateau. Once the God disappeared, Lucifer turned towards the demon and waited.

"Massstter…" The demon shifted closer. "The angel hass been in the bathings room again."

When the demon got no response, it continued, "Ssshe could not swwim and merge with the floor, sso sshe iss trying to empty the water in the bath, Masster."

There was a pause. "And how is she doing that?"

"By movingss the portal mirror, Masster, into the bath. The Dragarth iss not pleassed, Masster."

Faint sounds echoed below them. Haunting moans and low howls of a phantom wind.

"Masster?" From the lack of expression, the demon gathered his Master was not pleased.

"Make sure the portal mirrors don't move again," came the icy tone.

The demon bowed its head. "Yes, Masster."

***

I wanted to scream. I wanted to hurl all that water in the bath and dump it on Lucifer's head. The only thing was, I didn't have that power, and Lucifer would probably retaliate by lighting me on fire. It had been several days, and I still couldn't figure out a way to get to Rushton. All I could think about was him down there, trapped in a small cage, which continuously drained him of his Light. The Creator only knew how often Gregori went down there and what he did to him. I could barely stand it.

Short of pounding my head through the bathroom floor, there was no foreseeable way into Lucifer's underground torture chamber. My attempts to access the lower grounds had resulted in the Dragarth half tearing the room apart, and that strange, silent demon hovering around, vanishing the portal mirror I was using. It was a good plan, too, and it had worked. But now, the portal mirrors wouldn't move from the wall, and any other efforts had resulted in me being stuck in the floor.

I was out of options.

The room had been restored to its original condition. The disturbingly beautiful paintings of creatures, some I had never seen before, were back to their pristine state.

I paced around the bathing pool for the 23rd time in the past hour. My fists clenched and unclenched like they were restless to do something. Anything. The thing was, I wasn't entirely sure what I was going to do when I got to Rushton. There was the malevolent dark energy trapping him, the Hell Hounds, and potentially a Fallen angel.

I called up a white sphere of Light and let it hover in front of me. I let my intent mould it into a curved disk large enough to cover half of my body. The fact that I could manipulate my Light to create a shield was a recent discovery. Would it be enough to protect me? Probably not.

There was also the current understanding that my soulmate didn't really want to hurt me. If Gregori did come after me, I was pretty sure Lucifer would intervene. At least, I hoped so. After the Dragarth incident, I was becoming a little more confident that I wasn't going to be physically tortured for eternity.

But he had still left me with that threat, one that urged me to be careful. If I annoyed Lucifer, he'd take it out on Rushton. My soulmate had easily found my weakness and effectively used it against me. Maybe I was already annoying him by trying to get to Rushton. Maybe my attempts were only hurting the warrior angel.

I frowned and stopped pacing. What was I going to do?

You cannot give up, that voice in my mind whispered.

"I didn't say I was going to give up," I growled to myself. "I just don't know the best course of action."

My white dress gleamed in the dim lighting, making me feel like one of those lost spirits roaming around in the Underworld. Like them, all I could do was keep moving, constantly seeking a way out. But no matter what direction I took, I always ended up at the same place.

"Maybe I could just ask Lucifer if I could see him?" I said to the empty room.

The silence that followed was an indicator of how brilliant that plan was.

As I had expected, as soon as we had a confrontation, the Lord of Hell vanished, disappearing like a wisp of smoke in a dying fire. I wondered if he knew what had occurred between us the last time our wills clashed. The impact of that meeting still shook me to my core. Like a creature of the night that had lingered too close to dawn, Lucifer had left, sensing danger or finding a darker place to remind himself of who he was. Was he so steeped in darkness he hadn't realised the small crack of light that reached out towards me? It was so fragile and thin I was afraid I'd snap those gossamer threads by breathing wrong.

But I knew. He had a soul.

Even if he denied it. Even if he fought against it. Even if he had forgotten it existed at all.

He had a soul, which meant he wasn't completely lost.

I let out a slow, unsteady breath. But why did it show itself then, at that very moment? He had saved me from the Dragarth, but then again, he had saved me from Hell, and our link hadn't formed. It wasn't the fact that we kissed... was it?

Why do you want to keep experimenting?

I glared at the empty space in front of me and decided that question wasn't worth an answer. I pondered the train of thought a little more. I was still Light, so it couldn't be about me; it had to be about him. Something had shifted inside him. Just enough to let a little light, though. I just didn't know what it was yet.

I threw my hands up in frustration. "By the Spirits, my soulmate is driving me crazy!" I couldn't find a way underneath the pool room or ask Lucifer to let me go see Rushton... so, now what?

I wandered around a few more times, adding another five laps around the bath to my current total, then contemplated the intricate paintings on the wall. This one depicted a serpent rising violently out of the sea, annihilating boats and creatures of light with its massive body. It conveyed terror, hopelessness, and fear from those on the side of Light, and viciousness, strength, and power from the monster that sought to crush them.

I pursed my lips, touching the painting. It was typical Hell decor, but strangely I suspected the event was true. This did happen somewhere, at some time.

How many other rooms did this place have, and how many could I access?

If anything, maybe I could find my elusive host and prepare myself for another clash of wills.

***

The demon floated across the liquid surface of the floor, noticing its own darkness was so deep it barely reflected back at him. He could feel the threads of their spell-bond and followed its trail. Deciding to take the shorter route, the demon faded out and then back into a large hall.

The glint of metal flashed its teeth, varying in different hues and textures. The prickle of dark magic called to him, vibrating off the walls. Like a caged beast, it moved around the room with contained violence, just waiting to be released. He'd only have to feel the room to know what it was. The Mur' Shard. The Weapons Room.

His master was standing next to a gleaming block of onyx stone in the centre of the room. In front of him was an exquisite box of gold, inlaid with runes and spells. Whatever lay inside would have to be extremely valuable to be warded so heavily.

"Masster," the demon hissed, stopping on the other side of the rectangular stone.

Lucifer carefully closed the box and pressed his hands down on either side. He lifted his eyes slowly and let out a soft, "Yes?"

"Itss the angel."

"What now?"

"Ssshe's found the apple tree."

The solid stone table cracked, parts of it falling to the floor. Then in the flickering space between the beat of a dying heart, Lucifer vanished.

Chapter 16

My past had suffocated me since the moment I left The City of Light. It didn't seem to matter if I was awake or asleep; every night I was slammed with some feeling or memory that reminded me of another life. A life saturated with extreme emotions, as bright and sharp as coloured pieces of glass. A life that confused me because the warrior angel in it had never left but had found me once again.

If only the past had remained frozen. I could have looked at it from time to time, trying to understand the feelings it evoked and the layers of meaning revealed at every glance. Like art on a wall, I would have immersed myself in the moment and then put it safely away. I didn't want that picture to move, to become alive, pulling me into its world and trapping me there. Because that's how I felt now... trapped in a frozen moment.

I was in a large circular cave with no exit or entry points. Rough, brown rock climbed high over my head, disappearing into the darkness. I wouldn't have been able to see a thing if it wasn't for the circle of fire suspended high up in the air at the centre of the cave. Like a glorious crown, it served to highlight the importance of the single object below.

An apple tree.

I knew that tree. If I closed my eyes and had to mould it out of clay, it would look exactly the same.

Gnarled roots draped over the ground, sinking into the rich earth below before a few surfaced again to touch the heated air from the firelight above. I remembered tripping over them occasionally, trying to find a gap to press my back against the strong trunk. The bark was dark and rough, swelling only once to form a knot in the centre. I used to love placing flowers in that little hollow. It used to be my way of thanking the tree for its bountiful offerings.

Red glossy apples, swollen and ripe, hung from slender branches. They smelled sweet and tart, reminding me of baked apple pies, afternoon strolls in the dappled sunlight, licking syrupy juice off my fingers, and... him.

I stared and wondered if what I was seeing was an illusion or something impossibly real. Slowly, I walked towards the tree... and lost myself once more.

My back hit the tree as warm lips covered mine, making my eyes close and my toes curl in their worn cloth boots. I was grateful for the solid surface holding me up. My temperature was increasing quite rapidly, and I was sure I was going to form a pool on the ground like warm, sticky sap. I fisted my hands in the back of his vest, scrunching the soft material against my palms, and stretched it tight against the muscles that shifted slowly as he pulled me closer.

That golden hum danced along my nerves to a rich, feverish song. Notes thundered its way through my blood and vibrated down my bones, only to pluck a sweet melody along the edges of my heart.

Luce, my mind whispered in a soft sigh.

He answered by rubbing his thumb over the arch of my cheekbone and deepening the kiss until my sigh became a breathy moan. After a couple of mind-numbing moments of being pressed tightly against him, he pulled back slowly.

"I have something for you," Lucifer said huskily, untangling his other hand from my hair, pausing briefly to smooth the long strands over my shoulder. "Wait here, I won't be long," he murmured, his cerulean blue eyes warm and mischievous.

I smiled up at him, my lips still tingling from his kisses. I had been getting all sorts of gifts lately. Some from lands I had never even heard of. The last time Lucifer had given me a gift, it was exotic-looking sweets with foreign flavours that burst in my mouth in little explosions of delight. It was delicious and had me eager for the next surprise.

With a quick press of his lips against mine, he took a few steps back, spread those glorious white wings, and flew up into the clear, blue sky. My smile widened as I watched him disappear from sight.

A wave of dizziness passed over me.

I braced my hand against the tree and waited for the world to right itself once more. After a few minutes, the dizziness funnelled into a heavy sensation in my stomach, like the *weight of a large stone. I shook my head and rubbed my stomach.*

My appetite had not been the same since the night I met Lucifer; the thrill of meeting him had driven most things from my mind. But it was clear by these increasingly common dizzy spells that I needed to eat more and be less distracted.

I leaned fully against the apple tree again and stared up at the sky through the thick branches. It was becoming harder to ignore the desires that built up in me when I was with Lucifer. I couldn't help but want more.

Every touch was like a drug, a deep craving that could only be sated by replacing it with something more intense. He would hold my hand, and I wanted to slide into his arms. He would kiss me breathlessly, and I sought the touch of his skin. And then more skin. It was beautifully maddening.

I wanted more and was struggling to remember the reason why I should not have more. All the women in the surrounding villages were taught to only surrender themselves bodily under the sacredness of marriage. A union of the body had to be blessed by God first, and yet that simple statement only heightened the ridiculousness of my situation.

I was with an angel. Surely that meant God's blessing was a forgone conclusion?

It had occurred to me that I could get Lucifer to ask God, but it just seemed so trivial and utterly mortifying. Would God really care? I couldn't imagine Lucifer having that conversation with God. What would he even say? The more I thought about it, the less I wanted him to.

And if he didn't ask God, would there be consequences? I knew from the village that some couples did join together without being properly wed, but nothing really happened to them. They didn't get struck down by lightning or lit on fire. People just shunned and talked about them and said they had sinned. And sinning was wrong. But what I gathered from my conversations with Lucifer, God didn't get mad or angry about things humans did.

It was so confusing. I felt like everything I had been taught to believe was more complex than it actually was. Life was apparently simple.

And that simple truth was that anything done in the energy of love was pure.

Every action, every thought, and every decision made in that frame of mind was the highest, truest thing you could do. If you just asked yourself, 'What would 'love' do in this moment?' all the choices you could make would boil down to just one. And that was the path you should follow.

Though, it was harder than it sounded.

Carmine, the miller's daughter, always had something snide to say about the shabbiness of my clothing. I hadn't bought anything new in more than a year because I couldn't afford to, and she knew it. So she taunted me, and often in the hearing of others who whispered and made their own sly comments.

"Nadia, I was wondering where my kitchen rag was!"

"God, what's that smell? Must be the same dress Nadia has worn for the past two years!"

Love would not want to smack her in the face with a mud pie or wish she'd trip and fall into a pile of dung. Love would probably forgive her, as her father was forcing her to marry a man she despised for social standing, and she had probably just taken that frustration out on me.

But I still wanted to smack her in the face with a mud pie. So very badly.

I frowned and drew a circle in the soft earth with the front of my shoe.

If anything done from love was pure, how could being with Lucifer be wrong? Because I did love him. It was impossible not to love a being such as him. He was so perfect in every way, and most of the time, I didn't even feel worthy to be in his presence.

How do you hold a dirty piece of glass next to a diamond and compare the two?

Being human meant I had so many flaws, so many life lessons still to learn, whereas Lucifer was in tune with the deeper currents of life with every breath he took. He listened to a symphony that my ears had not been built to hear. I was so grateful for my time with him, for every single second, and I knew I didn't want to waste it.

I caught the shimmer of white in the distance, slowly coming closer, and I knew I had made my decision.

The vision ended, leaving me shaky. My hand trembled as I ran it over my face, pushing back my hair. I was me again... Sandriel.

I stared at the tree only a few metres in front of me. There were so many memories, so many feelings permeating the air, and I was breathing it all in like fine mist. It was like I could hear the ghosts of the past, snippets of conversation too soft for me to grasp fully in my hands. Fragments of memory flashed like light, but only the strongest beams hit me. I wanted to touch the tree, I wanted to see if it was real.

But I was scared. There was a memory hovering here, and it was dark.

I took a few steps closer.

"No, the one on the right." I pointed to the shiny, red fruit just begging to be plucked.

Lucifer stood on a platform of air, dutifully picking out the apples I wanted to bake for the fair.

"How many do you need?" he called down.

I squinted against the sunlight and spun in a slow circle. "I think there are only two more I can use."

There was that soft musical laugh. "You know I can get you some more from other apple trees."

I placed my hands on my hips and stared up at him. "I can't use those."

"And why not, my lady?" came the amused response.

"Because they are not from my tree."

"Is there a difference?"

"Yes, this tree is special, simply because it's mine." I gave him a wide smile. *"Which means everything is going to taste better... unless, of course, I burn all the pies."*

"And if you do, you're still going to sell them, aren't you?"

"Of course."

I shifted out of the memory. Close now. The tree was close. There was the scent of apples...

Another step.

I crawled along the grass, nails sinking through to the dirt below. Every breath I took felt like sand scraping down my throat. The tree was in sight. If I could just make it there...

My body spasmed, and I screamed through gritted teeth. I clawed the ground, tearing at it like I wanted to tear the flesh from my bones. Pain gripped me like the jaws of a monster, tossing me around with a cruel, calculated viciousness. My pain sated the thing churning deep within me, a dark shadow that had slowly solidified during the past week. I could feel the oily blackness whispering through my veins, becoming stronger as I got weaker, trying to kill everything it touched.

I vomited, spilling the meagre amounts of water I had managed to get down during the day. The spasms stopped, giving me a brief respite. I hauled myself back up on my hands and knees, exhausted, and slowly crawled, fell, crawled, fell...

This was the third time I had collapsed since Lucifer had left, and it was by far the worst. He didn't want to leave, but I made him. Especially since it was another demon attack... Oh, by the spirits, I wished he was here...

It had started again with the dizzy spells, followed by the bone-weary tiredness. Something was sapping my energy, but I thought I was just coming down with a common season sickness. But then came the visions... the tentacles lashing out at me in the dark, popping out my bones from their sockets and squeezing the liquid from the pores of my flesh. I could hardly sleep, tormented, scared, and alone.

The sunlight and fresh air helped, but not enough. It was consuming me, it was killing me. I was dying, and I didn't have long.

My hands touched the roots of the apple tree just as another wave of pain slammed into me. My back arched, bones creaking, wanting to snap from the strain. I fell forward again, my fingers curling around a root that had surfaced and dipped back into the ground. I pulled my body closer, dragging it over the ground. Tears blurred my vision as I sobbed harshly.

I called to whatever was out there. God, Goddess, the spirits...

Please don't let me die yet. Please. Just let me see him one more time. I beg of you. If there is any mercy, let me see him one more time.

"Lucifer," I whispered hoarsely.

My heart clenched in my chest, and the agony inside eclipsed the darkness that rode my body. I thought of his beautiful white wings, that slow, easy smile full of warmth and light. My lips curled slightly as I imagined those stunning cerulean blue eyes looking into my own.

Just one more time. Please.

I reached out blindly in my mind until I thought I felt the faintest gold hum. I clutched at it with the last bit of strength I had left as hot claws scored the inside of my chest.

Lucifer...

My forehead touched the bark of the tree, and my finger curled around the trunk as the memory faded. Tears dripped silently down my face, spilling over my chin to the floor. I slowly bowed my head and sank to my knees. I stared at the ground, breathing deeply, trying to calm myself down and failing miserably.

I knew he had been standing there for a while. Even in the midst of my visions, I could feel him in the background, like a satin touch caressing the corners of my mind.

"Did I die here?" I whispered.

He took a long time to answer. "No."

I sucked in a breath and stood up slowly. I still didn't face him. Couldn't yet.

"Did... did you find me?"

I felt the tension in the air. "Yes."

I knew he didn't want to answer, but strangely he did. Still not ready, I turned around anyway, bathed in the firelight above. When I saw him at the edges of the light, I trembled. That still aching part of me drank him in greedily, taking in every fascinating hard line and stunning curve. I felt more tears slip down my face.

He retreated further back into the shadows. "Stop that," he said harshly.

My voice shook as if a ledge was crumbling beneath it. "I... she... really loved you."

That tiny thread of our link became another.

I craved his touch, yearning for comfort I knew I wouldn't receive. My body swayed forward with the need as if pulled by an invisible string, but before I could move, his voice reached out to me, cool in the darkness, like a layer of thin ice at the start of winter. "You are dwelling in a time that no longer exists, little angel."

I took a step forward and gestured towards the tree behind me. "But it does," I answered quietly, my eyes wet and full. "You have my apple tree."

I felt him move in the shadows, carving his way through the ghosts of the past. "And you think that means something? Maybe once, little angel, but not now." His voice took on a deceptive edge under its smooth silken tones.

"When I descended into Hell, I took certain things with me. Things to remind me of my angelic side." The edge of his cloak slid into the light briefly before disappearing back into the shadows. "But I found I didn't need them anymore. The pale colours of your City no longer warmed me. I bathed in the fires of Hell with far more ease than I did in the Light."

His eyes glowed in the dark, a violent, deep red. "Time has a way of making things matter less, of making feelings and beliefs you once thought were important... obsolete. The tree meant something once, it doesn't anymore."

I studied his words in my mind, weighing the sounds of truth in them with the silence of things unspoken.

"Then why are you here?" I finally asked

He stared back at me.

"Why did you come here?" I asked again and wiped the tracks of tears from my face.

"I think you are forgetting, little angel, that I live here, and I go where I please."

"I didn't forget. But why here? Why now?"

Lucifer's face bled slowly into the firelight, casting his unholy beauty in flickering lines of red and gold. "Because... I can. Why?" he crooned. "Did you miss me?"

He emerged from the shadows, his ebony cloak flowing over his muscular frame to form a dark pool around him. Red eyes had darkened to black, and his skin gleamed in the firelight like molten gold. Lucifer moved towards me, his movements, the deliberate flex and shift of his body, a seduction all on its own.

"I... I was looking for you."

I felt his power reach out as he came closer, dark and sensuous. It flowed in the space between us until it touched the curve of my stomach. My eyes widened in shock. Phantom fingers trailed a delicate path over my navel and then higher, between my breasts. Slowly his power pushed me until my back hit the tree.

"Well, now you've found me." He closed the gap between us, bracing his forearms over my head and leaning into me. "What is it that you want, little angel?"

I closed my eyes and then slowly opened them."I've been trying to get into the room underneath the pool."

His eyes glinted. "So I've heard."

Did he really have to be so close while we had this discussion? Part of me knew what he was doing. He was using seduction for control, a way to sidestep the emotions that permeated the air around us. And if I pushed him, he'd leave.

"Has your pet demon been telling tales?" I didn't realise that annoying creature would be reporting my every move.

"They are not tales if they are true."

"Are we really going to talk about truth? When you liberally throw that concept around like grain in a chick yard."

I caught the glimmer of amusement behind his obsidian eyes. It warmed the darkness, making it seem like a starry night instead of a barren wasteland. "I think you've been spending too much time with your former self."

I sighed, not wanting to acknowledge where the farm reference came from."I want to see Rushton."

"I don't think you've earned that pleasure. And it is a pleasure," he said cruelly, "to see him wilting in the dark."

I glared at him, not liking the visual he had created in my mind. "What do I have to do to earn it?"

His lips curved, and I knew he had been waiting for me to ask. I groaned inwardly. The scent of apples wafted around us, sweetening the sour taste I had in my mouth.

"You look concerned, little angel." Lucifer brushed his lips over the corner of mine. I shivered and felt the weak, pale threads of our link flicker to life. I tensed, hoping he hadn't noticed the faintest of hums. If he did, he didn't show it in that sleepy, half-lidded look.

"Come find me in the bathing room tomorrow, where you have been spending so much time, and I'll take you to him."

I narrowed my eyes suspiciously. "That sounds too easy."

"Doesn't it?" he asked with a bored nonchalance.

"What are you going to do, make the room disappear?" I asked sarcastically while hoping this wasn't the case.

He smiled slowly, and my breath caught. "If I tell you, I'll spoil the surprise." He moved his hand and skimmed a finger down my neck. "There is also a price for asking."

I frowned. "What price?"

His lips slammed into mine hungrily, pressing my head back into the rough bark. Shocked, I rode the intensity of his feeling like a turbulent wave. The struggle of his control had cracked, and I was feeling the results.

I felt his tongue slide against my own with a carnal heat, making me feel like he was touching other parts of me with wet, slow strokes. I shuddered in his arms.

He took me down a road of deep, dark pleasure, and I blindly followed. His power caressed my skin with excruciating finesse, sliding over the curves of my breasts and down the dips and hollows of my hips. I felt the hot, open kiss of a phantom mouth at the base of my spine, skimming upwards between my shoulder blades and up the back of my neck. I arched in pleasure, the air slamming out from my lungs.

He was a master musician, playing my body with consummate skill. Every note he strummed drove me higher, made me want him more. It was a fast, burning passion, and I didn't try to stop him. I didn't want to.

I moaned in his mouth as desire spiralled deep inside me, tightening my muscles. I was so close to the cliff edge of pleasure, and all I wanted to do was fall into the abyss.

Then he stopped.

He eased back, the fire in his eyes brighter than the flames above. I saw the need in them that mirrored my own, but still, he took another step back, sealing the cracks in his armour with an impressive display of will. I saw the flash of satisfaction as my legs wobbled, and I slid down the tree, gasping for air. Tension still coiled within me, almost to the point of pain.

"Tomorrow," he crooned and left me there.

If only I had a mud pie. I knew exactly what I'd do with it.

Chapter 17

Sepheroth watched as the demons under his command gathered around him. Those in front avoided his eyes in case they incurred some particular form of torture he might be in the mood to dole out. Others shifted amongst the edges like feral animals, sensing the potential for violence, and waited to unleash their own brand of darkness that howled inside of them.

It was a constant battle for dominance and power, and those at the top never usually stayed there for long; but unlike many of his brethren, he had taken time to weave his threads of control amongst the hoard and had waited until he had enough strings to pull. Those who had the capacity to dethrone him had already been effectively neutralised, long before he stepped out of the shadows.

He slammed his fist down on his throne of bones, shattering the thick, yellowish fragments that his arm had rested on into hundreds of pieces.

The snarling and hissing silenced.

"The Warden of Hell has held us here for far too long." His deep voice resonated throughout the caverns, piercing the ears of all the inhabitants.

There was a resounding roar of agreement and insatiable anger. He silenced them again with a penetrating look from his crimson eyes.

"He is not infallible, he is but one being. A Fallen," he said with contempt. "An angel from the Light who thinks he can rule us. He is powerful, but not without weaknesses." His lips curled over the serrated edges of his teeth.

"Others have tried before and failed. What makes you think you can do any better?" a hooded figure from the centre of the gathering interrupted. Sepheroth knew him instantly. Markos, the demon sorcerer.

His pale, white hands curled around a staff made up of bone and pieces of the dead. Markos had many dangerous abilities that had secured his position close to the top of the hoard. By choosing to stand in the centre, trapping himself in a circle of violence, he sent a message that he was either foolish or extremely deadly.

As Sepheroth leaned forward, the demons around Markos edged away. "Others were impatient." His eyes glowed with fire, "Our Warden is holding something of value within his domain. You have just volunteered to find out exactly how valuable."

Markos straightened, holding his staff closer. A smoky haze formed around him, obscuring his form. "I did not say I was going to be part of your plans, Sepheroth. You do not rule me." The circle around Markos became wider, except for one or two demons who stayed pointedly close. Interesting. It appeared this interruption had been planned, even anticipated.

"If you are not with us, then you are of no use to me, sorcerer."

Sepheroth didn't have to wait long. Five swirling dark orbs shot out towards him with deadly speed just as Markos disappeared into mist. Sepheroth stood up as they hit him, exploding dark fire against his skin and hitting the floor in a sizzling rain. He barely felt it. A demon launched out at him from the left, and he grabbed it by the throat.

As it struggled, he squeezed slowly until its tongue flailed frantically out of its mouth in panic. His mouth elongated, and he crunched the demon's head between his jaws, spitting out bits of his skull and bloody flesh in front of his throne.

The other demon tried to attack him from behind. Sepheroth reached back with one arm just as the demon landed on his back and pulled him forward, slamming him forcefully on the carcass of his friend in front of his feet. With one foot, he crushed the demon's throat.

When a stream of dark metal shot out from an empty space to his right, Sepheroth tilted his head, letting the deadly tip slide just passed him. In a blur, he latched onto the metal lance with his hand and bent it with his fist. Twisting the weapon around his wrist, he continued to wrap it around his arm, bringing whatever was on the other end closer and closer to him. The metal tried to slide back, it even started to burn, but it couldn't compete with the unrelenting force that held it.

Markos flickered back in view as he got closer to Sepheroth. To his credit, the dark sorcerer's face was strained with determination, even as he saw his own agony etched in the long hours before him.

Embedding his claws into Markos' skull, the sorcerer screamed in raw, agonising pain.

"In a few hours, you will reconsider, Markos. Then you will do exactly what I say."

Some described Hell as a realm of fire, others described it as an icy prison, but Hell was really just about pain. It was about all the exquisite ways one could inflict the greatest amount of damage on another being. It was about finding that weak spot… and then stabbing, carving, and clawing again until that being was shattered to its very core. Then they were yours to do with as you will.

**

The food stall was simple this week. The only things that perched on my mother's faded cherry coloured tablecloth were several apple pies. Some were what I would have generously called "crisp," but they still smelled delicious. I would have made some lemon tarts, but I had run out of time.

My food for the week and general living expenses were dependent on my earnings at the stall, but ever since a particular angel swooped into my life, I had been abundant with all sorts of palatable riches. Therefore, the

222

need to bake and trade for ingredients had taken a lower priority. If I was honest, my lack of preparation was due to my utter distraction from Lucifer, even when he wasn't there. Washing clothes and mid-morning sweeps of my cottage were halted by foolish daydreams. There I was, staring out at the sky, a sloppy smile on my face with my wet underthings dripping onto the ground. I must have looked like an imbecile.

Being around him made me see things differently. Like a vine stretching towards the sun, I had suddenly grown past the fence, realising the world beyond was much larger than the world I had been confined to. Maybe it was just being around the energy of a greater being, whose wings frequently touched the stars above and whose mind delved into the great mysteries of the universe, tying the mundane to something more meaningful. Whatever it was, I was forever changed.

I hooked some auburn hair that had escaped my modest hairstyle behind my ear and watched the mix of people walking by. Everyone was familiar to me as I was to them. I had gone to the village and stood behind a food stall ever since I was a little girl. First with both my parents and then with my father before he passed away. It took some time to come back after that, to see the pity in everyone's eyes... at the poor orphan girl. But I had no choice. I needed the money.

I scowled as I saw Jacob, the chubby baker's boy, stuffed with pride, arrogance, and probably bread, kick at a stray cat that was unfortunate enough to get too close to his fat little legs. Then his gait changed to a slow, confident swagger, and I rolled my eyes as he passed by Jacinda's clothing stall. He could only catch glimpses of her voluptuous form as his view was blocked by the swarm of other men buzzing around, vying for a look from her honey-coloured eyes.

She flirted and laughed, and I wondered just for a moment what it would be like to be her. Jacinda was one of the great beauties of the village, and it seemed to me that she never lacked for anything. She had money, and her father was well-respected in the village. Having things didn't make her kind, though. She wasn't as cruel as Carmine, who laughed and mocked me, but she didn't say anything either.

"Hello, Nadia," came a sweet voice, breaking my reverie.

I smiled at the young woman with pretty chestnut curls. "How are you, Hannah? Is your brother back from his mining trip?"

She laughed. "Not yet! Mamma thinks he isn't going to come back. He has found a life of adventure, meeting new people, and seeing amazing things. He writes to us all the time and also sends us some money."

I smiled. "Well, that's nice of him. I'm glad he's happy."

She gazed down at the table. "Can I have a pie? They look great!"

Beaming, I placed two pies in a paper bag. She passed me a few coins.

"You know," she said with a sly smile. "Christopher would have stayed if you encouraged him."

"Why?"

"Nadia, he liked you! Everyone knew that!"

I flushed and stumbled over my words. "Oh. Well… you know. I'm not looking for anything. I wasn't… before… either."

Hannah gave an exaggerated sigh. "Well, I think you both would have been great together. But we'll never know now." She paused. "Are you happy?"

Something warm fluttered inside me. I smiled slowly. "Yes," I said softly.

She seemed surprised, then shrugged and smiled back. "Well, that's good then. I'll talk to you later. I have to buy some cotton for Mamma's sewing."

I waved goodbye and pocketed the coins, hearing them click reassuringly together with a few others.

Mr. Nash, the local doctor, walked past and smiled with a glint in his eye. He gave me a little wave with his fingertips that made me recoil slightly. That was odd.

"Nadia!"

I started at the loud sound of my name and turned to my right to see Mrs. Bedford ambling up to me with the pace of a broken wagon. It's not that I didn't like Mrs. Bedford; it was just that once she started talking, it was almost impossible to get her to stop. Most of the time, my lame excuses and highly contagious colds were my most effective means of escape, but here at my stall, she had me effectively trapped like a chicken in a pen.

I smiled politely. "Mrs. Bedford, how are you today?"

"Good, good child. You look well, clean at least today from the last time I saw you, if not a little pale." My smile took on a strained quality. True, Mrs. Belford had last seen me when I had tripped on the way home and fell into a line of bushes.

"I was just talking to Mrs. Anderson," she continued, the loose skin of her throat waggling to and fro as she talked. "And we were just saying that it was high time that you find yourself a husband. It's not proper for a young girl like you to be living by herself out there in the hills. Why, you could run into a manner of things and find yourself in trouble! And, what? With no one to help you?"

"I'm fine, I-"

"God knows some men could stumble across your home and," she whispered, leaning closer over my table so I could smell the overpowering scent of lavender she had doused herself with. "Do something untoward."

"I assure you I'm fine, Mrs. Anderson. I can perfectly take care of mysel-"

"There are many fine, eligible men in the village that would make a suitable match. Why, there is young Jacob over there, he..."

Oh, kill me now. I tried to tune her out and nod blankly, praying my silence would end the conversation as swiftly as possible.

~ Let's not wish for your death so soon, little one. I, for one, would miss your company. ~

The smile resurrected on my face and went into full bloom. I twisted my head around, trying to spot that perfect face.

"...Mr. Nash may be long in the years, but he has been looking for a wife for quite some time. I told him you might be quite agreeable. I'm glad you seem happy at such a..."

I strained to look through the throng of people. ~ Where are you? ~

~ Around ~ came the teasing response.

~ I can't see you. ~

~ Shhh... Mrs. Bedford is talking to you. ~

I scowled.

"Why, Nadia!" Mrs. Bedford admonished. "Don't look like that! It's very unbecoming. Mr. Tupper only has ten children, and they so need a mother to look after them. Why you and Mr. Tupper could have a couple more of your own and..."

Please save me, I implored in my head. Or better yet, save Mrs. Bedford before I stuff a pie in her mouth.

She is only trying to help you find a suitable man.

I raised my eyebrows. And you would be okay with that?

There was warm amusement to the voice in my head. A man isn't what you think about when you wash your wet underthings.

I gasped, slapping a hand over my mouth.

"It's true, I'm sorry to say, Nadia."

I had no idea what she was saying, but I replied quite firmly, "Mrs. Bedford, thank you for your concern, but I am quite fine on my own."

"I know you think so, child. But if you were married, then you and your husband could have looked after your father, and maybe he wouldn't have left this world the way he did. In fact..."

I stilled. A surge of anger passed through me, shooting like fire up my body and clouding my mind. Something inside me resonated with that anger and fed on it. How dare she. How dare she blame me. My fists clenched then...

A warm hand slid across my shoulder, followed by a rich, golden hum that sank soothing under my skin, distracting the darkness inside me with its sweet fire. My fists unclenched.

"Mrs. Bedford," came the rich masculine tones of the finest tuned instrument.

Mrs. Bedford's mouth was agape, her eyes practically larger than the circumference of my pies.

Her reaction was completely understandable.

Behind me was a creature made from some sort of pagan sorcery, designed to enchant your mind and bewitch your senses. He was Lucifer. No one's eyes could ever be prepared for his beauty.

The air wheezed out of her mouth in one long rush.

I think she's dying, I said in my head. His fingers twitched on my shoulder.

"Would you mind if I steal Nadia away?"

She continued to stare. When the moment stretched on to painfully awkward levels, Mrs. Bedford finally shook her head no in several jerky movements.

"Thank you, Mrs. Bedford," Lucifer murmured. "You are very kind."

He held out his arm to me, and I looked up over my shoulder. Even my breath stuttered in my lungs, and I had been seeing him for months. His rich, dark hair was pulled back, emphasising the perfect symmetry of his angelic face and the mesmerising deep blue of his eyes. This time, Lucifer wore a loose white shirt that still failed to conceal his broad, muscular frame and dark brown pants. He was trying to fit in. I smiled.

I slid my hand over the curve of his arm, and he led me away from the stall. I heard the whispers and hushed gasps. The reactions were mostly the same as Mrs. Bedford's; shocked into silence. Part of me revealed in the awe and envy that flowed like a thick current around us, but as I flicked my gaze up and caught the eyes of the women around me, I could also see their bewilderment openly on their faces. Why her? They seemed to whisper. What could he possibly see in her?

The corners of my heart withered as self-doubt took a pick and hammered away at the edges. My insecurities found their voice and spoke to me cajolingly. You will never match him. You are plain and simple. You are not beautiful enough, or intelligent enough, and you have no skills that make you stand out. There must be some mistake. There--

"Don't," Lucifer said out loud.

He stopped, turned, and gripped my arms gently. His eyes blazed with intensity. "If you could see what I do, you would not be asking yourself such questions. Do you think beauty to us is defined in the shape and colouring of the flesh? These vessels of blood and bone are just that. Vessels. They change their shape and size through every incarnation. Why would we place so much value on something so temporary as a body?"

"The only thing that remains the same is your light. The goodness, the compassion, the empathy, the generosity that flows from the heart and lights up the eyes. That light is carried through from lifetime to lifetime. And you've made a choice to feed that light, to make it stronger instead of dousing it in darkness. For those aware enough to see the strength and purity of it, it's the most beautiful thing in this world."

I didn't realise there were tears on my face until they fell from my chin, hitting the tips of my fingers that were resting lightly on his chest.

"But you're an angel," I whispered. "I'm just... me."

He rested his forehead against mine. "I'm in my highest incarnation. You have yet to grow into yours." Lucifer smiled, and it was like the warmth of the sun touching the shadowy corners of my heart, piercing through the dense foliage of inner doubt that had wound its way through my childhood and into my adult life. "And when you do... what an incredible force of nature you will be."

***

There is a moment, even in sleep, when you know you're in danger.

Your body becomes aware moments before your mind has fully comprehended the threat around you. You feel it like a sharp prickle along the skin, a coiling tightness in your chest, a low humming in the back of your mind. Breath accelerates to the beat of a galloping herd, and panicked sweat forms along your skin, dripping down your spine.

I opened my eyes… and moved, throwing myself to the floor.

Something slammed into the bed where I had been. It sounded large and heavy, and I could feel the heat radiating off it. There was something else… a particular clicking sound that made my blood curdle inside me.

I summoned a ball of Light and fought the scream clawing from my chest.

Eight eyes reflected my horror back at me. It was the size of a pony. It was covered in thick, dark, bristly hair. It was the largest spider I had ever seen. It clicked menacingly at me, raising its front two legs up in preparation.

Channelling more energy into my hand, I blasted my ball of Light at it. My aim was true, and the white orb shot out, hitting the side of its body. I heard its clicking scream as it fell sideways.

I ran. I managed to get one arm through the wall before it gathered itself and launched. Eight legs and a set of dripping fangs hurled in my direction. I blasted another stream of Light with my other hand and hit it again, flinging it backwards. There was no way I was going to make it through the wall in time.

It came up on its legs again and moved cautiously around.

"Lucifer!" I yelled.

I threw more Light, but this time it dodged fluidly and moved towards me once more. Fear tightened my throat. Where in the seven hells was Lucifer? Didn't he know this thing was inside attacking me?

"Lucifer!" I yelled again as I watched the spider's legs ripple with energy.

Ice ran through my veins. Of course, he did. He wanted it to. He didn't want me to reach the bathing room.

I was too scared to be furious.

I moved around the room, and the spider moved with me. Waiting for me to slip up. To fall.

What could I do? What could I do? WHAT COULD I DO?

I focused my fear and willed Light, in a short rapid stream, to shoot out like bullets. They were small and hard, but they made a bright electric spark on impact. Some of them hit, sizzling the hair on its body, and the spider screeched in pain. But it was also quick, jumping on the wall's smooth surface and scuttling towards me. When it threw itself at me again, I picked up the chair and whacked it as hard as I could.

A mistake.

It had gotten close to me. Just as its body hit the chair, something wet and sticky sprayed all over my face and upper body. I couldn't see. My back hit the table, and I went down. I flailed wildly, clawing at my face, trying to get it off. I gagged.

No, no, no, *no*.

The substance stuck to my fingers like slime. It was too thick, too sticky. I couldn't breathe. I couldn't get it off.

My vision went from red to black. Sensation began to recede.

I couldn't breathe. I couldn't breathe.

Everything went dark.

Chapter 18

Candle light flickered ominously, reacting to the stirring energy building inside the small wooden hut. The scent of wild, smoky herbs slithered through the air in spiralling coils, forming intricate symbols before fading away. Ancient words in hissing tones, almost too complex for the human tongue, slipped from lips painted in blood.

Black grease smeared the thirteen witches' eyes, veiling their dark magic from the Gods. The ramifications from the higher beings were a dangerous thing to play with, but the danger inside the circle they had cast was greater still.

The chanting intensified. Fresh bones from children trembled from their patterns on the floor. The hint of sulphur hit their nostrils, a warning that they were accessing the forbidden realms.

Hell was virtually impossible to break out of. The locks of the prison doors were on the inside, preventing the strongest demons from breaking free and roaming the Earth. But accessing Hell from the outside was a different story. If you had the right tools and enough power, you could pierce the veil for a limited amount of time.

The pronunciation had to be precise. One mistake could call the wrong demon or worse, break the holding spell to contain it. But the power to be gained was worth the risk.

Raven, the head witch, felt the portal slowly start to open and focused the energy of the circle to call upon the demon they wanted.

"Belial," she hissed. She said the demon's name two more times whilst slicing the flesh of her upper arms, letting her blood drip down to her elbows. "I call you and bind you to this circle. I call you from the fifth level of Hell and bind you to this circle. I call you by your true name, Belialgarth Malkitch, and bind you to this circle. I call you by will, magic, and blood. I call you from the power of my dark ancestry, from the relics of old, and from the circle of thirteen. Come. I summon you to this circle. I summon you into this circle and bind you to it. I summon you. Now."

The air crackled with electric power. Smoke filled the circle as if something was burning. Then there was a loud *SNAP*, and all the candles extinguished.

Darkness infiltrated, suffocating the glimmer of the full moon that hung heavy in the sky. It was alive, malevolent, and rolled thickly through the small hut as if hunting for prey.

The breathing of the witches was fast as they sensed something more evil than them in the centre of the room. Raven calmed her nerves. She could sense the great power of the demon and was both cautious and elated. Cautious because the covens will and strength would be tested to hold onto the binding of the circle and elated for such power could be used and channelled for their ambitions.

Raven tapped into the circle's power to light the candles once more, casting the room into a dim glow. The smoke cleared, but the potent scent of sulphur increased, as well as something new… the beguiling fragrance of apples...

She should have noticed the obsidian steel blade dripping with demon blood, but all she could focus on was his face. The demon had the type of dark beauty that could steal a woman's soul from her willing hands, promise all sorts of sensual wickedness, then drive her to complete utter madness.

Raven took a deep breath, taking in all that smooth golden skin over hard muscles. Surely this was some sort of demon glamour? From all the entries in her family's grimoire, Belial was not known to cast a seductive guise. His main objective was to play on emotions and guilt. He preferred to take the form of a man, but this… was something else.

Her intuition, which always alerted her when something was wrong, was screaming.

She cleared her throat slightly, feeling for the magic in the circle and reassuring herself that it was still strong. "Belial, our coven wishes to negotiate a deal with you." As soon as she spoke, the demon locked his midnight eyes with her. He smiled sensually. She shivered.

He crouched down at the edge of the circle and said, "What makes you think I'm Belial?"

The witches stilled.

Raven tensed. "Who are you?"

She didn't want to take her eyes off the demon to look at the rest of the circle. She could already feel their fear and desire for the creature through their magic link. Instinct told her that if she moved her gaze for even one split second, he would kill her. Though, that was almost impossible. He was bound to the circle by ancient magic that even the Gods had to obey.

"Are you the one calling my demons out of Hell?" he crooned.

Her palms became clammy. "Your demons?" she whispered. Raven's mind raced. If the summoning had gone wrong, she could close the circle and send him back to Hell. It wouldn't be easy, though.

She didn't have his name. If a witch had a demon's true name, she had a measure of control over them. Without it, she would have to use the circle's raw magic against him.

They could do it. Belial was a fifth level demon, and this demon must be the same to take his place. He might have even assumed control of the fifth level of Hell from his implications. She just needed some time to channel the circle's energy.

"We just wanted to negotiate," she said, her voice coming out stronger. Raven slowly started to feed the circle's magic into her body. She felt her blood begin to hum with power. "We could negotiate with you, too," she continued coyly. "For a little bit of power, we could let you possess a human and have a few uninhibited nights away from Hell."

"Negotiate?" he purred. If it was possible, the demon's eyes darkened. The corner of that perfectly sculptured mouth lifted. "By all means, lay out your terms."

She hesitated, halting the flow of power. Maybe this summoning wasn't completely fruitless. "I'm informed Belial could increase the power of our coven by the power of his blood. If you can do the same – double the strength of our abilities and only that – I'm willing to offer you a host to possess."

Raven knew to be careful with her words. "The host will be a healthy, attractive male or female from the town of Attica and of my choosing. They will even be from the upper or middle class. You can possess them for three earth days and nights. You can do whatever you wish with their bodies during your possession, but you will not harm me, my coven, or our families in any shape or form. And, I require you to perform one service during your possession."

Now it was her turn to smile. "I have a nemesis I wish you to eliminate. A priestess by the name of Adrianna who resides at Ares High Temple. I want you to kill her in the most horrible way you can imagine."

She paused. "What do you say, demon?"

The demon balanced the blade of his sword on his knee. "I think I have a better offer, witch."

Raven expected as much. Most demons had a particular style, like a signature dish that was attributed only to them. They wanted to do something to be remembered during their short stay on Earth. And she had to admit, she was curious to understand what this demon's particular brand was. If she had to guess, it would be something sadistic. Sexually sadistic. For a brief moment, she contemplated laying with him herself. The thought of touching that dark beauty excited her.

She responded in kind."By all means, lay out your terms."

The light glinted off his blade. "I'll allow you two choices. One, seven of your coven members die, and I'll remove only one of your eyes. Two, six of your coven members die, and I'll rip out your tongue."

It took her a couple of seconds to process what he said. When she did, the sharp prick of fear wedged its way between her bones. It hadn't been what the demon said, it had been how he said it. With complete calm... like a fact. Rain falls, the moon rises, and she was going to suffer.

Raven continued the pull of magic into her body, accelerating the flow. Her blood burned. "Demon, you may have gained some power in the fifth level of Hell, but here on Earth, in this circle, you are in my domain. I hold the power. I do not agree to your terms, and now you are no longer welcome here."

With a deep, controlled breath, she unleashed the power of thirteen dark witches into the circle. She chanted the ancient words she had been taught by her grandmother and her great-grandmother before her, fused them with her will, and felt the portal into Hell open. Using every bit of magic channelling through her body, she banished the demon from the circle and back into the Underworld where he came from.

Except... he didn't go.

She folded over, sucking in gulps of air as the magic drained from her body. Cold sweat prickled her skin. She tried not to give in to the shakes, but her hands trembled like an old lady in her last hour of life. The witches around her groaned with fatigue, spent and near to exhaustion. The room stank of fear.

The demon stood up slowly and snapped his fingers. Just like that, the hell gate closed. He stepped over the circle boundary. Her mind stuttered.

He shouldn't have been able to do... he shouldn't have...

The demon's voice was like rich wine laden with exotic spices. He moved around the circle like an arctic breeze, freezing every person he passed. "Even if you knew my name, witch, your fate would still be the same. I am not bound by Hell, Heaven, or Earth. Certainly not by someone so insignificant like you."

With a flick of his wrist, Clara, the dark witch second to her right, went up in flames. It was quick, but the putrid smell of burning flesh made her struggle not to vomit. Ash fell to the floor, scattering over the witches on either side and like that, she was gone.

The screaming began, shrill and panicked, as her coven scrambled to their feet, intending to flee the horror they had brought upon themselves.

"If anyone tries to leave, you all will burn," he said coolly.

Some of her coven members, with enough wits about them, pulled the others back from the door. Hushing their screaming into trembling whimpers.

Raven pulled herself together. Now was not the time to expose the vulnerable side of her throat. "What do you want from us?"

"Stop interfering with Hell," he replied softly.

She nodded and opened her hands. "As you wish. We won't summon any more demons."

"Oh, it's not going to be that simple." The demon casually moved the small children's bones with the tip of his blade. "Your lust for power is an addiction you don't have the desire to overcome. If you don't see me for a time, you'll start to convince yourself that this night was akin to a bad dream. You'll start to question whether you could have changed the spell, called a lesser demon, added more protection... be unnoticed. Your confidence will build, and then you'll cast again, and I will have wasted all my time." His eyes locked on hers, and she flinched. "And that, witch… will annoy me."

The point of his sword aimed in her direction. "I gave you a choice. Choose. Seven coven witches, or six," his lips curved. "One is already gone. I'll even let you choose the rest if you're quick enough."

Raven panicked. Dark Goddess, he was going to take her eyes or tongue. She'd never be able to cast again. The idea was unthinkable… unimaginable. Maybe if she offered him eight of her coven, he would leave her untouched?

As if reading her mind, he spoke before she opened her mouth. "No more bargaining, witch. Choose, or I will choose for you."

When his wings came out, Raven finally knew what they were dealing with. She froze in terror.

Then her friends started to die.

Blood sprayed the room in arches, splashing against the windows and doors. Bodies thumped to the floor like puppets with their strings cut. Heads rolled like melons, smudging carefully placed runes and wards. Some of her coven members tried to fight back, but it was like throwing a pebble against the onslaught of an avalanche. She couldn't even fathom such power, and still, Raven knew she was only seeing a fraction of it.

Even as her witches screamed, the desire for that power rolled sickly through her veins.

He crouched before her once more, and her eyes travelled up the perfection of his form to the unrelenting beauty of his face.

"I chose six this time, witch." The Devil smiled as her tongue began to burn. "Don't say I'm not merciful."

***

I woke up with my insides on fire.

It felt like acid had been poured down my throat, burning a languid path inside my body and consuming my internal organs one by one.

Demon venom. More specifically, spider demon venom.

As my mouth opened in a soundless scream, I felt a sticky substance covering my face and contouring my lips. I tried to open my eyes, but my eyelashes caught in a spider web. It had loosened enough to let me breathe, but now it was encasing my entire body. Struggling, I found my arms trapped to my sides and my legs immobile. I also started to swing...

Oh, sweet Goddess.

I was hanging upside down from the ceiling in a cocoon.

Panic choked me as visions of being slowly consumed by a gigantic, hairy spider flashed in my mind. Where was it? Maybe it was above me, watching me from the ceiling with its multiple eyes. Was it coming for me, checking to see if I was dead?

Terror pounded inside my chest, threatening to sweep me away.

Panic is a poison of the mind, liquefying your will and strength until it falls numbly from your fingers. It generously helps you become a victim, sending you off into a mind maze with no way out. If I gave in to my panic, my body would die, and my soul would be lost in some tormented place in Hell.

I couldn't rely on Lucifer. I was on my own, and right now, my insides were dissolving.

Pain slid across the edges of my concentration like razor-sharp fingernails. I tried to hold it at bay and trembled with the strain. I lost focus twice before sending my awareness inside my body, seeking out the demon venom slowly destroying my angelic form. I could sense the darkness immediately. It had spread fast from my upper arm where it had bitten me to my chest and stomach. The lower vibration of Hell had increased the demon's potency and made my angelic form more human.

I quickly but carefully visualised green light channelling down from the top of my head inside my body. Weaving strands of green light with white, I pictured it cleansing the demon venom, banishing it from my body. The darkness recoiled from the healing light, but its inky threads still gripped firm, digging its thorns further inside. It wasn't enough. This wasn't just a physical wound, this was something far darker.

I coughed and sprayed blood from my lips. It clung to the cobwebs around me like liquid drops of ruby.

Healing physical wounds from the Dragarth had been easier with my basic knowledge, but I wasn't trained in Archangel Raphael's temple of healing; I had been trained in Archangel Michaels. My role was to guide souls in the mortal realms towards the Light, and that skill seemed pretty useless right now.

Though... I did have one other ability.

Channelling Light itself. Pure light, which was the light of the Creator and the soul. It might not be able to heal a myriad of wounds, but it did have enough power to counter the dark.

I could feel the energy of my soul like a flame inside the centre of my being. Reaching down towards my wellspring of power, I channelled it inwards, making the flame brighter and stronger with my intention and will. I could feel it strengthening, coiling with power.

There was a buildup of pressure... then the Light pulsed out like a wave, sinking into the darkness. It tried to fight, raking its claws inside, trying to find purchase in the battleground of my angelic body, but the Light was too strong. Its tendrils shredded and weakened its hold, dissolving rapidly under its force. The burning pain receded until I could take in breaths of air without wanting to scream.

I trembled from the aftermath of the violence within me.

Then something skittered above.

I froze.

There was a soft clicking sound... the demon spider was above me.

The cocoon I was in shuddered from the movements above. My hands were trapped uselessly in front of me. The panic that I was suppressing reached up through my chest to choke me.

Think Sandriel! Think!

I couldn't move, and I didn't have a weapon. "Lucifer," I whispered, and I hated myself immediately for calling him. He clearly had something to do with this. But...why? Where was he? Our tenuous relationship was riddled with uncertainty. One minute, I was convinced he wasn't trying to torture me; the next, a giant spider was in my room trying to eat my face.

If I was a warrior angel with elemental powers, I could have used air as a barrier that would encase the cocoon, making it almost impenetrable. I had heard about angels who were so skilled with air that they could summon hurricanes from the sky and blast demons into the horizon. If I had the power of earth, I could shatter the ceiling above the demon and incase it with rock.

I didn't have any of those abilities. All I had was Light.

I flexed my fingers within the cocoon and called up a ball of Light into the palm of my hand. I could see its bright glow encasing my hand all the way up to my fingertips. In response, the web shuddered around me. I tensed, trying desperately to see through the cobweb.

I still didn't know the extent of my abilities and what I could do. I knew I was strong when I hit Lucifer with a large bar of white Light. The Light I had was spiritual, a force of love to counter the dark, but it had also started to do other things. In the underground tunnel beneath the pool where Rushton was held, it had begun to form a shield.

My attention was caught on the area of light that illuminated the spider web. The interwoven threads had been infused with a small measure of dark energy, but my Light had quickly destroyed the oily film in that area, even though the threads remained.

The Light I held in my hand was warm. Very warm. In fact, the warmer I thought it was, the warmer it was becoming.

My breathing quickened as I saw the thick threads slowly start to fray under the heat. There seemed to be a point right in the centre of the light where the web was giving way more than the outer circumference. Eyes widening, I wondered if instead of making my Light larger to blast my way out, I could make it smaller and more intense.

Just as I had that thought and intention... my Light shrank to a small dot. It became hotter, and brighter, and started to burn like a small laser. A small hole formed in the web, and the epiphany finally kicked in.

There was spiritual Light and physical Light. My abilities allowed me to do both.

The cocoon shuddered again, and I heard the clicking sound come closer. I felt the spider demon touch the top of my cocoon.

I was out of time.

Concentrating, I moved my hand in an arc and burnt through the web. I fell, hitting the floor and cracking my knee painfully against the hard surface. Rolling on my back, I saw the demon spider a split second before it launched, fangs out and beady eyes reflecting back my horrified face.

My hands came up. I thought of a shield and my Light spread out.

Crack!

The force of the spider demon hit the shield, pushing me back against the floor. It sizzled against the Light and reared up, scuttling back to a safer distance. My Light had spread out into the shape of a shell covering the front part of my body. Keeping my hands up and not really knowing what I was doing, I fused more energy into my impromptu shield.

The spider darted sideways, trying to get around my Light. I shifted my body quickly, keeping the shield between us. It let out angry clicking sounds, its pincers like knives clashing together. Then it spurted a stream of sticky web at me.

It hit the shield and clung on.

The shield prevented the cobwebs from reaching me, but it was becoming increasingly difficult to see.

I didn't want to risk burning the cobwebs again as my Light would shrink, leaving me exposed.

The spider jumped to the side of me again, its hairy body raised. I just managed to see it before it spurted another jet of web. It added another thick layer to my Light shield. It was going to get me sooner or later. I scooted back quickly until my back hit the wall.

Now the spider couldn't get around me. I heard the angry clicking, and yet another spray hit the shield. I could try and merge through the wall, but I didn't know if I'd be able to maintain the shield at the same time.

Lucifer, where are you? You couldn't have saved me from Hell just to let me die here in my room.

Some part of me believed he was going to come. Any second now, he would emerge from the wall or a hole and destroy the demon.

"Omphhhh," my breath slammed out of my lungs once again as the demon hurled itself against the Light covering me. My head bounded off the wall, and I winced in pain. A burning smell infiltrated the air, followed by more furious sounds.

I couldn't hold this shield indefinitely. I was already weak from healing myself from the demon venom. I couldn't let it bite me again. Moving my hands slightly, I tried to see if I could glimpse the demon spider around the edge of my Light.

I peeked quickly sideways but couldn't see it. Shifting the shield to the right, I tried to glimpse the demon on the other side. I saw fruit that had fallen on the floor, a broken chair leg, and a silver platter leaning against the bottom of the bedpost. In the reflection of that platter, hair-covered spider legs shifted.

Gritting my teeth, I steeled myself, then moved the shield and blasted a strong stream of Light at the silver platter with my other hand. Light hit the silver surface and bounced off at an angle… straight at the demon.

Hearing the sound of impact across the other side of the room, I dissolved the shield and scrambled up. The demon spider was slowly moving its crumpled form up from the floor. Its eyes eloquently sang songs of my death as it shifted towards me again. I blasted another stream of Light at it, but it dodged, slower this time. My Light managed to clip its front legs, sizzling its skin and causing it to shriek in pain.

My Light was hurting it but not enough.

Screeching, it climbed up the wall, blending against the dark surface. Oh no, I knew what it was going to do. I brought my shield up just as cobwebs flung over me. Moving the shield I hit it with a stream of Light again, just as it was preparing to leap. It sizzled under the intense glow, but I could see its legs bending, tensing, and preparing to launch.

Burn, I thought.

My Light shrank to a white hot, molten beam. It cut through the air and hit the demon. My fingers flexed, and the demon fell to the floor. In two pieces.

Black blood exploded across my face and clothes, followed by a decaying stench that made me gag. I slumped against the wall, insanely relieved and exhausted.

I had killed it.

I had killed it, and Lucifer didn't come.

Chapter 19

The demon blended through the wall from the angel's room, its shadowy wisps trailing like shredded cloth along the ground. He had watched the fight between the spider and the frail one with hunger, eager to join the building violence and appease some of his hatred towards the Light. Unfortunately, his orders had been very specific.

These games the Master played with the frail one were confusing. Sometimes it seemed like torture; other times like he was teaching her.

If he had free reign, if he wasn't bound… he shuddered internally, imagining the ways he would dull that angelic glow until it flickered into nothingness. Every instinct shrieked at him to destroy, but he was trapped in a prison within a prison. His actions, his instincts, followed a different set of rules than the ones nature gave him. Sometimes he envied his brethren in the lower levels.

He thought the demon spider would have captured the frail one again. Its size, strength, and speed were by far superior, but the angel had surprised him. He had not needed to intervene. She did not scream and fall into a mindless mess, which those unused to the horrors of the dark realms were prone to do. She did not curl into a ball and wish it away, or mentally detach from her body, sacrificing her flesh as she lost herself in the lands of oblivion.

She fought back.

It seemed that the frail butterfly was starting to metamorph, giving in to another evolutionary stage it had not realised it possessed.

But what would it become? the demon mused. Her Light was surprisingly becoming stronger despite the lower-level energies that compressed her from all sides. And yet the darkness was also taking its toll. He could feel her anger, her confusion, her doubt, and most deliciously… her pain.

Maybe the Master's plan was to make her Fall.

The other Fallen usually had that pleasure, torturing the warrior angels they had captured in various ways, relishing their screams echoing in their private realm. It had become a game to see who could break one first. Maybe the angel was the Master's personal project. After all, there were many ways to break a being.

He followed the threads of his Master's energy towards the portal mirrors, clearing the mist from their gleaming surfaces, and waited. There would be no sinuous movement rippling within the walls as the Dragarth recognised the creature to whom the demon was bound.

The three-headed serpent was a formidable defence against those who weren't welcome into Lucifer's private realm, a sentinel of destruction that had weakened the resolve of even the most ambitious of demons. It was not used to, however, keeping beings in.

The frail one had possessed some intelligence, the demon mused, to outwit the Dragarth, but not enough to realise that one only left Hell if the Master willed it.

When the realm the demon was searching for flickered before his soulless eyes, he stepped through, following the pull of his spell bond.

Kryptos. The realm between realms.

The neutral place.

***

A gold shimmer dusted the air, catching the light from flickering flames held in ornamental sconces. The shimmer slowly formed into the shape of a woman, tall with an abundance of curves that drew the eye and captured the attention. Dark hair fell straight, like a waterfall of shimmering silk beneath her breasts, and was adorned by a golden headdress that rose high above her head in the shape of a sun. Her flawless caramel skin was covered by an ornate gold breastplate with ancient symbols etched upon the metal and a white cloth that wrapped tightly down her hips and upper legs in a semblance of a skirt.

Amber eyes flashed like prized jewels in an ancient city and looked cautiously around the room with keen intelligence.

Such was the Goddess Isis.

In husky, displeased tones, she asked, "Is this for my benefit?"

Lucifer walked passed the painted hieroglyphics and images depicting the gruesome murder of Isis's flame, Osiris, by her brother, Set. The dismembered parts of her lover were detailed exquisitely along the walls, as well as her rage and despair.

Images shivered and moved. Blood dripped from the walls. "I thought it a fitting backdrop for our meeting."

A gold staff appeared in her hand, and her fingers tightened around its circumference. Isis's gaze cooled like a night amongst the desert sands. "That sounds like a threat, Dark One."

"Perhaps it is." He stopped in front of her, his robes folding around his frame and absorbing the light. "You owe me a debt, Goddess."

The word 'debt' stung her pride, but she didn't show it. It had been millennials ago since she had asked him for a favour, and back then, in that moment, she would have given him anything he asked without considering what a creature such as he would demand in return. "And now you are here to collect." Her eyes narrowed. "What do you want, Lucifer?"

There was a pregnant pause as he drew upon the tension between them like a long discordant note.

He looked at her with sleepy, half-hooded eyes. "You're going to send me back in time."

She blinked at him in shock, mind racing. What havoc could this being of the dark create through the passages of time? Every tiny change in the past was like a ripple effect; it could seem innocuous at first, but even just a small alteration could potentially wipe out an entire race. To give such a being that kind of power…

She needed to know. She took a breath and focused her energy, illuminating the crystals embedded in her headdress. Images flickered in her mind showing her possibilities of past, present, and future. They came at her in a rush, complex with hidden meanings and blends of truth.

Some possibilities were stronger than others, glowing brighter than other threads, but she knew firsthand how the unlikeliest paths could still bear fruit.

Intuition guided her mind, and she stilled.

"Archangel Michael's Flame. You want to go back in time when she was in her human incarnation on Earth."

Lucifer said nothing.

"Why?"

"You know better than to ask me that."

Unwilling to accept his lack of response, she took a risk and looked deeper. Past and present merged together again, weaving a complicated story. She flinched, tearing herself away.

"Isis..." Lucifer crooned, his gaze like a knife edge grazing across the column of her throat. "Are your eyes looking at things they shouldn't? I would rather not remove them from your head before you've paid your debt."

She felt a flicker of unease at his easy tone. "I am one of the Guardians of the Gate, Lucifer. It is my responsibility to ensure that travel through time does not disrupt the balance of light and dark," she replied. And sending him back in time would. She was still reeling from the knowledge she had gleaned.

He tilted his head casually. "Do I need to remind you that this is not a request?"

"We all have a choice, Lucifer."

He flashed her a slow, sleepy smile, and she remembered why this fallen angel was also called *kalliantri*, the dark seducer. "True," he purred. "You certainly have the choice to ignore your debt." The room became a touch darker. "And one night, you might wake up and find Osiris's head in Hell, back where I found it."

Rage flared like a wild beast, and she could feel her skin starting to darken. Slowly, she caged the feeling, shutting it down as she had many times before. She had learned a lot about herself when her Flame went missing, what she was capable of, and Egypt had suffered greatly for it. But this was what the Dark One did. He made you lose control, he exploited weaknesses with unfathomable ease.

"Do not threaten me, Lucifer, or my Flame. I'm not one of your demons to be ordered around. You start a war with me, you start one with all the Gods."

The calculation that shifted across his face was disturbing. "I wouldn't be concerned with a war with the Gods, I would relish it." His eyes gleamed. "But we both know you will give me what I want. Tick... tick... Isis. My patience only extends so far."

She paused, debating with herself whether to continue. She didn't owe Archangel Michael anything, but she did respect him. "We have a saying in Egypt... to seek without finding is worse than eternal damnation."

"I beg to differ."

"Do you?" Isis raised her amber eyes to meet his, calm with knowledge. "You searched for your Flame for aeons without ever finding her." She saw him tense, the slight shift of muscle. "I've seen your agony, the bottomless depths of your pain, the lengths you went to, the sacrifices you made trying to heal-"

Icy fingers gripped her throat, strangling the rest of her words from reaching her lips. Suddenly he was next to her, lips by her ear. "They say you're one of the more intelligent Gods in the realm. I feel like that has been grossly exaggerated. I would consider very carefully what you say next. Don't you know it's dangerous to peek in dark corners, Goddess? You might regret what you find once the dust stirs."

There were rumours, words whispered in the dark, that a long time ago, the Fallen One had killed one of the Greek Gods. Their body had been reversed inside out in a sphere, organs pulsating on the outside with their intestines trailing loosely on the floor. The God had still been alive, their tortured screams muffled inside their rolling flesh. It had taken 380 days to die.

She did not want this creature after her.

But she was not helpless, even in front of him. Her staff coiled around his wrist and yanked his hand from her neck. It hissed at him like a snake before resuming its original form. He raised an eyebrow.

Power rolled through her like thunder, and a golden cylinder flashed up from the floor to surround him. "Touch me again, Fallen, and I'll send you so far back in time you'll only have plants for company."

He smiled, and in it, she saw the unspoken challenge.

There was a sudden pull of energy in the room, and a portal opened, a circular, pulsating black mass that hung in the air. A demon slid out of its depths like an oily spill on a clear lake. Its face was concealed beneath a hooded cloak, and its body floated above the ground in tattered whisps.

"Massssterrr…" it hissed.

She had seen demons when she had ventured into the Underworld. A few had also emerged in Egypt before Lucifer took his throne in Hell. They were horrors beyond imagination, and the echoes of that time were still embedded in her peoples' psyche. This one seemed deceptively placid. In her experience, those were the most dangerous.

Lucifer made a gesture with his hand, and the demon stopped speaking. He turned back to her. She released her magic.

"What will it be, Goddess?" he asked softly.

Acknowledging the situation was difficult. The Dark One did hold the power, and he knew it. For what would the world do if he decided to release his demons on Earth? What would they all do? There would be a mass slaughter, the Gods' powers would diminish, and chaos would reign. It was a wonder that he hadn't already done so and deeply terrifying that he still could. She doubted that even the angelic realm could stop him.

A circular amulet appeared in the air, vibrating with power. "My debt is repaid, Lucifer. Concentrate on where you want to go, and it'll take you there and back. Once you come back, it will disappear."

The amulet flew into his palm. She watched him dismiss her, turn, and walk towards the portal. Her lips moved before she could stop herself. "Use it to go back in time and save her. You could stop the demon attack. It would change everything for you."

Without breaking his stride, he slanted a look over his shoulder, darkness eclipsing the whites of his eyes. "Hell suits me just fine."

The room erupted in flames, surrounding her from all sides, rippling down the walls and across the floor as he disappeared into the portal. She cursed, feeling the singe against her skin, and just managed to shift out.

Archangel Michael better be prepared for the storm heading his way.

***

I left my room, splattered with demon gore and covered in perspiration.

The foul, black liquid dripped thickly from the bridge of my nose and through the heavy weight of my hair, clumping the strands together and sticking them flat against the sides of my face. The sludge, mixed with fragments of hard shell, rolled down my legs like dripping wax and left a gory trail behind me.

I breathed through my nose and then had to quickly clamp down on the urge to violently empty the meagre contents of my stomach all over the floor. It was better than breathing through my mouth and risking a drop of the demon remains to coat my tongue. The Creator only knew how that would affect me.

Exhaustion threatened to slam me to my knees, but I pushed forward, stumbling, and silently prayed there were no more "surprises" waiting for me outside.

I had used too much energy in such a short time. Being untrained in my abilities, I was blindly groping for power like a child in the dark instead of with the skilled finesse of a warrior angel. The drain of that much energy to heal and defend myself was taking its toll.

In the higher realms, I would have been able to sustain such a surge of power and heal at a rapid rate. Here, with the press of darkness slowly but surely smothering my light, it was a colossal effort to regenerate.

I could have been my dark self, covered in pieces of my enemy. Yet, instead of feeling gleeful viciousness at the demon's destruction, it was betrayal that sparked an electric current beneath my skin. I felt betrayed... which was ridiculous.

Somehow I had believed that, despite Lucifer's insistence on my infinitesimal value, he would still protect me from harm. Hadn't that display with the Dragarth been proof of that?

Perhaps this was still an elaborate game, one intended to destroy me so utterly by giving me the one thing I couldn't resist. Hope. For what would lure an angel more than the quivering promise of redemption? I was looking only a few metres ahead, not knowing the mind maze Lucifer had crafted extended far beyond the horizon.

Fool.

My vision blurred, merging the sinister paintings on the wall into a softer abstract. Blood red became tones of pastel pinks and soulless black into lighter greys. Maybe that's what I had been doing, looking at Lucifer as an abstract, a compelling blend of past and present, trimmed with the golden cord of a soulmate link. When in reality, he was just like one of his demons in Hell.

What about the soulmate link?

I leaned heavily against the wall, smearing it with demon gore. My eyes tiredly flicked over to the direction of the bathing room. Almost there.

What about the soulmate link? the voice in my head insisted.

I pushed myself off the wall and dragged myself forward, passing a luxurious settee that I considered tumbling into and shutting out the world. But nowhere was safe. How could I rest when danger stalked me like a well-seasoned hunter? I had no idea what I was going to do once I...

The voice in my head intruded. *WHAT about the soulmate link?*

"I don't *know*," I hissed out loud. That was the piece of the puzzle I still couldn't figure out. And clearly, my subconscious mind didn't want me to make up my own conclusions without at least considering a key element in the equation.

I just... didn't want to think about it.

Well, think about it.

I'm too tired.

It's important.

The problem with my theory of Lucifer being determined to eviscerate my sanity and break my spirit was the fact that our soulmate link had started to reform. That meant he was changing, and I was changing him. But if I was somehow connecting to the tiniest fragment of his soul, shouldn't things be getting better? Shouldn't I be seeing glimpses of his former self?

I managed to make it to the wall that led to the bathing room and leaned my forehead against the cool surface. A sudden wave of sadness broke over me, dragging me viciously under. I swallowed thickly.

"Why do I even care?" I whispered. I should be concentrating on escaping, on finding my way to the Earth plane, or Kryptos where we first met, or even the Elysian fields if I managed to find the portal in the Underworld. When did my focus start to change?

When you started to remember who he had been.

By the Creator, I was so tired. I summoned the tattered remains of my strength and merged through the wall to the other side.

My mouth dropped open.

What... in the holy crystal of Archangel Michael's temple? This wasn't the bathing room. Was it?

There were candles everywhere.

Thick pillars of smooth golden wax filled the room, making the darkness seem softer and more inviting. They decorated the floor in tiered heights and hung from chandeliers that dropped low from the ceiling. Tiny flames were suspended in the air inside cut quartz crystals, forming intricate patterns along the walls.

The effect was exquisitely beautiful.

The rectangular pool had also disappeared. In its place was a narrow strip of water, which started near my feet like a beckoning path and led to a perfectly circular pool where white puffs of steam rose in delicious waves. The scent of apples and cinnamon spiced the air, and I noticed platters around the water's edge with red fruit and dark berries mixed with an assortment of cheese and nutty bread. A single black towel lay folded, almost blending in with the tiles.

It was a seduction, an enticement to my battered soul that yearned for something beautiful. With soft words and warm touches, it persuasively asked me to crumble my walls, my doubts and fears, and... enjoy.

So I did.

My hands went to the stained straps of my dress and slid them off my shoulders. The material stuck to my skin, so I peeled it off my body and kicked it to the side.

I placed my foot into the long strip of water and wasn't surprised to find a step there, leading me down. The water was deliciously warm, and when I slid into its depths, I couldn't help the gasp of pleasure that escaped my lips.

The remains of the spider demon sloughed off me, and I ran my hands through my hair, dislodging the hard fragments and congealed blood until it felt silky smooth. I washed my face clean and slowly made my way to the circular pool in the middle of the room. The flames flickered as I got closer, and the temperature rose to a degree where my muscles started to unknot and finally relax.

I was still aware that I could be attacked. I was also aware that Lucifer could possibly appear at any moment. I just couldn't find the energy to care.

The circular pool had a smooth curve of rock jutting out under the water line in the perfect position to sit down and lean back. I dropped my head back against the edge of the pool and sighed, enjoying the feeling of the water lapping against my skin, washing away the foulness, the grim, and the past couple of hours of terror and fear.

My eyelids drooped. I was tired of thinking, I was tired…

**

"What are they?" I asked, amazed. "They are so beautiful."

We were lying together underneath the stars on an old knitted green blanket my mother had made. My head rested on the smooth planes of Lucifer's chest, and my fingers were entwined with his. The golden hum of our link ran sweetly through me, playing a soft melody that filled me with joy.

Above us were what looked like a canopy of glowing orbs in different colours; smokey white, and fire red that shifted to orange and back, deep rolling blue, and forest green. They danced in the air, zipping around each other playfully.

"They are elementals," he replied softly. "Every angel has at least one type; earth, wind, fire, and water."

"Are these all yours?" I asked, surprised.

"Yes, usually there are five that come to you when you master an element, but more may follow if you are exceptionally strong."

I rubbed my cheek against his skin and half-joked, "Are you the strongest angel in all of Heaven?"

"Yes."

I blinked. "Pardon?"

"I am the first angel that has come into being," he said calmly, as if he was discussing what types of vegetables grew in springtime. "Then my brothers, Michael, Raphael, and Uriel, and my sister, Gabriel."

"You... you..." I stuttered, my mind still processing who this angel was next to me. "Do you rule over them?"

He laughed, amused, his vivid cerulean blue eyes glancing down at me. "No, little one. We are all created for a purpose and have our own destiny to complete. Mine is to keep the darkness at bay on Earth, send the demons back into the Underworld, and close up the Hell holes. The abilities I have been gifted with make me the perfect instrument for this purpose. Michael helps from time to time, but he mainly keeps the balance in the other realms."

"Are there many demons on Earth?" I asked, concerned.

A flicker of unease passed across his face. "There have been more and more each passing year." He explained further, "When there is a war amongst people, suffering or death, the natural barriers between the realms weaken and tears appear. Demons can take advantage of these breaches in the barrier and slip through."

I pushed myself up on my elbow and looked down at him, my auburn hair fanning around his face in riotous curls. He smiled at me and reached up to tug on a few of the strands. I stopped breathing for a second, entranced.

I blinked rapidly. I was going to say something. Oh! "So why was there a Hell hole near my house?"

He cupped my face, brushing his thumb across my cheek. "It would most likely be because the area has seen trauma periodically through many, many years, before you were born. It wasn't something that happened instantly but gradually over time. The tear could have been caused simply by something as unfortunate as an animal dying."

~ You don't have to worry, Nadia. I've taken care of it. You will be safe. ~ he said in my mind. The expression on his face was as determined as I'd ever seen it.

~ I know ~ I smiled back at him. ~ I trust you. ~

Unable to resist, I leaned down and slowly pressed my lips against his, enjoying the soft firmness as he kissed me sweetly. The hum between us intensified, drowning out my thoughts until there was only a golden wash of colour beneath my eyelids.

He tangled his hand in my hair and pulled me closer, settling my body against his. I could feel his desire match my own, the yearning to be closer intensifying. It was always this way, the wanting between us, and when it was interwoven with the shining threads of love, the feeling became pure, utter magic.

I sighed and deepened the kiss, and this time I felt his breath catch.

"Luce," I whispered against his lips.

He looked up at me, the incredible blue of his eyes like lightning across an ocean.

"I... I want...."

His expression changed, shifting from something soft and tender to alert and cautious. Lucifer swiftly rolled me over, caging me with his body. "Someone is at your place."

"What?" I looked up at him, confused. "But it's so late." My eyes widened, and I put my hand on his arm. "Maybe something is wrong? Maybe something happened at the village?"

"I'll have a look." He kissed me quickly. "Stay here."

He moved off me and stood up, unfolding his glorious white wings from his body. They gleamed in the night as if they were glazed with moonlight. His muscles tightened and then released as his wings shot him up into the sky. I watched him disappear in mid-flight, as if he had found a hole in the sky and slipped into another world. All but one of the elementals disappeared, a smokey grey ball that fluttered lazily around me in concentric circles.

"Are you here to watch over me?" I reached out with my fingertips, but the elemental darted shyly away.

Still disconcerted, I sat up and looked around. Maybe there was a fire in the village? It had happened before when one of the baker boys left the oven fire on unattended at night. But I had only found out when making a trip to the village a couple of days later. No one came to tell me.

My mind swirled around with scenario after scenario until I got up and started to make my way down the hill leading to my house. The elemental followed me, a little agitated at first as if I was disobeying an order. Even though it was dark, my feet were familiar with the terrain, nimbly avoiding holes, rocks, and fallen branches. I had played here as a child when my father was still alive, making up games and imaginary comrades to have adventures with.

I never felt lonely or wished for another sibling. It was only until after my father passed away that it became hard to be on my own, having no one to rely on and facing a certain stigma that came with being a female without any family. I had always kept busy, there was plenty to do around the property, but life had lost a certain spark.

Then Lucifer appeared, and my existence was irrevocably altered. The spark didn't just return, it returned with a ring of otherworldly fire. What else was in this mysterious world that I didn't know about? Angels, demons, Gods, and monsters. Even if I had a dozen lifetimes, I believed I would barely skim the surface. If I had to tell anyone the truth about Lucifer's origin, they would think I was crazy. I had no doubt the villagers would be convinced I was a danger to myself and find a place to lock me up.

We only know what we know. And by the spirits, we don't know what we don't know.

I made my way down the hill until I could see a glimpse of my home nestled amongst a field of wildflowers that had sprung up magically during one of the nights. There was a warm light shining inside, illuminating the windows.

Concerned, I quickened my pace and weaved my way through the trees. Did someone break in? I stopped when I noticed a familiar broad outline filling up the tiny door frame. Lucifer stood with his arms crossed, leaning casually against the side of the wooden frame as if he owned the place. Outside were two men.

I crouched down, squinting, trying to get a better look without being seen. If I wasn't mistaken, it looked like the other two figures were young men from my village, Edmond and Kaleb. Edmond had a bottle tight in his grasp and was swaying slightly on his feet. His long brown hair, usually tied neatly back, was messy and half out of its leather strap. Kaleb had a hand on his shoulder, twirling something between his fingers that I couldn't quite make out. He had always been unusually tall and lean compared to the people in the village, which was why I recognised him.

A shiver rolled down my spine. What were they doing here? They had barely even talked to me before.

After another minute, they turned around and started to walk away towards the path that led to the village, whispering and nudging each other. They walked here? It would have taken them at least a couple of hours. Confused, I looked back towards my house, but the door was already closed. The elemental flitted around my head and then flew off. Knowing what came next, I stood up, dusting the dirt off my pale blue dress, and leaned back against the nearest tree.

A few seconds later, there was a soft impact on the ground. Dust and leaves stirred, and the air shimmered like parts of it were made from water. He appeared looking serious… and disappointed.

"What is it?" I closed the gap between us and reached up to touch the side of his face.

"They were some men from your village."

I nodded. "I know. I recognised them. What did they want?"

He brushed his fingers lightly over my hip. "They said they had heard there were strangers in town and wanted to make sure you were okay."

I frowned. "That's odd. Did they say anything else?"

"They just asked how you were, then apologised for disturbing me and left."

"That doesn't make any sense. We've had strangers in town before, and no one bothered to check up on me." I gestured with my hands. "And why would they come now, so late?"

"They weren't telling the truth, Nadia."

The breeze picked up, sweeping my dress around me and flicking my hair into my face. I dragged it impatiently back behind my ear, even more confused.

I stared at him for a long moment. It took a second to click. "Oh." I took a step back as shock slowly crept up to my throat, holding me tight. "Oh." My heart rate kicked up. "Why?" I asked hoarsely. "Why would they do that?"

The disappointment in his eyes turned to sadness. "Because they are lost. They have forgotten who they are."

My fists clenched. "They are evil!" I burst out, my voice echoing through the tree, disrupting the birds above.

"No, little one," he shook his head, compassion softening his voice further. "They may do evil deeds, but they are not inherently evil."

"How can you say that after what they were thinking of doing!" I stared at him in disbelief.

"I have seen evil, Nadia. There are creatures from Hell that would simply destroy your mind just by looking at them. There is no soul to be found there, no conscious to guide them to a better path. There is only darkness."

Lucifer took a breath and looked up to the sky. "Humanity will always have a choice, in everything they do, to choose light or dark. That choice is made in every moment of their lives. They have the capacity for incredible goodness, love, and empathy as much as they have the capacity for hate, fear, and greed. There is always a path of redemption, even amongst the most lost of your kind."

"They just seem like demons to me," I said, almost in tears.

Lucifer folded his wings into his body. He took a seat on the ground and held out a hand to me. I walked over, and he pulled me down to sit in front of him. I leaned my back against his chest, feeling our golden hum and the soothing beat of his heart against my back.

"I will always keep you safe. You don't ever need to fear. I will always watch over you."

"But you have to watch over the whole world, not just me."

"And yet, to me, you're the most important person in it." His love wrapped around me through our link, and I breathed it in like it was sunlight, warming the parts of me that had gone cold with fear. Sighing, I relaxed into the depth of that feeling.

After a moment, I said, "I'm just angry that they could even think..." I sighed. "We don't need demons to hurt us, we hurt ourselves."

"Do you want to know a truth?" He rested his chin on top of my head.

I nodded. I had learned that some of Lucifer's truths filled me with joy and others with dread. The other week he had revealed to me that there were creatures called nymphs that could make dresses out of flowers. Other truths were not so pleasant, but I always wanted to know, if not for my own curiosity, but to give this beautiful angel someone to share his thoughts and burdens with.

"As you are by now aware, humans are no contest for demons. Demons can kill, maim, and possess, and no human on Earth can stand in their way once they are released. But... they rely on the very existence of humans to survive."

"What do you mean?"

"How do you think demons are created?"

"I don't think I've ever thought about it."

"Demons have always been the physical manifestation of the negative thoughts and deeds of humankind."

I sat there, stunned. "Are you saying we created them?"

"Every thought is energy, every action is energy, and all that energy channels somewhere. A single person might not create too much harm, but a village whose beliefs injure its people can create smaller creatures in hell. A war, definitely. All that blood, violence, and destruction can manifest in chaotic spirits that feed on pain. But it's the collective consciousness of countries and the world that creates the darkest of demons. When there is greed, hate, lust, and anger in the hearts of mankind, those emotions as a collective whole are unfathomably powerful."

I turned to look at him. 'The demon I saw that night when you found me, was that one of the worst ones?"

"No, little one, unfortunately, there are far, far worse."

"Are you trying to make me feel better?" I asked wryly. "Because I'm not sure this is doing it, Luce."

His lips curved. "This is a truth, remember. But if you want me to make you feel better, then I'll say that even though humanity created them, they also have the power to destroy them."

"I thought that was your task?"

"I may temporarily destroy them and send them back to the Underworld, but to truly wipe out their existence, that power lies in mankind."

"How?"

"When humanity starts to choose love instead of fear, darkness won't have the capacity to survive."

I pondered this. "You're right. It really doesn't make me feel any better."

***

I woke up in a daze, my body loose, warm, and relaxed. I wanted to drift back to sleep. I wanted to return to the arms of the angel who loved me. My eyelids opened slightly, and shapes of different colours shifted in front of me. The water lapped higher against my skin as I sensed another presence in the bath with me.

My eyes flicked open.

"Hello," my darker self said with an enigmatic smile. "I was wondering when you were going to wake up."

Chapter 20

My body jolted awake as fear punched a hole in my chest, crushing my lungs and squeezing my heart tightly. My rational mind started to shatter like glass. Short, sharp breaths escaped my lips. The room spun. I wanted to haul myself out of the bath. I wanted to blast her with Light until she exploded. And yet, I couldn't seem to act on either.

She laughed, a rich, vibrant sound as if she were at a fancy ball instead of a chamber in the dark recesses of Hell. "Oh, calm down. If I wanted to hurt you, I would have done so while you were sleeping. Plus..." droplets slid down her skin as she raised a shoulder from the water, "it would be a little silly to hurt myself now, wouldn't it?"

"You've done it before." Oh Goddess, what was she going to make me do?

She sighed dramatically. "Are you still holding a grudge? I didn't *hurt* you, I was helping you. Surely, you could tell the difference."

Her face was identical to mine, but the contours seemed sharper as if the cool calculation had whetted away the softness like a knife. Her golden hair shone brightly in the candlelight, making a stark contrast against the deep, soullessness of her eyes. The darkness I saw there reminded me of the spider demon but with infinitely more cunning and intelligence. I couldn't trick her. She knew me because she had *been* me.

"You're not really here." I took a deep breath and closed my eyes. *Go away, go away, goaway goawaygoaway.* Wake up, Sandriel. You're still sleeping. *Wake up!*

I opened my eyes again.

My darker self raised an eyebrow back at me. "We're not back to this, again, are we?"

I gritted my teeth. "What do you want?" The drum of my heart was deafening inside my head. I must be in a deeper sleep than I thought. Unless I wasn't dreaming. Oh please, by the Light, let me be dreaming.

I thought about Rushton. Was she here because of him? Was she going to make me torture him?

She rolled her head back slowly and stretched her arms out sensually along the edges of the bath. There was a hint of something feral in her dark gaze. "Power. What else is there?"

Liar. "No. You want me to be like you."

She gave me an amused look. "Well, how else are we going to escape? You're not strong enough, and you never will be if you dabble with the lighter spectrum of powers. And that's what you really want, isn't it? To escape?" She curved her lips knowingly. "Or have you decided to tumble into bed with the Master of the house?"

I didn't rise to the bait. "And it's only going to cost me my soul." Narrowing my eyes, I stared into her black ones. "I'm not interested."

She flicked a bit of water at me with her fingertips. I flinched.

"Now, now, let's not be too hasty." As she considered me with her disturbingly familiar face, her hand curved over a glossy, red apple. With slow deliberation, she picked up the fruit and took a large, juicy bite. Then she struck. "Archangel Michael sent you here. He *sent* you straight to Lucifer, knowing your history with him. Have you considered, that maybe, The City of Light doesn't want you back?"

I stilled. "I think they would want me to make my own choices."

"Maybe they gave you a mission and by leaving you'll be failing."

That hit too close. I slapped my hand against the surface of the water. "Stop it! You think I don't know what you're doing? I know what your agenda is, I know your ultimate goal. By staying here, I become like *you*."

"Temper, temper." She smiled at me pleased.

If I had the ability of fire, I would have drawn all the flames in the room together in one blazing inferno and burnt her out of my existence. My fist clenched and I almost felt a spark of power sizzle along my fingertips. "I'm going back. I *will* find a way."

"What's there for you anyway? I'd be so very disappointed if you sincerely believe everything would return to the way it was. You're different now. You know too much. Are you really going to be satisfied fluttering around delivering messages to the temples? They've hidden so much from you, your past, your abilities. They *lied* to you."

I stood up abruptly. Water streamed in a rush from my body and the cool air bit into my skin like tiny, sharp needles. I had enough. "All for a reason," I spat out. "I have the knowledge of my past now because it was the best time for me to know. Do you think I have so little faith in the Light that your words would make a difference? Do you really think I'm that weak? Maybe you really don't know me at all, which is why I will *never* be like you!"

She rose up from the water with more innate grace than I did, like a slender sword rising from the depths of a lake. Her body moved with a confidence and purpose that was completely alien. My darker self used her physical body in a way I never had. Like a weapon.

It took a will of steel that I didn't know I possessed to hold still and let her cup my face in her hands.

"Then why am I here?" Her voice was a soft caress.

I blinked.

"I'm here because you called me. You needed me."

"No," I denied.

"Yes. Shhhhh…" she said when I opened my mouth to speak. "You out of all people should know how powerful your thoughts are. How powerful your *fears* are. I am as real as you are. Don't be scared. You fought well today, but you don't have to go through this endless suffering. I am already as strong as you want to be. You don't need Lucifer to save you, you don't need *anyone*. With my help, no demon will touch you ever again."

I quickly knocked her hands away from my face. "Leave me alone. I can be strong without the Dark."

"In this place? Not likely." The corner of her lip curled up. "I'll be here when you need me again. In the meantime, I suggest you grab that towel. The Master of the house is coming." My darker self leaned closer and whispered in my ear. "Though, if I were you, I'd stay just the way you are." She pulled back and winked.

Then vanished.

It took me a couple of seconds to process her disappearance, then her words. I lunged to the left and picked up the thick, heavy black towel that was rolled neatly on the side of the bath. Opening it, I quickly wrapped it around myself.

He came like an eclipse on a warm, summer's day. His presence infiltrated the room slowly, raising goosebumps across my skin. The candles flickered, then dimmed as if the fire was anticipating the will of its master. I shivered, feeling the fragile threads of our link spark to life.

"Lucifer…" His name rolled off my lips like a curse and a promise.

"Did you enjoy your bath?" His voice wound its way through the room like the softest of silks.

"Where are you?" In the candlelight, the shadows were plentiful and the Ruler of Hell was practically a shadow himself. Everywhere and nowhere.

Not wanting to ask again, I decided to try something new. I drew my awareness within myself and sought the faint hum of our soulmate link. With care, I followed the delicate threads. I tugged ever so gently. There.

I turned to my left and waited.

The shadows clung to him unnaturally as he parted from them. Even now, with the confusion and betrayal churning sickly within me, I found him staggeringly beautiful. His silky dark hair was loose and untamed, and underneath his usual heady scent was the faintest traces of smoke.

"You're late," I said flatly.

"My apologies." There was a shimmer of amusement in the night black of his eyes. "I had assumed you might prefer a bath before you saw our guest."

I stepped out of the water with the towel secured firmly around me. "I'm surprised you thought I'd make it to the bath at all."

He took a step closer to me. "Oh, I had every confidence."

"You tried to kill me," I ground out.

His voice had the cool certainty of an unwritten prophecy. "If I wanted to kill you, you would already be dead." Pieces of white cloth materialised in his hand. He held them out to me. "Death is such a definitive word. We both know there is no death, only transition."

"And what are you hoping to transition me into?" I took the clothes from his hands. Our fingers brushed against each other and I felt the hum of our link thrum a note deeper. My eyes flicked up into his. Surely he could feel it now?

"Well, little one," he purred, his midnight eyes an infinity of possibilities. "That's entirely up to you."

I waited. "Can you please turn around?"

I could feel the heat radiating off his skin as if his body could turn into a column of flame. He smiled at me with a hint of that fire and turned his back to me. "As you wish."

I unfolded the clothes. They were a pair of long loose cotton pants and a short sleeve top that allowed for the opening for my wings. My towel made a wet sound on the floor as I dropped it. I quickly slid the clothes on.

"Are you trying to turn me dark, Lucifer?" I asked softly.

"I don't try, Sandriel, and the answer is no. As it is for any angel, that choice will always be yours."

I stared at his broad back, the contour of muscles exquisitely detailed in the candlelight. "But are you try… torturing me to make me choose the dark?"

"No," he replied with a slightly different tone, as if he was still trying to get used to that concept. "If I was trying to inflict that particular service upon you personally, little one, you wouldn't need to ask. You would already know."

Little one. What do you want from me, Lucifer? I wish I could trust you, but I can't.

I pushed. "Then why did you send a spider demon to attack me while I slept?"

"You seem to have forgotten you are in Hell. There are all manner of creatures down here that you need to get used to."

"Stop deflecting. Do you think I don't know that nothing can enter this place without your will?" I sighed wearily. "Just tell me, Lucifer. I just want to know why."

"Would it make a difference?"

"Yes."

"I'll make you a deal. I'll tell you after your trip to see Rushton."

Gesturing impatiently, I demanded, "Why can't you just tell me now?"

He raised an eyebrow at my outburst. His tone dipped a few degrees cooler. "Because I choose not to. Do you really have to ask?"

"So I might not survive this visit to Rushton, is that what you mean?" I sighed again, knowing arguing would get me nowhere. "Fine, it's not like I have a choice now, do I?"

"You always have a choice." He flashed me a smile and opened his fist. A current of magic vibrated through the room and a portal opened in front of us.

I frowned, confused. "I thought we were going to the dungeon underneath the bath?"

His laughter was sinister and amused. "Did you think that was a dungeon?"

The mist cleared from the portal, and all I saw was darkness. I drew back, alarmed. Was that the sound of screaming?

"It's time you saw the real dungeons of Hell."

***

Submission. There was nothing worse for a demon than having to submit to another. The humiliation of it burned deep, igniting a ferocious desire for revenge. There was little that Mardath wanted more. It was an all-consuming obsession that gave him the strength to endure the pain in Sepharoth's hands. And pain it was, layers of agony that raked across his being in endless moments.

He was excruciatingly suspended between destruction and the last gasp of life over and over again. The worst part was being led to believe the torture had ended just before it started all over again.

It had earned his respect, but it had also earned his hatred.

But for now, he had been given a duty, and he had to perform it well to gain Sepheroth's trust. To execute the plan, the timing was critical. Markos had found the perfect demon to help him with his plans. Stupid, eager, and unquestioning. There were plenty of them in Hell.

The upper-level demon blended through the barrier into the seventh level. They had scouted for days, making sure that none of the Fallen were on patrol in the upper levels. If one of the Fallen caught wind of a breach between the barriers then all their plans would be unravelled. It was the Warden they had to worry about now. That's why this meeting had to be quick.

The third-level demon hunched his body as soon as he saw Markos, mud-brown fur shivering with unsuppressed fear. Upper-level demons descended into the lower levels with trepidation, knowing boredom could make them easy entertainment for a couple of centuries. But the lure of power still brought them down, hoping for glory and alliances for the time when they would all break free from their prison.

"We don't have much time. Have you found the hidden portal to the Warden's domain?" Markos asked.

The demon twitched his head, one ear flickering rapidly. "Your map was easy to follow. I saw the false wall, but I didn't get too close as the Fallen are frequent in that area."

"Leave the Fallen to me," the dark sorcerer responded. "We will create a large enough distraction in the fifth-level to draw most of them away. I have spelled a vial of my blood that will cloak your presence and shield you from view if you come into close proximity to any of them. We chose you for your natural stealth. Don't disappoint us."

The rat demon preened.

Markos retrieved a miniature black vial from the folds of his cloak and a dull silver amulet with obsidian stones embedded in the metal. The amulet hummed softly with power. "Take this," he said, handing over the vial, which the demon snatched eagerly, "approximately a minute before you need it. It will last the whole journey and back... unless you get caught."

He let the amulet hang by its red demon skin cord. It swayed hypnotically back and forth, and the rat demon's clawed hand spasmed as if aching to snatch the object and dash off with it.

"Is that... is that the weapon?" the demon asked eagerly, spiked tail lashing out behind him.

"This will kill the Dragarth."

"How do I use it?"

"It needs a drop of your blood to connect the spell to your energy vibration. When it senses the Dragath's attack, it will confuse the serpent heads to kill each other." Markos gestured to the demon. "Give me your hand," he ordered.

The demon held out his furry arm in anticipation. Markos moved his finger above the skin. Invisible blades drew a shallow cut releasing black demon blood to the surface. He pressed the amulet to the wound and chanted the spell. The amulet grew warm in his hand, glowing softly before returning to its original state.

"Now, place it around your neck. You must have it on you when you face the Dragarth, otherwise, it won't work."

The rat demon hastily put it on, stroking the cool metal with its claws. "That is all?"

"That is all," Markos confirmed. "You will be rewarded beyond measure. The true Ruler of Hell will count you amongst his legion when we break through to the Earth realm."

The demon nodded enthusiastically. He bowed, turning to scurry off.

Stupid, eager, and unquestioning.

"Neezen," he called the rat demon by his name. Neezen paused, his beady red eyes unblinking over his shoulder. "The rewards are bountiful, but fail, and we will tear you apart."

***

I didn't know what to expect. It was probably because my mind didn't have the imagination to conjure the ways a being could truly suffer, or the slightest understanding of how to crush a spark of light into nothing until it chose to become everything it abhorred. To know how to twist a soul into dark dimensions it had never experienced before took the most sadistic of minds, a shade of evil so black that a single drop of it would blot out the sun.

But the Devil knew. He had written the instructions.

The portal Lucifer had conjured closed with an audible snap behind us. We were in a tunnel, lit by long metal torch stands lining either side of the wall. The air felt different here, it hummed with anticipation, edged with violence. I could hear noises not too far up ahead, faint echoes of screams and shouting... though the tones had a different quality to them. I realised it wasn't the sounds of pain I heard but those of excitement.

Was Rushton here somewhere?

As we walked ahead, the sounds changed to a low drumming chant. I flicked a glance up at Lucifer. "What is this place?"

"This is where we keep the warrior angels. We are in the Fallen's domain."

I sucked in a breath. The Fallen. All the angels of Light that had been turned by Lucifer. I never knew how many we had actually lost to the Dark, and as far as I was aware, once an angel fell into the abyss, there was no pathway to bring them back.

Warrior angels, once captured, were rarely ever returned, but that didn't stop The City of Light from trying. Gregori was the only other Fallen I had encountered, and from that brief meeting, I knew I would never want to be alone in a room with him. I had never encountered him before he turned, but I knew Rushton and couldn't imagine him becoming so twisted into something unrecognisable. Much... like my soulmate.

I couldn't let that happen.

The chanting increased in volume, and I noticed what looked like a ledge up ahead, facing the inside of a massive cave. As we got closer, I saw other openings facing us from the other side, a few of them occupied with Fallen. Their dark wings fanned out from either side of them, and their bodies glinted with metal. It was like a flash of teeth in the depths of the ocean, belonging to a predator other predators feared. If Lucifer wasn't here beside me, I had no illusion of how they would use those teeth.

We got to the edge of the ledge, and I could feel them, eyes raking me from head to toe, violence, hunger, hatred, and lust making my head swim with the faint stirrings of panic.

We could take them. We could take them all. You only have to ask. My darker self whispered her words sweetly into my mind.

Eyes widening, my nails left grooves in the palms of my hand. Why was I still hearing her? Then I looked down, and all thoughts of my darker self fled.

Fire ringed a large pit at the bottom of the cave. Long, metal spikes rose high from the flames, curving inwards, forming a wicked barrier. In the centre stood two figures facing each other. One was clearly a female angel dressed in a brown tattered shift, her short dark hair falling around her shoulders in different, jagged lengths. She held a small round shield strapped to her forearm and a short black dagger. Both had symbols etched upon their surface. They glowed red as if volcanic lava flowed beneath.

She looked exhausted. Her shoulders were hunched over as if she carried a great weight. I could almost see the strain marring her face. Swaying slightly, she stumbled to the side before finding her balance again. I didn't recognise her. When had she been captured? How long had she been here?

The creature that faced her was clearly a demon. Bruised purple skin stretched tightly over a tall, bulky frame covered in boils and scars. Its head was wide at the top and narrow towards the bottom like an upside-down triangle. One horn twisted out the side of its head like a spiral, and the other was broken, leaving a sharp uneven edge.

There was a flurry of movement from above, and a flash of dark wings obstructed my vision. A beautiful fallen angel landed lightly between them. He was dressed in coal black armour with two curving blades strapped across his back. There wasn't anything to differentiate him from the other

Fallen, but he radiated a confidence that bespoke of authority and power. Cinnamon skin moulded over exotic features betraying his heritage of the Light, despite the darkness that cloaked him.

"Pathetic," he jeered at the angel. "Is this The City of Light's finest? I have never seen a warrior angel so easily captured, so weak and unskilled."

She flinched.

"Look at you, worm; you're barely even able to stand on your feet." The angel was slammed backwards by some invisible force, skidding across the floor towards the ring of fire. She jammed the point of her dagger into the ground, managing to stop her momentum before she hit the flames. Laughter and taunts echoed from around the arena, the disturbing clash of musical tones forming the basest of language.

The tips of his wings swept the dusty ground as the Fallen angel turned towards her. "Every time you fail and display your lack of reason to exist, I destroy one of your friends. You know how painful it is to reform in Hell. You know how much weaker you become." He cocked his head to the side like a raptor studying his prey. "I'd like to see Tristsolin step inside a ring with a Manticore when he finally reforms. They still like the taste of flesh, even with their little human head."

The angel got shakily to her feet, using the shield as leverage to haul herself up. "No, don't hurt them. I'll fight. By the Light, I'll *fight*!"

"There is no Light here. Surely you've realised this by now," he sneered. "Please try and last more than a couple of breaths this time. We came here for a bit of a show, not to watch your carcass be tossed around like a chew toy for the upper-level demons."

"No," I whispered, horrified. "Stop this, please."

Lucifer's face was impassive.

This warrior angel wasn't going to make it. Clearly, she was too weak to fight. I couldn't just stand here and do *nothing* and watch her be slaughtered. I tried to think quickly as I looked around this cave filled with the Fallen. Maybe I could fly down, grab her and come back up...

No, I wouldn't make it. There was no way they would allow me to take her without a fight. And I wasn't deluded enough to think I could last in combat with trained warriors imbued with powers of the Dark. Even one would be one too many.

But maybe I didn't have to...

I flicked my eyes to my soulmate. Was I willing to rely on his help? Lately, he hadn't been too generous with his intervention, but surely he wouldn't let the Fallen touch me? Considering I had almost been consumed by a spider demon not too long ago, did I really want to take that chance?

I looked down at the warrior angel, trembling with fatigue. Yes, yes, I would.

How good were my energy reserves? I gathered my-

"Don't be foolish, little angel," Lucifer said mildly. "You wouldn't make it halfway down before being swarmed by the Fallen. Or hadn't you noticed them yet? You are not here to interfere, you are here to observe."

I glared at him as if he had lost his mind. "You can't expect me to stand here and watch you torture one of our kind." I felt my power tingle across my palm. "I can't do nothing."

"You will if you want to see Rushton."

I froze, the power draining from my hand. "Where is he?"

"Wait and find out. Or fly down and try to enact a rescue that would most certainly fail, forcing me to intervene and wasting my time as the angel will still fight anyway."

I fumed. At least he said he'd intervene. Logic and emotion didn't marry well in this situation.

But it was too late anyway, the fight had begun.

The angel made the first move, pushing herself forward with her shield and dagger out. The demon... tried to run away...

As she got close, she skidded on her knees towards the demon's right side, holding her shield high and slashing at the tendons of the demon's leg. It let out a howl of pain and stumbled to the left, trying to get away. Flailing, it limped, dripping black blood on the ground, and turned to face her, arms up defensively over his face.

My lips parted in confusion. Why wasn't it trying to attack?

Some of the Fallen cheered, yelling out suggestions and encouragement on what she should do next. Others hissed their disappointment, hurling insults, and threats. The angel got up slowly from her knees, then spun around snarling, blade dripping with blood. She charged the demon again, who swung frantically with his claws as she approached. She leaped up high in the air, smashed his flailing hands aside with her shield, and landed on her knee across one shoulder, pivoting to straddle him from behind.

Locking her legs around his shoulders, she tried to stab him in the neck, but the demon deflected, thrusting upwards with its arm. It managed to reach around and grab her torn shift, throwing her away from him. She tumbled through the air and skidded across to the other side of the arena. The demon turned and stumbled close to the barrier as if seeking a way out, but the flames rose high, trapping him within. Its eyes wide and panicked, it prepared to launch itself through the flames, but more spikes rose from the ground forming an impenetrable barrier.

The whole thing seemed wrong. I didn't know what I was watching. Was the angel the tortured or the torturer?

The angel picked herself up again from the ground, unsteady on her feet as if the burst of energy had completely drained her. Her hand holding the knife trembled like a leaf in a storm.

A voice called out, a slithering whisper in the dark full of derision. I knew it was the Fallen from earlier. "Weak. Just like I thought. Only one of you will leave this place alive. Your failure, angel, will be deeply felt amongst the rest of your comrades."

Her face twisted in a mixture of rage and desperation. It was as if those words pushed her over the edge.

She flew at the demon, who again tried to scuttle out of her way. Vaulting up, she grabbed him by his unbroken horn, pulling him down backwards like a lioness felling a wild boar. Landing hard on his side, he let out a roar and scraped at her with his claws, rendering a terrible gash along her leg.

With a feral scream of her own, she kicked him in the face, snapping his head back sharply. Still screaming, she raised her arm high and brought her dark, tainted weapon down into the flesh of his wrist. He arched his back in pain and tried to tear his arm out, but she kicked him brutally in the face again… and again… and again.

I recoiled. The way she was hurting the demon reminded me too much of my dark self. It wasn't clean, and it wasn't quick.

As if the thought had its own effect, the angel dropped her shield and grabbed the demon's horn with both hands.

I stiffened. "No, no, no…" I whispered. "Don't do it."

Muscled bunching in her arms, she bore down at an angle. The area echoed with the audible snap, and the Fallen screamed their approval, drowning out the demon's cries of agony. I watched numbly as she impaled his other arm to the ground.

Picking up her discarded shield and wiping the sweat and grime from her face, she stood over the pinned creature, shaking. With a caterwaul of fear and pain and despair, she brought the shield down over his prone form again and again and again. Tears streamed down her face as blood splattered in arches all over her, but still, she kept going. The demon went still, but the edge of her shield kept slamming, cutting him into pieces. The grunts of her exertion were the only sounds to be heard.

Throwing the shield aside, she collapsed onto the ground, sobbing amid the scattered remains of her… prey. For that was what he was, not her opponent, but her prey.

"Good, good…" came the Fallen's voice, as smooth as a drop of honey melting on the tongue. "Well done, angel. You have earned your rest."

A bottle was thrown at her, and she snatched it from where it landed on the ground. Pulling it open, she drank down the contents greedily. The Fallen landed by her side and gently helped her to her feet. Before he could lead her away, she turned towards the bloody remains on the ground and picked up her knife, holding it almost possessively against her chest.

The fire that ringed them lowered slowly, then winked out, leaving a cloud of smoke that rose up, spreading thinly like mist. When it dissipated, I couldn't see them anymore.

Emotions churned nauseatingly through me. This was how they turned them. I didn't know how long it took, but looking around at the black silky wings and serrated steel, like an unholy amalgamation of dragon and raven, I knew it worked.

"I... you... this..." I pointed to the ground, unable to find the words. I wanted to cry, and scream so loud my voice could be heard in every layer of Hell. I wanted to hate. I almost could hate. Maybe I did hate.

His voice was like an empty night sky. devoid of any emotion. "This is Hell, little angel. What did you expect?"

"This is wrong!" I shouted.

"By your definition, yes."

"By *any* definition," I ground out at him.

His head moved in the negative. "There is no right and wrong, only choices we make."

"And every choice has a consequence. Isn't that what you told me before?" My eyes swam with tears I refused to shed. "Isn't that what you said before when you were Light? So what is *your* consequence for all this, Lucifer? What are *you* doing to balance out the scales?"

His smile was cruel. "I thought you already knew? Hell is my consequence, one that I accept gladly. Is there anywhere lower to go, little angel?"

"You don't seem to be suffering," I snapped at him.

He took a step closer and purred with a seductive edge. "The beauty of being Dark, little angel, is that there is nothing left to lose. Pain becomes just a state of mind."

I stepped back, realising we were surrounded by watching eyes assessing our little interplay. "Where's Rushton?" I demanded again.

Invisible ropes pulled me to him, pressing me into his skin. The contact made me shiver, as did the low golden hum that ran between us. My fingertips grazed his shoulders. "What are you doing?" I hissed.

His wings spread out from his body, and my breath caught at their beauty. Obsidian black, yet if you looked closely, it almost seemed like every colour was absorbed into its depths. Arms curling around me, he took a step backwards towards the ledge. My eyes widened.

Then we fell.

Chapter 21

My hair whipped wildly around my face as we plummeted towards the ground. Instinctively, I desperately wanted to furl out my own wings, but I resisted, knowing that, in a strange paradox, I was safe.

Well, as safe as a butterfly trapped in a lion's jaws, surrounded by wolves.

My physical destruction was an imminent threat that already left a flourish of bruises on my body and mind. It was only a matter of time before Death became too eager, holding me down underneath the water for just a second too long. Beings of light weren't meant to survive in Hell. I understood that now. You had to adapt, and devolve or... be destroyed.

Finally, his wings spread out like the width of the horizon curving through the night, slowing our descent for us to land gently in the centre of the arena. I felt the roughness of sand beneath my feet and the enmeshed scent of demon and angelic blood. It was a heady combination, a violent signature scrawled across the first pages of creation.

A bloody war that was destined to continue until humanity chose a side. We were fighting mankind's darkest deeds and intentions, and they had only become stronger and more insidious over time. Maybe the side had already been chosen. Maybe the war had already been won.

By the love of the Creator, I sincerely hoped not.

Pushing my tangled hair away from my face, I extricated myself from Lucifer's grasp. There was the sound of several feet hitting the ground behind me. Tensing, I turned to face the Fallen, moving slightly, so I was by my soulmate's side. Five of them formed a pattern in front of us, much like a formation in an army, arranging themselves to either strike or defend. Like a bad omen heralding the apocalypse, I felt an instant surge of dread overcome me.

The leader in front was the same Fallen who had orchestrated the fight between the angel and demon. His skin was the colour of cinnamon bathed in sunlight, his features almost feline. The swollen darkness in his eyes was like an alien creature had crawled beneath his skin, peering at me intently like I was an insect that needed to be dissected with meticulous care.

The other Fallen around him were equally imposing. Like jagged pieces of stained glass, they would have been exquisitely beautiful if whole, but now with their very essence shattered, they had been reduced to a singular, purposeful function. To destroy.

And here I was, dressed in white, an embodiment of everything they despised.

"Warlord," the leader addressed Lucifer. "Is this our newest recruit to train?" His quick assessment, coupled with the slight curl in his upper lip, clearly expresses his opinion. "She doesn't appear to be a warrior."

He already knew I wasn't a warrior angel, and he already knew I wasn't here to be "trained." This was more of an unspoken question to Lucifer. I hadn't considered how highly unusual it would seem to others in Hell that I was in Lucifer's domain. I doubted anyone else was aware that he was my Flame, and it was clear that I had been treated differently from the others. Were they all waiting for an answer? Would the Ruler of Hell even deem to give him one?

"That's because she's not." He held the Fallen's gaze for a second. "Is Rushton in the lairs?"

"Yes, my lord," the leader replied slowly. "Did you want us to bring him out? He has already been through several battles earlier, but we can make him fight again if that is your wish?"

"We will go below."

They parted like a bear trap, straining to snap around us again. As we walked through them, I could feel their hostility scraping along my skin. We approached the edge of the arena, and the ground gave way ahead of us, forming sandy stairs that led below.

Lucifer paused at the top of the first step and turned his head. "Stay."

I flicked a look behind me and caught the lead Fallen bristle slightly. His eyes moved, caught mine, and in that split second, there was a promise made. Taking a deep breath, I turned back and followed Lucifer down the stairs, leaving the Fallen behind.

Our descent was eerily quiet. There were no moans of pain or struggling gasps of air. I couldn't hear the echoes of violence or the shouts of desperate rage. There was only a cool breeze that twined around my legs, dragging me further down like the hands of a lonely spirit condemned to eternal isolation.

My gut clenched. My intuition tingled. An overwhelming feeling filled the air, unexpressed by voice or sound, and it threatened to choke me with its intensity. I felt it infused in the very molecules around us.

Agony.

Not the physical agony of being cut, bruised, or beaten, but a deep, hollow emotional pain of one's spirit being ground slowly into dust. If it had a face, it'd be one of starving children, shivering from cold, foraging for food as their bodies slowly wasted away. It would be the look of a mother trekking through a barren landscape with her critically ill child, desperate for medicine and knowing she would never make it in time. There was another name for it, a name I had unfortunately started to become familiar with.

Hopelessness.

But not just hopelessness; this was slightly more complex. It was also layered with the bitter taste of futility. Knowing that whatever action you might take, there was still only one inevitable outcome.

My feet hit the bottom of the stairs, and my eyes were forced to adjust to yet another level of darkness. We were within an underground chamber, but this wasn't made from the harsh, jagged rocks from above. The ground felt smooth underneath my feet as if it was made from marble.

It was much cooler here, too, bordering on icy. If I'd let out a long breath, I knew there would be a ring of condensation drifting away in front of me.

Lucifer walked ahead, a deeper shadow sliding through the darkness. I followed with trepidation, trying to block out the chaos of emotions battering my senses. Being a creature of Light, I was naturally sensitive to the hum of energies around me. This was my sixth sense awakened, alert, and as active as any of my other senses.

Having an active sixth sense allowed me the ability to energetically read people, places, and situations. It gave me a glimpse of intention, a fingertip dip into the current of people's thoughts and emotions. It was a powerful tool, some people even called it magic. Most humans were born with this sense, too, but they lacked the awareness and training to develop their abilities to their fullest potential.

My sixth sense, however, didn't prevent me from smacking into something hard and electric. Body spasming, I let out a short scream as my skin was ignited with invisible fire. Stumbling back, I instinctively called my white Light into the palm of my hand.

Gratefully, the power came.

Light illuminated the area surrounding me, and I was confronted with what looked like a large cube of pulsating, dark power. It seethed at me, flicking tendrils in my direction before settling back into its shape. Something else caught the corner of my eye. Turning my head, I saw another cube about the same size. I spun slowly in a circle. Another one. Another one.

They were taller than me, and about two wing spans in width and length. I knew the room would be scattered with them. I also knew the answer to the question as soon as I asked it.

"What are these?"

His voice curved like a throwing dagger to hit me in the chest. "Cells."

My whole body tensed. "They're all in these cells?"

"They can't hear or see you. They have no awareness of what is occurring on the outside. There is only the arena and this place below," his voice travelled closer to me. "For them, it's like being in eternal night... but a night that burns."

I sucked in a breath and held it for a long moment. "Do you truly hate us that much?"

"Hate? No."

The ball of Light flickered in my hand. My fingertips were starting to go numb from the cold. I shook my head as I stared at the cubes, imagining being inside. "Then why are you *doing* this?"

How many of them were here? And how long had they been here? Every time I thought I had reached a state of horror that I couldn't descend further, Lucifer showed me another depth. How could this creature be my Flame?

"This is just a consequence. This is what happens when you get in my way."

I struggled to speak. "That's a pretty harsh consequence to be tortured endlessly, kept in isolation, and deprived of any contact until you become Dark."

"Well, I do have a reputation to maintain."

Spluttering inside my head, I focused my will, moving the ball of Light from my hand to float up ahead towards the left. The edge of wings entered my vision, followed by the high slash of his cheekbone and those midnight eyes.

"How many angels do you have locked in these things?" I asked, letting the revulsion drip through my voice like acid. I wanted to claw at these dark cages, and drag them down until I freed them all. The frustration boiled up inside me until I felt the answering prick of tears in my eyes. I blinked them rapidly away.

"Only one that you came down here for." He turned around, and I was forced to follow. I tried not to think about the angel locked inside those dark walls.

I tried not to imagine a face or a name because if I did, I wouldn't be able to move.

We shifted through the maze of cells. There was no obvious placement of each one, they seemed to me like they were scattered sporadically without any sense of order. Some were close together, others were metres apart. With so much dark energy in the room, I wondered why I didn't sense it before. Maybe by consistently being around so much negativity, I couldn't differentiate between the varied levels anymore. It was just another stone added to the oppressive weight I was already carrying.

Lucifer finally stopped. The cells looked like all the others, but my blood turned cold as I realised who was held inside. He lifted up a hand, and where the darkness lashed out at me, it caressed him as if it was welcoming back home a lover. The black energy moved, moulding and shifting like oil on water until it formed vertical bars similar to the cage I saw Rushton held in before.

And there inside, I saw him.

He had changed drastically since the last time I saw him. Huddled in the centre of the cage, his body was almost equidistant from all four sides. His head was on his knees, which were drawn up and pressed against his chest. His clothes, which were once a pristine white, were smeared with dirt and blood. There wasn't much movement from him except for his fingers. Wrapped around his upper arm, they were white with tension, clenching and unclenching in a rhythmic fashion.

"Rushton…" Eyes wide, his name left my lips in a soft mixture of hope and sorrow. Please, Creator, let him not be broken.

At the sound of my voice, his head snapped up from his knees. He looked confused at the sight of me through the cage bars as if I was a mirage conjured from his mind, but then his gaze focused on Lucifer. The warrior angel moved swiftly to his feet as if the ground had started to cave under him and glared at the Lord of Hell with a feeling I could only attribute to as sheer hatred.

It was a shock to see that emotion mapped to the angelic beauty of his face. It was a base, lower-level emotion, a feeling that had never belonged in The City of Light or to the higher beings who lived there, only to those who lived below and had forgotten the interconnectedness of all things. But with all that he had experienced and witnessed in this soulless place, was it any wonder that those feelings encroached on his peace and angelic centre?

Even I could feel myself slipping further and further away from my true self.

Now that he was standing, I could see that he carried wounds that had yet to heal. There was a painful, ragged slice down the side of his chest, curving towards his navel, and small sharp slices that cut through his pants and upper body like small creatures had crawled up him with razor-sharp blades strapped to their feet.

Rushton was still oozing blood as he glared at Lucifer. No, he wasn't broken yet.

"You," he spat. He strode forward and reached out as if to grab the bars but paused just before he made contact, his fingers curling into fists instead.

"Me," Lucifer agreed.

"Are you finally going to step into the arena, or are you going to send another of your lacky demons to do your work for you?"

"As amusing as that would be, I'm afraid I will have to decline," came the languid response. He turned away from Rushton and walked forward until his shoulder brushed mine. A spark of gold flickered between us both. I struggled not to flinch away from it. "I have things to attend to upstairs. I will collect you when I'm done."

The raging fire dimmed slowly in Rushton's eyes as he walked away, leaving a bleak emptiness that flashed quickly away I almost thought I imagined it. Finally, he turned his attention back to me. His gaze took in my clean clothing and washed hair, and his lips pressed in a hard line.

There were no more traces of demon gore that I had worn, almost like another layer of skin, or of the poison that had burned through my insides like a forest flame. And the slight tremble in my body could have been from the arctic air that blew through the room from an unknown source, not from fatigue bordering on exhaustion.

I essentially looked like a guest taking a stroll through the pits of Hell.

"Why are you here?" he snapped. I flinched.

I could feel the anger. Anger at me. "I came to see you," I said softly. "I've been worried. I tried to see you earlier, but I couldn't find a way to get inside the room I last saw you in." I rushed to explain.

I saw him struggle with the emotion, wrestle with it. Rushton closed his eyes and then took a deep breath. After a couple of seconds, I saw his body relax.

When he opened his eyes again, his gaze held mine and whatever he saw there made his face soften. "Sandriel... are you hurt?" he asked gently.

That he should ask me that when he looked the way he did... "I... no, not physically. No, no, I'm fine. Have they..." My gaze snagged on his torn and bloody clothing, and my mind flashed back to the arena. "Are you coping?"

The silence all around us, especially the empty, desolate one emanating from the other cells, made my question sound ridiculous. I suppressed the urge to wince. I might as well have asked, 'Does that gaping cut down your chest sting?'

His eyes dulled from gold to brass. Restless, he walked to the corner of the cell and then back again. "You know that I've been down here before with the others. The Fallen only released us because we were relatively new. They won't let go of angels who are close to breaking." He glanced at me. "Is it hard being here again for the second time? Yes. But I know I'm still better off than all the other angels locked in here. I know I still have time."

Time. He meant time before they broke him. Was it inevitable, then? There had been no escapes from Hell, no successful rescues... maybe they all knew that once they were down here, there was no way out. Except, I managed to free some of them. It was only now that I knew why.

Rushton suddenly made a sound, his eyes fixated on something behind me.

I reacted. Spinning around in a panic, I conjured another ball of white Light. It flared brightly in my hand. My whole body braced for some sort of attack.

And I saw nothing.

My other Light was still hovering in the air, so I moved it further down, trying to see, or sense any movement coming towards us.

"You're a Light angel," he whispered reverently.

I turned back around, following his gaze to the white flames licking up and down my fingers. He was looking at me as if I had turned into a portal mirror to the higher realms. "Yes."

Rushton's hands reached out to touch the bars again and stopped. "Sandriel, do you know how rare that is?" he asked urgently.

Realising that my Light was what startled him, I relaxed a fraction. "Lucifer said not many angels had that ability."

His face twisted, his lips bordering on a snarl. "Usually, I would say don't believe a single thing out of that lying Demon King's mouth, but in this case, it's true." His eyes latched onto mine. "There is only one other Light angel in existence besides you, and he is still young and in training. The only one before that was… him."

He meant Lucifer. I mentally reeled. How had I not known this before? Was this yet another reason I was sent here?

Despite having been fighting in the arena, Rushton seemed reinvigorated. "You have no idea…" he continued intensely, "if I had that ability, I could free everyone down here. Do you know how to use it properly?" He paused. "How are you even using your abilities down here?"

My power was still limited as I had used an extensive amount of energy in a short period of time, but I could still draw upon it even in my weakened state. "What do you mean? Can't… you use your abilities?" My mind raced ahead. "And what do you mean by *free* everyone."

His brow creased. "My element is Earth, but I am unable to call my elements in this realm and, therefore, am unable to access my powers." Rushton shot me a considering look. "Your abilities might work differently for you. Sandriel, you are one of the strongest weapons we have against the Dark." He gestured. "Let me show you. Bring your Light closer."

Hesitantly, still cautious from my last run-in with the dark magic cells, I inched closer, extending my hand out. The Darkness recoiled, thinning out as if trying to minimise its exposure to the light. Emboldened, I took another step forward.

It lashed out.

The Darkness hit me like a giant arm with twelve fingers engulfing my flaming hand. I felt the pressure as the magics fought each other, struggling for dominance. My Light winked out, and I screamed. Lightning pain jolted down my arm, cracking through my bones. I stumbled backwards and fell to my knees, snapping the contact. I cradled my arm against my chest, breathing hard.

I heard a snap in the air, followed by a sizzle and a harsh curse. "Sandriel! Are you okay?" Rushton's voice was distraught. "I'm so sorry, I didn't know it would do that."

"I'm fine," I winced, standing up, and taking a moment to steady my feet "I'm still a bit weak from earlier."

"Show me your hand," he insisted.

I held out my arm, still keeping a safe distance away. Even though it stung something fierce, there was no burn upon my skin.

"I'm sorry." He ran his hand through his hair in frustration. "Light is the counterforce of Dark energy. Technically, you should have been able to dissolve it in a way the elemental abilities of other angels can't. But it takes strength, focus, and training, and you have had neither. I'm so sorry; that was completely foolish of me. I endangered you, and that is unacceptable."

My smile was like a thin piece of string fraying at the edges. "Considering where I am, I don't think that can be helped." I shook my head, strands of damp hair sliding across my shoulders. "No, if there is a way I can help, I'd do anything. I've been trying to experiment with my abilities, but as you've indicated, I'm not a warrior. I barely understand what I'm doing. I can create orbs," I gestured above, "And I can throw them at demons, which causes them some damage."

Rushton's face darkened. "You've been fighting demons?" His fingers twitched. I could see the tips were stained with blood. "What does Lucifer want with you? Why did Archangel Michael send you here?"

How could I explain to him a past I was only just beginning to understand myself? There was no easy answer to his question. I wasn't just his Flame, I was the beginning. I was the origin, the reason why one of the greatest angels of Light to have ever existed turned into the deadliest creature to walk the lower realms.

"I've met him before in a past life when he wasn't Dark. He…" I hesitated, looking momentarily away, then forced it out. "He was my soulmate. He *is* my soulmate."

If a horde of demons suddenly rushed out screaming towards us, I don't think Rushton would have noticed. It was as if all the muscles in his face had frozen solid, all except for his jaw, which gaped open. His tawny gold eyes were equal parts stunned and dismayed.

"It can't be possible."

I rubbed at my arms, trying to absorb some warmth from the friction. His expression made me want to melt into the floor. "It's true," I whispered. "He remembers me, Rushton, which is why he has brought me here. It's also the reason Archangel Michael sent me, or at least one of the reasons."

"Listen to me; whatever he wants you for, it cannot be good. Lucifer being your..." he stumbled over the word, "soulmate only means he has the ability to manipulate you. Don't let him." Rushton suddenly tensed, his body instinctively going into a half crouch. "We don't have much time," he hissed. "If you can find a way out, take it. If not, practise your abilities, get stronger, and *free us*."

The last two words were said in a plea. It was the dying breath of a fading sun as it fled from the encroaching night. It was a sliver of hope, and it was pinned all on me. My eyes darted around. I half turned so I could look behind me. Reaching out through our soulmate link, I tried to sense Lucifer's presence. If he was on his way, I couldn't feel him yet.

"Rushton, what do–"

I felt them. They surrounded us in the shadows, moving slowly, blocking off every route of escape. Their eyes shone eerily like a pack of Adaryian wolves hunting at night. The air crackled with violence scarcely restrained and hunger barely repressed.

More than that, I felt their hatred.

The Fallen. They had come.

Chapter 22

The Adaryian wolves were a technical advancement gone horribly wrong.

The people of Iceolsis wanted to create a genetically superior pack animal to pull their supplies across the ice and assist with hunting in their harsh environmental conditions. The wolves they had currently been training could no longer endure the ever-increasing frigid temperatures and, as a result, were on the brink of extinction. That meant the Iceolisis people were also on the brink of extinction.

Their men of science experimented for years with different DNA from species all over the world. What they engineered was a hybrid wolf the size of a wild horse, coupled with the muscular physique of a black jaguar. This new species had the strength and endurance that their predecessors lacked. Their size meant that they could take more than three times the load of ordinary wolves and hunt larger animals.

They called them the Adaryian wolves, after the man who first created them. The Iceolsis people celebrated, and for the first few years, their communities thrived.

Then things started to change.

What the scientists didn't intend to do was to elevate their cunning, intelligence, and prey drive tenfold. The Adaryian wolves, for the first few years, had been learning their new masters, absorbing their communication style, communities, strengths, and weaknesses.

The people of Iceolsis barely survived.

They descended upon the communities first, massacring men, women, and children. For the few that were killed, more bred in overwhelming numbers. The people who survived the initial attacks scattered across the land, seeking refuge in distant places. The Adaryian wolves hunted them down, tracking them relentlessly for days on end.

Once they had your scent, they didn't let go. It mattered not if their bellies were full or the distance was great; they would track you and kill you.

Surrounded by the Fallen, watching the way they moved and acted, I couldn't help but make the comparison. They had my scent now. For them, it was only a matter of time before they got me.

And I was practically alone now.

The shadows shifted like layers of dark fabric, and the Fallen leader stepped forward into the edge of my Light. I could tell he was enjoying this moment, capturing his prey by surprise and watching the fear creep slowly into their eyes. To say I wasn't afraid of them would be ludicrous. The Fallen were the greatest fear of all the angels.

Not that we experienced that emotion surrounded by the peaceful crystal glow of The City of Light. But those who went down to Earth and encountered the suffering their darker brethren brought to the world and to others of their kind felt that fear. Not just confronting them as they wielded powers gifted by the Dark, but becoming just like them.

If angels had a horror story, this was it.

Watching the leader, I moved slowly, so my back was against Rushton's cage. His dark eyes flicked up to my orb, hanging in the air like a star in the sky. If he was affected by the Light, he didn't show it.

"A Light angel. How... unusual." His voice was a soft hiss, like a blade sliding quietly beneath the ribs. The armour he wore was like a dragon's scale with subtle shades of colours that made him blend into his surroundings. Smooth like the surface of a still lake, there was no gap or bindings to determine how it was put on. In the darkness, he could have been right next to me, and I wouldn't have seen him.

"Ezriel," Rushton said tensely from behind me. "She is under Lucifer's protection."

"Tisk, tisk, little worm," interrupted a sharp, feminine voice. "You're not supposed to speak to your betters."

A female Fallen emerged from the right side of Rushton's cage. Her hair was a long rope of coral pink, braided high at the top to fall in a complex knot just above her hips. There were glints of metal shining between the strands, which tinkered slightly as it brushed against the metal of her armour. She was shorter than me but corded with muscle that left no doubt of what she was trained to do.

Her fingers curled along one of the bars, and a tendril of dark power wrapped around her wrist. "You don't need to see what happens to Lucifer's pet. Don't you have enough to think about already?" She smiled wickedly. "Or have we been too soft on you?"

Opening her other hand, she blew gently on her palm. A stream of grey mist jetted out from the centre of her hand, flowing into the cell. I turned my head and saw Rushton's eyes widen as he scrambled backwards. In his haste, he moved too far back. The air sizzled as he hit the opposite end of the cage. Body spasming violently, he gritted his teeth in pain and fell to his knees.

The female Fallen and a few others surrounding us laughed mockingly just as the mist engulfed him.

I saw it pour into his mouth and nostrils, filling him up like an empty vessel until it overflowed. His eyes widened and strained as if they were trying to escape by themselves. The mist spilled over the contours of his face, sliding down to the ground in waves. Then my vision was obscured as the fog surrounded him... but I heard the choking and the laboured groans of pain.

Without thinking, I slammed my orb of Light straight into her face.

I had the advantage of surprise, but I wasn't prepared for her reflexes. The Light was like a flaming punch, snapping her head sideways and searing the right side of her cheek. Even though it must have hurt, the Fallen didn't make a sound. Instead, as my Light hit her, she reacted by immediately throwing something small and sharp right at my chest. The movement was so fast I almost didn't see it.

I watched it spin towards me, a play of light and shadow, and felt nothing but a vague sense of dismay.

Then a hand reached out between us and plucked it out of thin air. My lips parted, and I breathed out a small, surprised sound. It was a small, wickedly shaped throwing star less than a metre away from my heart.

Ezriel brought his hand down and turned towards the female Fallen. "Imraide, *no*. There are rules."

"Sandriel!" My eyes flicked up, and I saw that the mist had dissolved in Rushton's cage. He had gotten to his feet, and I glimpsed the fear on his face. Not for himself, despite what the female Fallen had just done; it was fear for me.

Imraide straightened up and narrowed her eyes at Ezriel. The dark energy was still wrapped around her wrist like a coiled snake. She gave it a quick tug, and the cell holding Rushton went dark. And just like that, he disappeared.

"The rules can go to the *below*," she hissed. The skin on the side of her face had turned to a dark brown streaked with veins of white. "This one needs to be taught a lesson."

There was a low murmur of agreement around us. I had attacked one of them, therefore, I needed to be punished. Despite the cold, sweat trickled down my spine as I processed my situation. I reached out through my soulmate link and felt nothing. Once again, I was left to my own devices.

Numerous scenarios passed through my mind, almost all of them not ending well for me. To my credit, my voice didn't waver when I spoke. "I don't think that would be a wise idea."

Ezriel snapped his head in my direction, and I flinched. I knew in a split second that he wanted to backhand me across the face. Every line in his body screamed suppressed rage, which made me believe his feelings extended beyond this current situation. This rage had been building up for a while, and unfortunately, the foundations didn't seem so steady. One wrong move, and I could topple the whole thing.

"Let's put her in a cage," a voice growled out.

Another voice spoke up from the darkness. "In the arena, let's see how good she is." Laughter followed the suggestion.

"Give her to Selaphiel to play with or Diagar... he'd enjoy that."

Ezriel lifted his hand for silence. After the suggestions died down, he spoke. "No, no, we were told not to interfere, brothers and sisters. We can't disobey our esteemed ruler."

I stiffened as he walked around me slowly. He didn't have the sensual grace Lucifer possessed in abundance but something colder and more calculating. Even though Lucifer had turned to the Dark, he was bewitching to watch, like poetry in constant motion.

When he was Light, it was like witnessing sunlight weaving through a waterfall, reflecting a myriad of colours that were beautifully hypnotic. Even though that beauty had changed, it didn't disappear. Every expression, sound, and movement Lucifer made was like a dark melody that could lure and compel even the strongest of sirens to drown in their own waters. Enziel had none of that colour or dark fire. He was as flat and cold as the stones that surrounded us.

"No..." he mused, "I suggest we leave her be."

Imraide's body shifted as if she wanted to throw herself at me and teach me a lesson herself. My orb of Light was still burning brightly near Rushton's cage, but I resisted moving it, unwilling to fuel the aggression that was already suffocating around me.

Ezriel continued. "Let's not harm Lucifer's angel, and in turn, we shall also not help her." His lips curled, and in it, I saw the stirring of anticipation.

Another line of sweat curved along my spine.

When he spoke again, the words were guttural, dripping with the despair of a thousand tortured souls and sealed with hellfire. It was a language that was excruciating to my ears, causing my head to pound as my mind struggled to filter the sound.

I blinked and it was like shards of ice had formed underneath my eyelids. Unable to understand it, I still knew what it was.

Demon tongue.

I heard a snap in the air, and my chest tightened. I could feel the dark amusement from the rest of the Fallen, as if they knew what would come next. It was only until I spotted the distinctive blood-red eyes that hovered low to the ground that I knew what Ezriel had called.

A Hell Hound. He had called a Hell Hound.

It entered my small circle of Light, the spines on its back bristling. If those spines touched my flesh, I knew it would rip right through me as if I was made from silk. The floor beneath the creature steamed as saliva made contact with the floor. It prowled back and forth, watching me.

When I had first seen Rushton, I encountered a Hell Hound, but it was held back with some invisible leash. This time it was free, and it had all its attention on me.

"Looks like you are in a bit of trouble. A pity there is no one here to help you." Ezriel walked over to the Hell Hound and patted it on the head as if it was an eager puppy he was trying to calm down. "Shhhhhh…" he soothed. "Soon."

Not comforting at all.

I couldn't outrun a Hell Hound, and my little ball of Light would probably only aggravate it further. If I had more time to rest perhaps, I could destroy it the way I did with the spider demon. But it was too soon. I already felt the last energy reserves I obtained from my short nap in the bathing pool slowly run dry.

All these thoughts flicked across my face, and I could tell the Fallen leader was enjoying my dilemma.

"Don't despair," he turned to his fellow Fallen. "We can be merciful." They all laughed in response, a clash of harmonies that echoed all around. Turning back to me, he flashed his teeth. "There are several open cages in this room. If you go inside one, it will close, and you will be safe, otherwise… feel free to run."

Ezriel gave the Hell Hound a short, hard tap on the head. The Hell Hound growled, and I felt the sound run right through me. Its nails grated along the floor, making a high-pitched sound. Then it leapt, but I was ready. Directing my will, my Light slammed into its body, knocking it sideways.

I turned and ran.

I figured my best option was to try and make it to the stairs that led back up to the arena. Maybe Lucifer was still up there. Then again, maybe he had left me deliberately. I choked down my anger and increased my speed.

The laughing taunts of the Fallen followed me through the maze of cages.

"Turn around and fight, angel, or are you one of those singing ones from Gabriel's temple?"

"Can we get you a harp? Maybe you can sing it a lullaby?"

"Red would suit you much better."

Was this what it was like in the arena? I passed several cages, all of them closed, all silent, all still.

Need some help? My dark self whispered coyly. I ignored her.

As my feet hit the smooth floor, my ears were tuned to another sound. I heard the click of nails and the soft thud of paws following me. I turned, running in a jagged line through the cages. The sound started to pick up speed and gain momentum. I didn't know exactly where the stairs were and I was merely guessing the general direction.

The cold burned across my face as I ran. My breath came out in short pants. The sound got closer. Closer, closer, and then...

My wings furled out, and I leaped into the air. I heard the snap of teeth that was way too close, and smelt the rancid breath. There was a skid of nails on the ground. Pumping my wings, I managed to get higher. The ceiling was low but high enough that if I flew, I could just see over the cages. I looked frantically around.

There. The stairs leading to above ground.

Flying as fast and as carefully as I could, I manoeuvred my way through the dark energy cages. The Hell Hound growled, its fury flaring at my escape. I could hear the drops of acid hit the floor, sizzling along the surface as it followed me.

It started to run again. I chanced a quick look behind and saw the Hell Hound bunch its lower muscles in its legs, preparing to leap.

I screamed as it vaulted through the air, higher than I anticipated. Teeth and claws came right at my back, and I had to throw myself sideways to avoid being dragged down. My wing hit one of the cages. Body jerking in shock, I crumpled to the floor.

Get up, or you're going to die. I could crush this thing in an instant. You're foolish not to call on my help. Do you like being prey?

I scrambled back to my feet, my Light still above, still illuminating me. It was like having a beam of sunlight announcing my presence to everyone in the chamber. But I had little choice. Without the Light, I was practically blind. There was movement to my left. Red eyes were slits in the dark. I saw the flash of jagged teeth, and I ran.

I wasn't far from the stairs. If I could make it… just a few more turns.

The Hell Hound was closing the gap. Thinking quickly, I brought my Light down, and as I turned the corner, I spread it out behind me like a hovering shield. Seconds later, I heard the impact and a high pitch yelp. That bought me a fraction more time. Just enough.

Calling my Light back towards me, I rounded the last cell and headed towards the stairs.

Finally there… then I skidded to a stop.

Three Fallen stood, blocking the exit.

In the centre was Imraide, arms crossed with a smirk painted across her lush pink lips. Two other male Fallen flanked her on either side. One looked indifferent, the other bored, as if he would rather make a tower of feathers than be in my presence a moment longer.

"I didn't think you'd last this long." Imraide fingered the hilt of a knife strapped to her hip. "In fact… oh, look out," she said mildly.

Instinctively, I raised my arms to block my face and crouched low to the ground. I felt the skin of my arms shred under the claws of the Hell Hound. Its hind legs raked across me as it landed in front, twisting around to come at me again. I screamed, channelling my pain and fear as it bounded towards me, eyes frenzied with rage.

Another shield formed from my open hands just as it hit me. I struggled to hold onto it as the Hell Hound snapped at the shield's surface, determined to get through or around despite its fur smoking away under the Light. The smell of my blood had made it mindless. All it could think about was the kill.

With will, I gritted my teeth and bent my shield backwards, wrapping the Hound up in a cocoon. It howled, going crazy in the small confines of my Light bubble. I felt its muscular size stretch the edges of my Light, building pressure as it violently thrashed. The shield wasn't going to last long.

I got up, staring at the Fallen in front of me, blood dripping down my hand, bright and vivid against my clothes. Imraide's smirk was replaced by a grim line.

My wings unfolded, luminous in the dungeons of Hell. Spinning around, I flew, not wasting any time. Another howl came from behind me, not too far away. The shield didn't have enough power to hold it for long. I also had never trapped a creature of the Dark before, and I had no idea how my abilities worked when there was distance between my Light and me.

And there it was. I found what I was looking for.

I flew down towards an open cell and landed lightly on my feet, facing the gaping black hole where many of our warrior angels were currently trapped. Taking a deep breath, I turned around and waited.

I didn't have to wait long.

The Hell Hound flew out of the shadows, fur charred and smoking, eyes blazing. Its lips widened at the sight of me, and rows of stained razor-sharp teeth flashed in anticipation. Blood dripped down my arm in a steady stream, and I could feel the darkness at my back, eager and straining to swallow my Light within.

Fear crawled up my throat, blurring my vision. I shoved the feeling back down and mentally sat on it, pinning it in place. It was like trying to hold down a wild animal. Fear is an emotion that helps you survive. It serves to stop you from doing stupid things, taking uncalculated, unnecessary risks like catapulting off a cliff or trying to fight a losing battle. But when you have limited choices, it just gets in the way.

I could sense movement around us, and I knew the Fallen were there to watch what I would choose. I was in the final act of a play, and bets were on me dying. Would I lock myself in a prison or try to fight a Hell Hound?

Watching the Hell Hound's spines bristle up as it prepared to launch, I wasn't sure what I would choose either. My foot came up to step backwards into the cell.

Let me, my dark self called sweetly. *Let me, and no one will ever hurt you again. My power is yours. Let us show them what fear really tastes like.*

I hesitated.

Then the Hell Hound came at me with incredible speed. I saw myself reflected in its red eyes, frozen and afraid. Looking at myself covered in blood made me angry, being put in this situation by Lucifer again made me angry. I set my foot back on the ground and braced myself. I would not run, not in front of them.

I don't need you, I told my darker self.

As the Hell Hound closed on me, I did several things all at once.

I called my Light into my right hand and shone the bright white glow directly into the Hell Hound's eyes. At the same time, I flung my left arm back and sprayed my blood into the cell behind me. Then I threw myself out of the way.

Blinded by the Light and distracted by my scent leading into the cell, the Hell Hound bounded forward into the cage. I landed hard on my hip and watched the Hell Hound disappear inside.

My heart pounded. The cage wasn't closing. Why? Why??

The answer came to me in a flash. Light. It needed to trap Light. With desperation, I blasted my Light inside just as the Hell Hound jumped out. Sensing a trap, it leaped, but my Light knocked it back into the air and into the cage.

Dark energy sealed the cage shut. Everything went dark. I let out a breath I didn't know I had been holding and started to shake.

There was a slow clapping sound.

Weakly, I called up another smaller ball of Light. Ezriel walked forward and gave a swift mocking bow. "You exceeded my expectations, which, to be fair, weren't very high." He looked at me coldly and mocked, "You outsmarted a dog. Congratulations. A warrior angel barely formed could probably do the same. Don't think that this was a real challenge."

His eyes glittered. "*This* is a real challenge."

I cringed as he spoke in Demon tongue, curling my fingers into my palms so I couldn't cover my ears. There were several snaps in the air and then… growls. More than one.

Four Hell Hounds slowly circled me, inching closer. If that wasn't bad enough, the front of the cell door dissolved and the Hell Hound I had already trapped stepped through. My eyes widened, and Ezriel's lips curled.

Then… the Hell Hounds sat down, wagging their tail.

Confused, I watched the Fallen's face smooth over, stripped of all emotion. I reached for my link and felt a light, golden thrum. Intense relief slammed into me, and my shaking got worse. I pulled my knees up to my chest and wrapped my arms around them.

"Someone seems to have forgotten his place." Lucifer's smooth velvet voice echoed around the room, coming from everywhere at once. "It seems I have been negligent in reminding you who you serve. Who *owns* you."

The Fallen stirred in the shadows, finally aware that a more dominant and infinitely vicious creature prowled amongst them. If they were the Adaryian wolves, Lucifer was something else entirely.

"Have you forgotten who owns you, Ezriel?" he crooned.

"No, my Lord." Ezriel's voice was cool as a distant lake. If he was concerned about Lucifer's presence he didn't immediately show it.

"I believe your actions make you somewhat of a liar."

"I did not touch her," he intoned. Ezriel's eyes flicked carefully around the room, searching.

"But you played with things you shouldn't be playing with. And... she got the better of you."

From my position on the floor, I could see the slight tightness of Ezriel's jaw. He went down on one knee and lowered his head slowly. "I apologise, my Lord. It will not happen again."

"Ezriel, I don't think an apology will be sufficient this time. Do you?"

The tension spread to the lines of his back. "I will do what you wish, my Lord."

"Yes," came the silky reply. "Yes, you will. That's exactly what I want you to understand, Ezriel. You will always end up doing what I wish."

The Lord of Hell stepped into my Light, which was miraculously still hovering above me. Even surrounded by all this dark beauty, he could still make them seem like rough, unfinished sketches. Not even glancing my way, he walked slowly up to the Fallen on his knee. His hand came out and he placed it on top of Ezriel's head as if he was a God bestowing his blessing upon one of his subjects.

Darkness flowed from Ezriel up Lucifer's arm in a long, curling stream, disappearing into Lucifer's body. Ezriel's head snapped up, and for the first time, I saw unfiltered emotion. It was a look of pure shock and terror. And there was something else. The darkness which had once encompassed all of his eyes was now reduced to just the irises.

"What have you done?" Ezriel whispered.

Lucifer ignored him and addressed the rest of the Fallen in a voice frosted with ice. "Ezriel seems to have turned partly back into his former self. I suggest you start correcting this lapse immediately." After his statement, I sensed another emotion filter in the air, blending into hopelessness and despair. Fear. And it was coming from the rest of the Fallen.

He looked down at Ezriel and said, almost kindly, "Your cell awaits you."

Ezriel got up stiffly, a range of feelings moving across his face like storm clouds in a night sky. He wasn't turned back all the way, I could see that. But he had been turned back enough to start to feel, and perhaps to even start to care. He forced himself to walk towards the unlocked cell in front of me.

As he moved inside, the darkness started to close around him, eager to squash whatever goodness had formed inside of him. Lucifer's voice rang out clearly and precisely. "Who owns you, Ezriel?"

The darkness engulfed him, but not before a whisper escaped.

"You, my Lord."

Chapter 23

The Fallen left the underground cells wrapped in a layer of fear they were not used to wearing. If Ezriel was one of the first turned, it was a devastating display of power to strip that away from him; humiliating even, as now he would have to be retrained by his subordinates.

Another event that had left me reeling was the fact that up until now, I and the rest of The City of Light had believed there was no possible way to turn a Fallen back into their angelic form. And Lucifer had done it with the ease of a wind angel directing a breeze. If, by some miracle, he was ever inclined, I knew he could revert them all back in a matter of heartbeats.

Coming to that realisation made me furious. It was another layer of anger on top of all the other layers of anger I had been harbouring since I'd been attacked by the spider demon. The layers boiled like a lava pit, finally merging together in a melting pot of seething rage.

He turned to finally look at me, and I energetically threw all that rage into our link. It left me like a bolt of dark flame, burning down a long tunnel to strike its target with deadly precision.

An eyebrow slowly raised.

I glared at him intensely as blood pooled around me on the floor. "I hate you," I growled out, my voice echoing in the quiet.

Lucifer moved over to where I lay, coming further into my Light. Dark energy wrapped around me like warm fur pulling me gently off the floor. As my feet touched the cool ground, the energy disappeared… and my knees buckled. His hands were there, curling around my waist, holding me up, and I felt the soft, honeyed thrum of our link wind its way through my body at his touch.

My eyes met his, and my rage fractured slightly, then held.

His expression was thoughtful. "No, you don't."

"Get your hands off me," I snapped. I was exhausted, but I willed myself not to pass out.

"If I let go of you," he explained patiently in that velvet-smooth voice, "you will fall to the floor."

"I don't care," I ground out, too angry to be rational.

A portal opened up behind him, a shimmering narrow oval hovering in the air. "Neither do I, little angel, as to what you currently want." He lifted me up in his arms, turned, and stepped through, leaving the dungeons behind us.

***

When his cell went dark, Ruston panicked.

"Sandriel!" he yelled, knowing that she wouldn't be able to hear him. He wanted to rip the bars apart and get to her, but that was impossible, too.

They might as well have been in a different realm or on a different planet. He tried not to imagine what the Fallen would be doing to her. He knew firsthand the insidious ways their mind worked, inflicting maximum damage as they progressed their plan to break you. There was no mercy and no rest. If you revealed just a moment of weakness, they were there, ripping the wound wider, so it was virtually impossible to heal.

In The City of Light, they didn't train to withstand pain. Pain wasn't an experience that even entered the purity of the upper realms. That was a physical sensation, and physical sensations could be controlled and even dismissed when your mind was centred and your will strong and steady.

The City of Light was all about mental strength, as mastering the mind was where true power was created. Therefore, it wasn't exactly pain that broke the warrior angels, it was the slow draining of that mental strength that really lay in the certainty of who you were.

If you start questioning that, that's when the cracks began to form, and the darkness slides in.

There was no possibility that someone as innocent and inexperienced as Sandriel would survive long. She had no training that taught her to endure, no experience on the Earth realm facing the creatures of Dark.

Even being a Light angel.

It still floored him. Her abilities were as rare as a gift of immortality from the Gods, but she had no understanding of how to use her powers, and she wasn't a warrior. Her only hope was the one person that could inevitably be her destruction. The last person anyone in existence should trust. The monster who made other monsters avert their eyes with trepidation and scurry off in fear.

Lucifer, her soulmate.

He wouldn't wish that on anyone.

The darkness pressed upon him, and he knew it was time. Rushton took a slow, weary breath. What was unbeknownst from the outside was that these cells were all linked to each other through a small conduct of energy. These conducts channelled an extraordinary amount of pain to each of the occupants. The agony was constant and profound.

But there was a choice. A cruel, sadistic choice.

Each occupant, or warrior angel, could push their pain back up the conduct, and their load would channel into the other cells, effectively increasing all the other angels' suffering. He had just done this in order to communicate with Sandriel, but now he had to take his share back.

He mentally sent an apology to the warrior angels who had to endure the extra weight of pain and sincerely hoped they had not just returned from brutal games in the arena. The arena was enough to slowly break your will, making you choose things you wouldn't normally in the right frame of mind. The constant suffering without rest only made those choices easier.

Reluctantly, he opened himself to the pain. He felt it flood in like a wave made of broken shards of glass. Sitting down in the centre of the cell, he tried to put himself in a meditative state and just… endure.

One indication that an angel was starting to turn to the Dark was when they started to offload their pain… continuously. Not because they had just returned from the arena and desperately needed a few hours to partially recover or communicate clearly with the Fallen. It was because they had simply stopped caring about others. That's when they started to forget who they were and began to lose their Light.

As he shouldered the burden of pain, feeling the additional wounds that had been inflicted upon his physical form, the temptation rose up in him like a sly beckoning hand. He pushed it back down and noticed it took just a fraction longer than before.

Not yet. Not yet.

***

We appeared in Lucifer's bedroom.

The fire running along the walls cast the room in a sultry, intimate glow. Light and shadow played with each other, forming interesting curves and angles against the threaded gold walls and across the wide bed of midnight silk. The subtle scent of jasmine and exotic spices filtered through the air, the source originating from long curing sticks of incense in metal stands.

Warmth infused my skin, easing my shaking down into minor tremors. All feeling in my right arm had disappeared. I looked down and was dimly amazed at the mess of flesh and bone. I hadn't noticed the extent of the damage during the Hell Hound attack, but now looking at it made me dizzy.

Lucifer moved to the bed and deposited me in the centre, blood soaking into my clothes and now onto the sheets.

I was still furious. I lifted my upper body up awkwardly by my left hand and hissed, "I prefer my own room, thank you."

He watched me through slitted dark eyes as he straightened up. My eyes widened a fraction as he whispered a couple of words that rang painfully with power, stealing the breath from my lungs.

Reaching into the air, his hand disappeared, making it seem as if it had been severed at the wrist. After a second, it reappeared with a small wooden box inlaid with burnt engravings. The engraves shifted and changed on the box's surface as if it was telling a story.

The whole time he did this, his eyes never left mine. They pinned me to the bed with the unvoiced command to remain exactly where I was. That expressed desire made me want to launch off the covers just to spite him, even though I'd probably end up flopping on the floor like a dry fish.

Lucifer opened the box and a radiant white light rose up from the inside. At least, I thought it was a white light. As I looked closer, I realised it was a small cut crystal about the size of half my thumbnail. It glowed with a radiance so pure it reminded me of the central crystal in the heart of tThe City of Light. We called that crystal the Creator's Crystal, as being close to it felt like touching the origin of love and of all creation.

My lips parted with wonder, and I struggled to comprehend how Lucifer had obtained this. Or even how he could be near it. His expression was neutral, but I also realised that he was very careful not to touch it.

"Where did you get that?" I breathed out.

It floated in the air, lifting higher and higher until it hovered just under the exquisite mandala inlaid above me. I had forgotten about that mandala. It also looked like something belonging to The City of Light.

Then it melted, dissolving into swirling, intricate patterns and designs, making the complex lines burn feverishly with bright light. The light spread out like a spider web, illuminating all the jewelled patterns in vibrant tones. Gold, tangerine, garnet, amethyst, and sapphire glowed intensely and then beamed brightly directly onto me.

My eyes closed shut. Every molecule in my body slowly filled with light, diffusing my pain, my rage, and the weight of despair I had been carrying inside me. The bed moulded to my back and head as I lay back down. My lips parted in a sigh, and I felt like I was floating, weightless and free, even though I knew my body was still on the bed.

My mind started to haze away. Before I sunk into blissful nothingness, I murmured, "How?"

A moment of silence, and then, "It's my Light."

And that was all I heard before I drifted off to sleep.

***

Soft sunlight, cool wind caressing, heated skin, the light beading of sweat. Fresh scent of grass, strong oak, and wild jasmine. Breaths mingled, words whispered soft sighs and softer moans. Fingers twined, nails lightly scraping, teeth grazing. Warm, golden hum, feelings and thoughts merging, offering, giving, and oh so sweetly taking.

Lips, warm and sweet, cruising gently over rounded curves, hollows, and hard lines. The feel of skin on skin, silky smooth, soft and firm, touching, pressing, moulding together sensually, invitingly.

Pliant and yielding, muscles deliciously coiled, moving, rolling, curving. Hair tangled, spread over and under, auburn and jet black. Lashes tremble, lips part, breaths deep, heavy, wonderfully strained.

Nerves shimmering, releasing, merging, bodies dissolving, reforming, transforming. Pure light. Cerulean blue eyes, full, tender, protective.

Love.

The dream shifted...

Pain. It came crashing over me, trying to drown my soul so I'd lose the fight to struggle to the surface once more. I tried to hold back from making any sound, but it whistled through my teeth in a low groan.

I felt Lucifer's fear spiral through our link.

I was sheltered in his arms, but I could still feel the wind shifting through my hair as we flew in the sky. I wished I could see what must be a heavenly view below, but I was fading in and out of consciousness.

~ Hold on, we are almost there. ~

I was dying; I could feel it. The thought provoked an inordinate amount of fear. I wasn't ready to end this life. Not now, not after the world had been opened to me in a way I had never conceived before.There was too much beauty to see and experience, too many questions with mind-altering answers I could ponder for hours, days, and years. And the most magical, wonderful part of it all was that I was sharing it with an angel made from impossible daydreams and secret, wistful hopes.

And he loved me.

And yet, from the moment I met him, our time together had been shortened. A demon poison ran through my veins, infecting and spreading inside me. The Archangels refused to help us, so we were desperately trying to find another way, which resulted in us heading to Asclepius's temple in Olympus, the Greek God of healing.

Lucifer's feet touched the ground. There were shocked gasps and whispers all around us. My eyes slitted open and I glimpsed white pillars gleaming in the afternoon sun and blue stone walls. I felt Lucifer fold his wings back as his muscles shifted.

"I need to see Ascelpius," Lucifer's voice rang out in clear, melodic tones.

There were murmurs of, "My Lord," and swishes of cloth and the light patter of feet. My Lord? They must think he was a God. I wasn't surprised.

"Please, follow me, my Lord," came a soft feminine voice.

We moved swiftly through the temple and down several corridors. There were more surprised sounds, and murmurs from the people we passed. My eyelids closed and I stifled another moan.

~ Just hold on. Please. ~

I was gently placed on something cool and hard. Moments later, a soft pillow slipped under my head. I faded in and out.

"...infected by a demon."

"Is she like you?"

"No, she is human."

"I don't heal humans unless they are one of my followers."

"I was hoping you would make an exception, Ascelpius."

"We don't usually deal with the Light realm. Why do you not go to your own to seek help?"

"...say she is not meant to be healed."

There was a scoffing sound. "Angels are governed by laws from a God no one can see. If they gave you that reason it most likely means they just didn't want to assist you."

Lucifer hid his impatience but I could feel it through our link. "Will you help her?"

"Hmmmmm… Mayhap…" there was a thoughtful pause. "I will need something… perhaps the blood of the demon who infected her?"

"I destroyed that demon and sent it back to the Underworld."

"Well… that is certainly unfortunate. You see, if I had that demon's blood, I could perhaps work on an antidote…" his voice trailed off.

I felt hope filter to the link. "I see." There was a slight rustle of movement. "If I were to attempt to retrieve such an item, would you be able to keep Nadia here and monitor her. I want her somewhere safe."

I could detect the slight eagerness in the healer God's voice. "Absolutely, I shall look after her myself."

More movement. ~ I have to go, little one. ~

~ Where… you going ~ I thought through a haze. I realised dimly that I must have been given something to block out the pain.

~ Away for awhile. But I'll try not to be gone too long. ~

~ Don't do anything dangerous ~

There was a light brush of lips on my forehead, and I felt the gentle but fierce love flow through our link.

The dream shifted

"The samples were good but I need more."

My consciousness surfaced from the deep sleep I was in. I was vaguely aware of being poked and prodded occasionally but I hadn't heard Lucifer's voice in what felt like a long time.

~ Luce... ~ I said in my mind.

Fingers curled around my hand, and I felt the warm golden hum of our link. Though, it felt a little different. Not as vibrant as it was before. As if it was made from darker tones.

"I gave you several cup fulls." His voice had an edge to it.

"And they have been excellent in making a decent headway to find a cure," Ascelpius said carefully. "But I need more."

"What progress have you made so far?"

"We have experimented on different combatants, and are currently working through a list, eliminating the non-responsive ones as we go."

"The demon blood is spreading. There isn't much time. Has there been anything that has come close to repelling it?"

"No, not yet, but if you get me more samples…"

Lucifer's fear increased through our link. With the energy I had left, I sent him a wave of reassurance.

~ I'm still here, Luce. ~

The dream shifted.

There was screaming down the halls. Panic reverberating off the walls. I struggled out of unconsciousness, fighting the drugs that blurred my senses.

~ Luce? ~

I could feel him through the link. And he was angry. No, he was furious.

I heard his voice. "Where is Ascelpius?" His voice was as dark and threatening as a thunderstorm. "Tell him if he is not here soon, I'll burn his temple to the ground."

I faded and came back.

"…bartering the blood I gave you to dark fae and witches. Were you even trying to heal her?" More fury simmering to the surface.

"…don't deal with humans who don't follow me. You're lucky I allowed her to remain here. She isn't in any pain, so by my calculations, you owe me." Snide laughter. "What are you going to do? You're an angel."

I felt my body being scooped up and held close. The golden hum soothed me, though again, it felt different.

~ Luce, are you okay? ~

~ I'm sorry, little one, but we have to leave. I've found another place that might be able to help us. ~

"Ascelpius, fortunately for you, I don't have the time to deal with your betrayal. But the witches and fae don't deal kindly to those who try and doublecross them," Lucifer continued softly.

More laughter. "And why should I worry about that?"

"Because the last batch I gave you was animal blood," came the cool response.

***

Neezen, the rat demon, crept through the fifth-level of Hell with mixed feelings of apprehension and excitement. Being in the lower levels was fraught with danger. If a fifth-level demon found him here, he'd be forced to serve at their pleasure until he managed to escape. But he was quick and quiet, and he had the natural ability to blend into his surroundings.

Demons created from fur, horns, leathery skin, spikes, blue fire, and several large eyes moved past him as he hid against the rocky walls of Hell. He was getting close to the portal, but he would move no further for now.

His long, boney fingers, tipped with curving brown nails, fingered the amulet hanging around his neck.

The power held inside prickled against his skin, making his fur shiver. When he killed the Dragarth, he would be well rewarded. He might even be able to stand beside the demon king, Sepheroth, and be counted amongst his inner circle.

When they all escaped from Hell, it would be a glorious night and he wanted desperately to be at the forefront, taking what he wanted, feasting on all sorts of delicacies from the soft lands above.

He pulled a bit of rotting flesh from his teeth with his nail. Food was very limited in Hell. His form had survived from scavenging and picking from the carcasses of other dead demons. He longed for sweeter meat and the hot spray of blood spurting from his own teeth.

His long pointy ears pricked up. Commotion in the distance.

Markos had created the distraction. The Fallen in the area would be drawn to investigate. Now was the time to make his move.

Quickly, he opened the vial the demon sorcerer had given him to avoid detection. The blood felt thick and oily as it slid down his throat. He felt the magic take hold of him quickly, and when he lifted his arm, it was blurry, as if he was looking at something deep under the water.

Yes, it was time.

Scurrying along the ground, he headed towards the false wall that led into the Warden's realm. It looked like any other wall in Hell, set a little out of the main walkway leading to an obvious dead end. There was no reason for anyone to venture in that direction. Even if your intention was to hide from the larger predators, it was too open to give you any decent cover.

Rubbing the amulet again between his clawed fingers, he made himself move by picturing the victory before him. Nezeen checked first to make sure no one was around or watching him. He couldn't afford another demon blundering in and ruining his one opportunity. Seeing no observers, he approached the false wall with caution. Tentatively, he reached out a hand and pressed it against the surface.

The surface bent inwards as if it was made out of soft sand.

Nazeen jumped back as he saw a ripple of movement in the wall. He fumbled with the amulet around his neck but managed to hold it in front of him by the red demon skin cord, trying not to flinch.

When the Dragarth emerged it was glorifying and terrifying. The three-headed serpent was as fierce as anything he had ever seen. Black, emerald, and cedar scales glistened in diamond patterns. Several rows of enormous fangs, wide and dripping. He watched in awe as it came at him at lightning speed, intending to tear him apart.

He held the amulet up higher, waiting for the magic to take hold on the serpent heads, waiting for the confusion to appear in their slitted eyes as they started to attack each other.

That never happened.

The Dragarth attacked him in unison, each head tearing him apart and swallowing him whole.

***

In the seventh-level of Hell, Markos felt the amulet activate. His pupils changed to slits as he accessed the Dragarth's vision.

A long, decadent bathing pool, a room of weapons…

What the Dragarth saw, now he, too, could see.

Finally, they had access into the Warden's realm, and to his secrets

Chapter 24

I woke up with memories of my former self scattered softy over me like autumn leaves, intensely beautiful and slowly fading away. My eyelashes fluttered open, and the deep ache of a hopeless love reluctantly left my heart, returning to the ghost it had once belonged to.

Taking a deep breath, I felt light, clear-headed, and more like myself than I had for nights. Or had it been months? Time was abstract in Hell. My original bargain with Lucifer had barely entered my mind. There was no way of knowing how long I'd been away from The City of Light, and like my soulmate mentioned during my first night, I was free to leave... if I managed to find my way back.

Sitting up, I looked around the room. From the corner of my eye, I thought I caught a flash of movement – black, wispy smoke – but when I blinked again, it was gone. I frowned, thinking it was the servant demon checking on me as Lucifer was predictably absent.

A sense of unease filtered through at the thought of a demon watching over me as I slept. Though, with the healing energies that had charged through the room, it was more likely to repel an attack than invite one.

My eyes caught on the mandala above me. The dazzling brilliance had faded away, and it was now reverted back to its muted colours that were still stunning in their complexity. The rage I felt towards my Flame had dissipated, the loss of it making me feel strangely empty. But the need for answers still churned deep within me.

The Devil had made me a promise, and now I was going collect.

I peeled myself off the rest of the bed, the drying blood making me stick wetly to the dark sheets. My injuries had been healed, though my clothes were ripped, and I was covered in blood... again.

His *Light*, that's what he said.

A lump of emotion wedged in my throat, but I swallowed it down before I could determine what it was. Too dangerous. Nadia was gone, but she still lingered in the corners of my mind, her fingerprints guiding me to things I wasn't ready to see.

"He's not the same," I whispered to myself. *Don't ever forget that.*

Somehow, Lucifer had preserved a piece of his Light powers in a crystal. I had a feeble amount of knowledge regarding crystals, but nowhere near the extent of angels from Raphael's temple. I was aware that crystals acted as conducts of energy to intensify healing and different vibrations. I didn't realise they could also store things, like power that wasn't inherently there.

Why had he kept it? And why was the mandala here, in his room?

I had so many questions, yet obtaining answers from Lucifer was like trying to move a tornado with a broom. His favourite distraction was seduction, and he was a master at it. With consummate skill, he blatantly diverted me from my train of thought, driving the notes of desire higher and higher with just a whisper of a touch or the burning heat in those midnight eyes. It became a constant struggle to resist, especially as I became more and more enmeshed in my past. Other times, when I broached a topic he was determined to avoid, he'd vanish for nights.

Lucifer was unpredictable and as elusive as a wisp of smoke in a dying fire, but by the Creator, he would answer me.

My feet padded across the floor to the door. I pushed the double doors open, and they released me into the rooms beyond.

I missed the slow, curving roll of the wall as I left the room.

***

Sindore's feet and those of her dark sisters climbed over the small, white boat and landed on the misty shores of the Underworld. With deft fingers, she quickly pulled out three blood-marked gold coins and tossed them to Charon, the ferryman.

He flashed her a grin, absent of several teeth, and caught the coins nimbly in one gnarled hand covered in seeping sores. Sindore felt the knot of tension ease from her belly. If she had been too slow at paying the ferryman, that deceptively frail form would have ripped the souls right out of their bodies and left them stranded on the other side of the shore for a hundred years.

She had seen it happen before. This was not her first trip down into the Underworld.

The ferryman ran his other hand down his long matted beard, then fluttered his fingers at her in a mildly flirtatious goodbye as the boat slowly drifted away. She fought to keep the disgust from lining her features. Best not to give anything away to one of the Underworld's denizens. Especially one as powerful as he.

When the boat submerged once again into the fog, she turned to her sisters, whose faces were partially hidden by their charcoal grey cloaks. She grabbed Endaya's ice-cold hands in her own and kissed her softly on both cheeks.

"May the Darkness be upon you, sister. I'll pray you return to us above."

Endaya's bottle-green eyes were fierce. She was much older than Sindore but didn't rank higher. Seniority was not determined by age but by power. "I will keep Hades off your trail for as long as I can. And if the Darkness wills it, I'll continue to serve above. Be swift, sister." She squeezed her hands. "May the Darkness take you."

She nodded and let go of her. Endaya caught Judith's eyes. "You too, sister."

Judith tilted her head back, her lips in a tight line to suppress their trembling. This was her first venture into the Underworld. She had botched one of the summonings by drawing the incorrect runes, and this was the last chance to redeem herself. The curvy brunette had put on a confident, cocky act before they crossed the threshold between realms, but now in the world of the dead, that facade was cracking.

They always came down in three but very rarely did three return.

Endaya slipped away, disappearing into the darkness and heading towards one of the many paths in the Underworld. As Sindore watched her go, she removed a dark orb from within the folds of her cloak. Whispering words of the spell, the orb split in two, revealing a bright purple flame. It floated up in the air in front of her.

Removing a small dark blade from a holster around her thigh, she sliced the meaty part of her thumb in a shallow line and waited for the blood to bead up. When it did, she flicked it at the flame, hearing it sizzle as the blood made contact.

"Take us to Osre," she commanded.

The flame shuddered, then moved jerkily up ahead.

They made their way through narrow pathways and slender crevices in the walls. They avoided the spirits wandering aimlessly around, not wanting to draw any attention to their presence. As always, Sindore grappled with the urge to bottle one up and take it with her. A soul could fuel a summoning without putting a strain on the rest of the coven. But she knew there was no way to cross the river if the ferryman sensed another soul on board that had already transitioned.

She had witnessed the consequence of that, too, from an overly ambitious witch. Sometimes she'd look down into the pale waters of the Underworld and wondered if she'd see her face staring at her, frozen in horror from their depths.

Stupidity always had its price.

Judith followed her lead quickly and quietly and made none of the nervous ramblings or asked multiple questions like new initiates were prone to doing. It almost made Sindore like her a little.

When they heard the movement of others approaching, she quickly cast a cloaking spell to conceal their presence and pressed their bodies against the rough walls so they wouldn't be touched by accident.

The demons that roamed the Underworld were few and weren't as horrific to look at as some of the ones they summoned from the lower realms. Most resembled humans in some form or another, whether it be their heads or their limbs. Though, she knew the most powerful demons could alter their form at will.

They passed one with the head and legs of a wild boar, the rest of its body very aggressively male. It sniffed the air around them, but Sindore had made sure they had covered their flesh with the dirt and grime at the river's shores. Whatever properties that soil had, it prevented the scent of their humanity from leaking through.

When the demon passed, she called back the flame and continued their journey.

After a couple of hours, they found Osre.

He was waiting for them at the end of a tunnel that opened into a small circular space. There was another smaller tunnel behind him, which led further down by a set of roughly cut stairs. Judith gagged as her stomach rebelled at the sight and smell. Sindore could hardly blame her, but she cast her a narrow look beneath the hood of her cloak, warning her to keep her reactions to herself.

If Orse was offended, he didn't show it. Instead, his fat, slimy lips curved up into a smile and his thick, porous tongue slipped out briefly, tasting the air in front of them. His four eyes were bulbous with no visible lids, and they roamed separately over them as if they each had their own lascivious thoughts. The rest of his body was made up of spotted, green rolls that bulged down to the ground, tapering off into a thin pointy tail like the end of a worm. Sindore was grateful that there were no obvious male appendages. Otherwise, she might have joined Judith in extracting whatever was left in her stomach.

"Orse," she greeted. She knew it irked him that she didn't use the appellations of 'master.' But dark witches who had even a sliver of respect never bowed down to demons.

"Have you brought me what I want?" The words came out in a series of low gurgles as if he was drowning from the inside and struggling to speak.

"Of course." She gestured for Judith to come forward.

Judith stepped in front of her and pulled out a stained white pouch from one of the internal pockets sewn into her robe. She untied the brown leather cord and reached inside, removing a heart, still fresh and wet with blood.

"We have brought you a–" Removing the blade from her thigh, Sindore stepped close behind her and slit her throat.

Hot blood sprayed in a wide arch, splattering across Orse's swollen face. Judith grabbed at the wound to try and staunch the flow, but Sindore had sliced through the major artery, and the blood continued to splurt between her fingers, dribbling down over her chest. She tried to say something through her sliced vocal cords, but the wheezing, wet sounds were unintelligible.

Judith turned to face her, betrayal burning fiercely in her eyes. Sindore kicked her in the abdomen, sending her sprawling across the ground to land just in front of Orse, whose lips were seeping with hunger. She landed on her back, body twitching from shock as her hands still slid weakly across her neck.

"Your payment," Sindore said, her voice devoid of any emotion.

Orse let out a high pitch, gurgling sound of glee, then bent his massive, corpulent body over and began to feast. Sindore wanted to look away, but she forced herself to watch. She was mildly grateful that she couldn't hear Judith's screams, but her fellow dark sister's face expressed everything she couldn't voice.

There was always a sacrifice. Unfortunately for Judith, she was unaware it was her.

The slurping, sucking, and occasional chomping continued for an excruciatingly long time until finally, Orse raised his massive head, covered in pieces of her former sister.

"Now, I want the names," she demanded.

Orse's tongue emerged again and wiped his face clean in a circular motion, leaving a sticky, pale residue on his skin. He smacked his lips once, twice, then replied, "One day, I might have you between my lips."

Her brown eyes narrowed, but her voice was as sweet as poisoned syrup. "If you ever find me inside you, Orse, it would be because my fingers were ripping out your puny, weak heart." She followed up with a smile.

His small tail lifted, then slapped back down to the ground. Sindore didn't know what that meant, but she held the demon's gaze. All four of them.

Finally, he let out a deep gurgling noise that could have been a laugh or even a war cry. She had a spell on the tip of her tongue just in case it was the latter. "Very well, since you have paid with a very tasty bounty, I shall be lenient and give you the demons' names."

She wanted to snarl but reigned it in. The demon acted like he was being benevolent, but in reality, he needed her more than she needed him. Yes, their coven relied on obtaining the names of powerful demons to summon and negotiate for power. Still, demons down here were plenty, and they were all vying for the opportunity to walk the Earth realm and create havoc.

Orse's arrogance was just a way to make him seem powerful in a realm where he was most likely the little errand boy trying to sit at the table with all the adults. Knowing anything she might say in response would most likely be a scathing insult, she inclined her head in acknowledgement and waited.

"I shall give you two demons of the third-level and two of the fourth. Any more requires additional payment." His bloodied lips split open in a smile.

"I am aware of our bargain." Level three and level four demons were standard. Any lower than that, and they would be harder to summon from Hell and control.

"Habory–" Orse started to say but then stopped, looking confused.

His wide mouth opened and closed, but nothing came out. It was then Sindore who noticed a thin, green line appearing around the demon's neck. Green liquid emerged and dripped down onto the demon's skin.

Orse looked down, his mouth still opening and closing.

And then his head slid off, hitting the ground with a large splat.

Above his neck was a black spear with a curved, silver blade protruding from the end. Orse's body dropped to the floor, like a bucket of lard slipping from a tray.

Sindore's heart pounded as she saw movement ascending from the stairs behind the fallen demon. Her fingers clenched around her knife, her mind racing. If it was Hades or one of the Fallen, she'd rather slit her own throat and join Judith on the floor than endure their particular form of questioning. She would not risk her whole coven.

In the two years she had been negotiating with Orse, they had never been found.

Three demons emerged from the stairs, one after the other. At first, they looked like ordinary human men, average in appearance and height, with grey armour moulded to their chests and arms. But then she immediately noticed their black eyes, the whites non-existent, like insects. The colour seemed to bleed around their sockets, like spilled ink in a vein-like pattern.

They stood in a line in front of her, feet squelching on the numerous, reeking fluids splattered on the ground. They didn't seem surprised to see her. In fact, they seemed... expectant.

The one with the spear was on the left, but it was the middle one with a scar curved diagonally across his face that spoke.

"Orse's dealings with you have permanently concluded," he announced. "You will now negotiate for demon names with us and only us." He spotted something on the floor amongst the carnage. Leaning down, the demon picked up the heart Judith brought with her. It must have tumbled from her hand when Sindore killed her.

The demon grinned and showed it to his companions.

Sindore assessed the situation quickly. It seemed like there was a new faction growing in the demon realm. Power shifted and flowed like the phases of a moon, but there had been no permanent changes in the demon hierarchy for a long time. She wondered how long it would last. It would take an exceptionally strong demon to hold the demon horde in its place.

"I have already paid for the demon names. I will not pay again." She watched them carefully, waiting to see how they reacted. Either way, it was critical that she not show weakness.

The one with the scar picked at the grit under his nail with a clawed, metal fingertip. "Then you will get no demon names."

"Then no one in our coven will trade with you. You have stolen what I have already bargained for before it was given. If you want us to trade in the future, you will give me four demon names now. If they prove to be worthy, I will come back and arrange payment for the four you gave and for four more."

His clawed finger pointed at her. "You will give me payment now."

Sindore sighed internally. This one wasn't too bright. "I have no payment for you now. There is no deal."

He took a menacing step forward. "I *will* kill you. Then I will rape your corpse and eat you."

"No," she corrected. "You will *try* and kill me. I will kill myself, and what you do with my corpse afterwards, I don't give a cow dung." Sindore lifted up her hand, showing her bloody blade. "But before you do, I will take at least one of you with me." Her voice was level and calm, her blade steady.

He scoffed. "You will kill yourself? You lie."

"I will not give you what you want. Even the satisfaction of my own death." She meant what she said, and by the flash of anger on the demon's face, he knew it as well. "And then," she continued, "you will have nothing to give your masters." They were working for someone in the lower realms, and these upper-level demons were at the bottom of the pecking order.

The quiet one on the right, who had yet to say anything shot a weighted look at the other two. He was identical to the one with the scar but without the marking. Harsh demon tongue lanced her ears as he conversed with the other two. She understood little, but a name rang out from the burning. acidic sounds.

It sounded like *Sepheroth*.

He finally faced her. "We will give you two demon names now, witch, not four. When you come back down, you will receive four more. In return, we require a child witch sacrifice and four virgin hearts."

Ah, finally, one who could think beyond their immediate desires. She was lucky. This could have ended badly. "We do not sacrifice our own children. I will give you a witch sacrifice, same as I did with Orse, and two virgin hearts."

The scarred demon growled at her, and his twin on the right shook his head in the negative. "Four virgin hearts."

She countered. "Apologies, I failed to mention, two virgin *child* hearts."

The demon paused, considering. Then he nodded. "We accept."

Sindore smiled. "Excellent." She flicked her knife back into its sheath. "Now... give me the names."

Sepheroth. She tucked that name in the corner of her mind.

It seemed there was a new king of Hell.

Chapter 25

The water was cool and soothing as I cleaned off the remnants of blood from my body in the bathing room. The room had shifted back into its former state, but the paintings on the wall had altered. Gone were the creatures of legend and myth resplendent in their cruel, gratuitous beauty. In its place was something more disturbing.

It was an eclipse.

The mural depicted the sun being eaten slowly away by darkness, the light all but fleeing the lands below. And in the shadows, the demons waited to rise, hovering on the bladed edge of an early night. In the distance, a sleepy town sprawled out across the horizon, its terracotta roofs and solitary bell tower catching the last rays of the sun.

The last glitter of safety slowly fading away. Disturbing, indeed.

As I tied my wet hair into a knot above my head, my mind drifted broodingly to Rushton and the warrior angels. While I had been sleeping, how many battles had he fought? How many more wounds had been inflicted upon his physical form? How many angels were still trapped in those cells with their faith being slowly syphoned away?

I had been so very angry by the way I had been treated by my soulmate when in fact, I was incredibly lucky.

I could be in one of those cages, forced to perform in the arena. Or worse, I could already be a Fallen. My darker self seemed to have become stronger, her whispered words and shadowy presence inching closer and closer like the demons in the painting. I was hoping the healing might have banished her back to the dark recesses of my consciousness where she came from, but I couldn't be too sure.

I left the water, drying myself off with one of the luxurious towels left on the side of the bath, and donned a silky white shift that was curiously a replica of the one I wore in The City of Light. Not wanting to put back on the stained slippers I wore before, I walked barefoot towards the doors and heaved them open.

And ran straight into Lucifer.

My body collided with his, soft meeting with hard. I let out a small sound of surprise and felt his hands curl around my upper arms, keeping me close. A thrum of sensual gold fire raced through us both as our link snapped on.

My head jerked up. Midnight eyes locked onto my green ones with an intensity I was unprepared for. His lips were soft but grim.

Unbalanced, I stared back.

And the world *shifted*.

My vision reorientated itself once more and landed on my soulmate, who was watching me with a carefully blank expression. Something was going on behind those dark eyes, but he had shuttered his feelings off, leaving me with that indomitable mask, which was always dangling from his fingertips, never far away.

I was so focused on Lucifer that it took me a second to recognise where we were.

I blinked, then tensed in Lucifer's grip, breath shortening in my lungs. In response, his fingers curled a fraction tighter. Our breaths mingled together, and my pulse hammered under my skin.

We were in Kryptos, the neutral realm.

The energy signature was unmistakable.

The room was stripped bare of all its lavish trimmings that were present during my last visit. Instead, we were standing on a sweeping length of short, white fur with wooden panelled walls surrounding us on all sides. There were no furnishings or decorations to create a sense of atmosphere or power play. The room wasn't designed for anyone to stay but for a short time.

I could literally shift straight back into The City of Light.

In a second. In a heartbeat. As soon as he let me go.

My eyes shot straight back to his, desperately trying to figure out if this was another elaborate machination designed to crush me further into the abyss. Wouldn't it be right out of the Devil's handbook to bring me so unbearably close to freedom, only to snatch it away, teaching me yet another lesson about the uselessness of hope?

Would he be so cruel? Of course. Of course, he would.

But then... he let me go. His fingers uncurled from my arms, and he took a single, significant step back.

My eyes widened, body poised on flight. I could leave. I could leave right now. But my lips formed one word, it coming out in a trembling note, quivering like a leaf in the wind.

"Why?"

His dark eyes were filled with veiled secrets and truths masquerading as lies. If I had a thousand lifetimes with this version of Lucifer, I still wouldn't be able to shine a light on all the twists and turns in the labyrinth of his mind.

"Isn't this what you want?" he asked softly.

Yes. Isn't it? Confused, I blinked rapidly. I didn't ever think there was a remote possibility that I would be set free. And now I had the option to leave the darkness and the horrors within and return to The City of Light. I should be rejoicing.

"I…" I took another step back, then halted abruptly like a puppet pulled by its strings. "You were supposed to give me answers."

My soulmate tilted his head to the side as if I was equally a mystery to him. His eyelashes lowered. "I thought you'd be in a hurry to flee."

I lifted my chin a notch, not liking the way the word 'flee' rubbed raw against my skin. "You promised me you'd tell me why you sent the spider demon after we returned from the dungeons."

"So I did."

I crossed my arms over my chest. "Well?"

I expected him to divert the question, to dodge or disassemble. He didn't. "The situations involving the arachnid demon and the Hell Hound were designed for you to develop your abilities."

My skin flushed with heat, then cooled to the temperature of a corpse. For a moment, I was speechless. "Are you saying you have been *training* me?"

There was a sardonic lift of his eyebrow. "Are you saying you haven't noticed?"

Anger flickered to life. "That's not training. That's trying to *kill me*," I hissed. I stared at my soulmate as if he was demented. Maybe he was.

"Just because the lessons are not what you are familiar with does not mean they are not lessons," he drawled out. "How do you think warriors are forged?" He looked at me and said with the calm certainty of one who had walked too many paths, seen too many things, "Pain makes you stronger."

He had taken me against my will, and had the audacity to wrap my tortured experiences in a neat bow of teacher and student. "I'm not a warrior! I never asked for this. You can't teach someone who doesn't want to be taught!" I yelled at him.

Lucifer's gaze dipped down to my hands and I could all but feel them crackling with magic. "In that, you are mistaken. You can teach a great number of things to the unwilling, to the resistant," he replied mildly. "The only constant thing is change. It just depends on what you change into."

"I was never trained to fight," I said fervently. "I was assigned to Archangel Michael's temple. If I was meant to be a warrior, they would have trained me."

The lighting in the room dimmed to reflect his displeasure. The Lord of Hell strolled past me, a combination of sharp lines and tailored edges with his hard jaw and ebony cloak, slit to leave his arms free. He still managed to look composed, but I imagined he'd seem the same way if he was leading a horde of demons through the gate of heaven. I, on the other hand, was experiencing a severe loss of the calmness I had acquired after my healing.

Now I wanted to beat him with a stick.

"You hone in on one part of your angelic life without looking at the entirety of it. Maybe you weren't meant to train in The City of Light. There is no one experienced with the ability of Light. There is no one there who understands the nuances of the power, how it transmutes, transforms, and impacts the darkness. It's not something you can study in scrolls and watch memories embedded in crystals. It's something you experience by fighting the darkness. There is only one person who can teach you that, and teach it well."

I shot him a mutinous expression even though he couldn't see it. "What if I don't want to be a warrior? What if I'm happy to continue my duties in The City of Light the way I once did before? Did you ever consider that?"

He turned his head to look at me reproachfully over a broad shoulder. "Every gift that you are born with is given for a reason. Failure to use it to its fullest potential insults not only yourself but the life you have been given."

I laughed.

It rang through the room like a bell with a slightly hysterical edge decorating its borders. "Do you know how ironic that is coming from you? You, the greatest of all angels who gave up his gift and turned to the dark."

Lucifer turned back to face me, his eyes glittered like coal threaded with silver. "Oh, but I am using my gifts and fulfilling my purpose far better with darkness flowing through my veins than strands of light."

"How is that?" I demanded.

"It sometimes surprises me to witness the utter blindness of angels. You are so full of Light, and yet most of the time, you truly can't see."

The angles of his face shifted, moved with terrifying subtly. The body my Flame wore turned predatory. The mask dissolved, and the thin veneer of civility in its place shredded, revealing the creature beneath. He prowled around me slowly in a circle, footsteps burning into the floor, causing a wreath of smoke to rise from the ground.

I could still leave. If I wanted to, I could leave in an instant.

"Why do you think demons aren't roaming the Earth like they were before?" he crooned.

I sucked in a breath at the tone of his voice. "I don't know," I whispered. I could barely see his face. The smoke covered the air like shifting veils.

"Why are they not ravaging the Underworld, tearing the barriers apart?" A flash of eyes, bottomless, consuming.

"I don't know," I gritted out. My hand tingled, energy coursing through my fingers, building at the tips.

"Why is there less chaos where chaos once reigned free?"

"I don't know!"

The smoke parted like silk, tearing down the centre. Suddenly, he was in front of me. "Because they are *mine* to command. I fought the demons before, battle by battle, fighting an impossible war. Now, I own them and the rest of the Fallen. They do what I say, and if they choose otherwise..." He smiled.

Hellfire eyes blazed as vibrant red as a blood moon on a cursed night.

Instinctively, I raised my hand, white fire exploding over my skin, rippling over my palms and down my forearms to my elbow. The power was bright and fierce, unhindered by the energy of the lower levels. It wanted to be used in the presence of such dark energy. It wanted to be free.

It crackled at Lucifer warningly.

"Finally. There you are," he purred.

The violent red faded slowly from his eyes, and he looked at me consideringly. "It's time for you to choose if you want to stay or leave."

I closed my fist, the light reabsorbing under my skin. "Why in Heaven or Hell would I *stay*?"

"Because in the time you've been here, you've learned more about yourself and your abilities than you ever have before. You have thought yourself weak, and you have found that you are not. You started with one mission, and subconsciously you have given yourself more."

Push, pull. There was always an angle to be played. The Devil was trying to flatter me. "I've almost lost this form several times over. That is no incentive for me to stay."

"You were never in any danger of dying. Of being hurt, yes. In pain, certainly." His lips curved, making a mockery of the poet's mouth. "But not death."

My eyes narrow to laser points. "Were you there, watching me this whole time?" I asked.

"Not me, but other eyes were."

The Dragarth? Or the servant demon? Or both?

"And you never intervened!"

All those times when I thought I was alone, I was, but it was cruelly deliberate. Did he enjoy my suffering? Was he trying to find the moment I would break?

"I didn't need to."

"And was that the plan? To force me to use my abilities?"

"How do you think I learned, little angel? You learn by doing. And just to be clear, in case you still haven't quite got my meaning. Doing is fighting."

A piece of information from my conversation with Rushton filtered in. "And yet there is one other angel in The City with the ability who is currently being trained. Who, I am sure, is not going through the same curriculum as me." I shot back.

If he seemed surprised or concerned, he didn't reveal it. "If that's the case, then the journey will be excruciatingly slow. They will not learn in one millennia what you have learned during your time in Hell."

"You could have just shown me how you have used your abilities." I pointed out. I shook my head suddenly, realising that I didn't even ask the most important question. "And why do you even *want* to train me? What do you get out of this?"

Lucifer gave me a sleepy, bored look. "I believe you have somehow forgotten I am no longer Light, therefore, undesirous to explain my motivations and also unable to show you an ability I no longer possess. Light isn't like all the other elemental abilities. The power isn't given to you by the elementals that you attract; it comes from you. You mould it the way you desire. It manifests differently according to your will. To teach you how I used it would, therefore, damage all the potential ways you could have used it. It's instinctive, limited only by the limitations we give it."

I frowned at him. "You may not tell me, but teaching me furthers your agenda, whatever that is. Why would I want to do that?"

"Of course it does. As it furthers yours," he replied coolly.

My chin lifts again. "How do you know what I want?"

"Little angel, your intentions are as visible as a rainbow in Hell."

I bristled.

When I didn't reply, he continued, "Your constant bleating about Rushton and his whereabouts gave you away," he said dryly.

I stiffened. "Of course, I want to free him. Them. Especially since I understand now what they are going through." I paused, the pieces clicking in place. "You *made* me understand. You wanted to show me!"

An elegant finger tapped his chin. "Let's call it an incentive to stay and learn about your abilities. Maybe you'll even learn enough to free them."

Was it really possible, then? Could I really save them? The thought fueled the desire, and I struggled to keep it from my face. I instead placed my hands on my hips. "Why would you want me to free them? You aren't making any sense."

"I'm curious enough to see if you can. If you possess the intelligence to work it out. And before you ask why I am even giving you a choice, it's because a willing student will learn faster than an unwilling one. If you choose to stay, your focus won't be divided on trying to escape."

"You can't expect me to believe you want me to free them," I scoffed. "That is ludicrous. Isn't that your whole plan? To turn us all?"

"Thank you. I was waiting for you to ask me, so I could explain to you all my intentions and motivations moving forward."

I glared.

"Stay and find out," he challenged softly.

Games. This was all a game, and this particular chapter had hidden meanings and indecipherable paragraphs. Whatever he wanted, willing participant or not, it would not be good. No, no more.

"No," I whispered. "I'm done." I tensed and looked straight into his dark eyes so he could feel the weight of my words. "I'm done."

Would he stop me now?

Lucifer didn't move. He stood back, shuttered and remote. "Then go."

My Flame turned away and a portal opened in front of him. Through the distorted surface, I glimpsed the bathing room I had just left.

My heart started to pound... and I didn't know why.

"Sandriel," he said, using my name on one of those rare occasions. He said it softly, like a caress. He also didn't look at me. "There is unfinished business between us, karmic debts to be paid. The scales have tilted one way, and they have yet to tilt back. And whether we right those debts now or in the future, in the end, they will be paid."

"We are night and day, yet we met on the edge of the horizon. You can run back to where the light glitters, but there will be a time again when the darkness will come, and you and I will face each other again. That is the truth."

I swallowed, feeling that emotion well up in me once more at his words, the feelings I had thought I had left under the mandala in his room. The feelings of the past.

He had kept his Light.

Without thinking, I reached for our link. The golden cord was about as thick as the width of both my fingers and stronger than the single pale strand that appeared when it first formed. He had a soul, otherwise, I wouldn't be able to connect to it. He had a soul. Wherever it had gone before, it was starting to come back.

My mind went over the times I had noticed the threads double, open to let more light through. It was always at an emotional crossroad, a choice to care or to push away. When he had chosen to care, to feel things he had previously blocked away, the link had become stronger.

And what had I been doing? Pushing away. Constantly.

It was an easy choice to make, looking at the monster he had become. But that didn't mean he would always stay that way. He could, perhaps, become something different. Maybe he already had.

Lucifer was far from being altruistic, and I wasn't foolish enough to believe that the choice he had bestowed upon me to leave wasn't just another cog in the wheel of whatever grand plan he already had at play. But as far as he was capable, and even a little further than that, he had loosened the noose of his control and allowed me to slip free.

But was that enough for me to stay?

I didn't move. I didn't call out. Though something inside beat at me, screaming, as I watched in slow motion, my soulmate, about to walk through the portal, back into the darkness where he came from.

Letting me go.

Lucifer's hand moved through the portal, disappearing to the other side. The rest of his body started to follow. He didn't look back.

Wait, I said in my head, directing the thought through the link with effort. The cord that bound us was just a shadow of what it once was, but that was also when I was in my human form. I was more than that now. I was his equal.

I closed my eyes tightly and opened them back again. Rushton. All the warrior angels suffering, turning, and dying, over and over. I looked down at my hands and saw them glow faintly with Light.

I looked up.

WAIT. I pushed again through the link again, my energy straining through the delicate fibres.

Crossroads. Choices. How far we'd come and how far we had yet to go. Did I have it in me to endure? Did I have it in me to hope?

He had kept his Light.

LUCIFER.

He froze. It was the first time I could see shock penetrate through that wall of ice. It disappeared quickly as he turned to face me, his face still a beautiful mask. The portal still shimmered behind him.

"Let's make a deal," I said.

The Devil smiled.

Bonus Chapter - Lucifers' POV

When Heaven called, the Devil rarely answered.

Though, when he was in the occasional mood to re-remind Michael of his position on certain matters, he let his wings cast a burgeoning shadow across Kryptos, staining the neutral realm with his presence like volcanic ash strewn across a cloudless sky.

The angel they had sent was already waiting. He could feel their presence in the space they had assigned for the meeting, a soft lightness that was expected of those who belonged in the higher realms. The last angel they had sent to negotiate with him had found himself bereft of an eye. The conversation had barely lasted a couple of minutes. He briefly wondered what state he should send the latest angel to brave his company.

If he sent them back at all.

He emerged inside the meeting room, wings out, the dark tips brushing against the midnight floor. The atmosphere immediately cooled, his energy reaching out and draining all the warmth. The lights flickered. His dark eyes locked onto the angel waiting for him.

Female. That was rare.

Light, blonde hair fell loosely around a pretty face. Her simple white dress fell softly to her calves in gentle folds, accentuating a long, slim frame. Wide, green eyes stared at him with a mixture of fascination and horror. He knew the effect his form had on those around him, and he used it decadently, enjoying the inner conflict his presence inflicted even amongst the stanchest of beings.

Desire. The scent, the feel and the energy of someone could creep inside your veins, changing the temperature of your blood and the cadence of your lungs by the barest of degrees. Fight it, run from it, ignore it… but sooner than later the temptation will weaken you.

"Angel," he crooned.

"Lucifer," she responded on an exhale of breath.

Her emotions flickered across her face, completely transparent and unaware of it. No, not a warrior angel. Not a warrior angel at all. They sent a fledgling to face his wrath. Which only begged the question, why?

"Heaven made an interesting choice this time," he said, blatantly studying her as he neared. "The last angel bored me with spiritual platitudes. Perhaps he thought I wasn't beyond saving. Do you think so?"

"I'm not here to indulge in games," she replied, on high alert at his proximity. Her instincts recognised him for what he was, a predator guised in the barest layer of civility. Her instincts told her to run.

She moved backwards and then around him, as if waiting for the rustle in the bushes to alert her that he was going to pounce. His lips curved, he rarely gave warnings when he intended to bite.

"No?" He mocked her. She thought she had a choice in how this meeting was going to play out. "What then, little angel, did you come here for?"

She looked at me coolly as if she could somehow diffuse the danger she had suddenly found herself in. "You know why. To negotiate."

He made a small, tight circle around her, making her increasingly more nervous like a jittery foal. She turned to face him, her wide green eyes full of trepidation. There was something about her eyes, the blend of forest and river green, that stirred something in the back of his mind. He let his energy curl out and slide against her energy field, seeking to unravel the reason she was here.

Michael didn't do anything without a cause. This angel was a deliberate choice.

"Stop that," she said.

"Why?" She couldn't possibly be a trap.

"It's impolite."

Lucifer smiled, slightly amused at her tone. Time to remind her of who she was dealing with. He gripped her neck harshly and squeezed, relishing the gasp of pain she let out.

"Is this also impolite?" he asked silkily.

She reached up and curled her hand around his wrist. Her eyes searched his, as if she was looking for something and was confused as to why it wasn't there. A vague sense of familiarity traced a delicate pattern in his mind, luring him closer to... something.

Distracted, the white glow of Light seering into his skin brought him immediately back into the present. His interest sharpened, and this time his smile was genuine as the nature of this angel was suddenly revealed.

What an interesting turn of event.

Then the Light exploded between them, the force and the intensity took him by surprise. Pushed back, he shook his head to clear it as the angel's *feelings* burned between them. Love, hope, joy... emotions that were inherently repulsive to him. The shape, the colours, the textures of them were all unique to this soul in front of him. The pain was inconsequential, a dim acidic burn in the background. The emotions on the other hand rippled through his body with force, flashing another face into his mind. A face that he had forgotten.

Forced himself to forget.

Untamed auburn hair. A slight, upturned nose and vivid green eyes. The same green now staring back at him with grim determination.

He moved without thought, crushing through the seconds between them. Her hand flared again with Light and he squashed the white fire with his own, the darkness bleeding against his palms.

Lucifer gripped her jaw in his hand and tilted it up. "That might have worked once, angel, but try it again, and I will crush the Light right out of you." Fear flashed across her face at his threat. Satisfied, he commanded, "Now, what is your name?"

"Sandriel," she answered reluctantly, trying to jerk away. He didn't let her.

"Sandriel..." He rolled her name in his mouth, tasting each unfamiliar syllable slowly, memorising the combinations of sounds in his mind. He released her face only to tangle his hand in her long, silky blonde hair.

The eyes. The eyes were the same, but every other feature was different, crafted with a delicate touch. It was a type of ethereal beauty that was reserved for those who lived in the City. The other one ... had imperfections. A dusting of freckles across the nose and cheeks, a faint scar across the underside of her chin, an unruly mess of hair. But despite the physical differences he couldn't dislodge the sense of familiarity.

"I came here to negotiate," she whispered defiantly.

She also didn't appear to recognise him beyond what she had heard. Lucifer smiled. "And how do you think you are doing, *Sandriel*?"

He saw her involuntary shiver. "Stop doing that."

"Stop doing what?" he replied, silky.

"You know what!" she snapped. She pushed back with her Light and her hands and he let her go, moving backwards to give her the illusion of safety.

Lucifer was tempted to take her now and unravel the mystery of her presence and its implications. But he was not one to let emotions rule him and he wanted to be certain that his instincts were accurate. He tucked the strand of her hair into his pocket before crossing his arms over his chest.

"You speak of negotiation," he said. "Negotiation for what, little angel?"

"I came here to negotiate for Devros, Elindara, and Rushton."

Of course she did. Or at least, that is what Michael told her. "Ah, the warrior angels."

She nodded. "Yes, for their release."

The Fallen's latest venture to Earth had been fruitful. Whilst containing some Jinn and playing with a travelling group of merchants, three angels from the City had intervened. Or at least tried to. It was never an even playing field when the Fallen were involved. Power and ruthlessness had a severe advantage over the concerned and righteous. Their feelings for their fallen brethren were their own undoing.

Lucifer shot her a contemptuous look. "And what is Heaven offering me this time? Another offer of peace?"

"Don't you want peace?"

He laughed. How naive.

"What do you want, then?" she pushed.

Lucifer tilted his head at her in consideration. He might not take her now, but that didn't mean he was going to let her go either. "What are you willing to give me?" he purred.

The shock on her face was amusing. "Me?"

"Yes, little angel. Is it not you whom I'm negotiating with?"

"On behalf of Heaven," she said firmly.

He shook his head slowly, as he planned their next encounter. "No, I think not. They sent you, so it is you I will negotiate with."

Her eyes narrowed. "That is not how it works."

Lucifer marvelled once again at how she spoke to him. At times it was with the terrified caution he had come to expect from those who had heard a sliver of his deeds, but at other moments, like now, she spoke as if she believed he wouldn't harm her.

Was that a conscious belief, or an unconscious one?

"If you want to free them, then that is how it's going to work," he continued.

"Fine. What do you want from me, Lucifer?"

"Your time."

Sandriel flinched back. "Why?"

He shrugged indifferently. "My reasons are my own."

Spluttering, she said, "Well, if I don't like your reasons, I might not agree."

Lucifer arched an eyebrow, even now she believed she had a choice. He played along. "Really? You would say no and leave the warrior angels you so bravely came all the way down here for just because of my *reasons*?"

She blinked. "Well…"

"As I said, little angel, my reasons are my own. If that's a deal breaker, go back to your City of Light and tell those who sent you to stop wasting my time," he taunted.

She frowned, and he could see her mind turning over the choices presented to her and finding them all unappealing. "How… much of my time?" She finally asked.

He suppressed the slightest of smiles. "A week."

"Three hours."

He raised an eyebrow. "Surely a life is worth more than three hours, little angel. Eight hours for each."

"Five for each." Too easy.

"Done."

Her shoulders dropped as if her wings suddenly turned to steel. She knew she had made a critical mistake but couldn't figure out how. She would. Soon. "Fine, five hours each for the release of the angels," she said, as if he had asked instead, to drink her blood.

"Excellent," he responded. "You will pay off one of your hours tomorrow." That would give him enough time to verify her identity.

"Tomorrow?" came the tentative reply.

"Yes, or would you like to make it sooner? Maybe you would prefer to stay here a little longer?" he taunted.

"No," she said quickly, taking a couple of steps backwards. "Tomorrow is fine. Where do I meet you?"

"Here," he crooned softly, a predatory glint in his eyes. "You can meet me here."

"And... what are we going to do?" Her voice shook like it was balancing on thin bones.

His lips lifted, but he said nothing, aware that his smile was unnerving.

Her green eyes widened. What she interpreted from his look, he couldn't tell. Then her form shimmered, fading away as she left Kryptos.

Lucifer slipped his hand in his pocket, letting his finger twine around the strand of her hair.

It was time to visit a witch.

Out Now

Obsidian Light

The Fallen Chronicles: Book 2

Please Help!

If you enjoyed reading this book, please help me continue my dream of being an author by writing a review on Amazon and/or Goodreads. To an author, reviews are pure GOLD as they help others decide whether they should purchase your book and if they will find the same joy in it as you did.

And if you REALLY loved this book, please consider sharing it on social media and to all your friends who love a mythical dark fantasy romance read.

Thank you for reading, and love to you all!

Vx

Author

Verusha Robbins lives in Sydney, Australia with her husband, Aaron and their sparkly ray of sunshine daughter, Ally. She has a cat called Odin who loves to sleep anywhere she is stationary, which isn't very long.

Verusha has written since she was seven years old and has always been drawn to fantasy and romance books. She has travelled all over the world but her most favourite places besides home are Egypt and Ireland. An introvert at heart, she loves nothing more than being warm and curled up with a good book with her family nearby.

You can follow Verusha's journey here:

Facebook: https://www.facebook.com/VerushaRobbinsAuthor/

Instagram: https://www.instagram.com/verusharobbins_author/

TikTok: https://www.tiktok.com/@verusha_robbins_author

Other books by Verusha Robbins

Much of Verusha's success in life can be attributed to her intense interest in Personal Development. She has compiled several books in this genre jointly with her dad, Virend Singh.

Verusha realises that when you put the effort into developing yourself, the rewards are amazing - you become happier, healthier, focused and more effective; your relationships improve; overall, you attract better outcomes in life.

If personal development is important to you, please check out Verusha's other publications at www. inkNivory.com